Serotine Press Australia
www.sereotinepress.com.au

ISBN: 978-0-6484918-5-9

Cover artwork and design by Jeff Brown Graphics
www.jeffbrowngraphics.com

Maps by Fictive Maps
www.facebook.com/fictivemaps/

Author website: https://markmccabeauthor.com

A catalogue record for this book is available from the National Library of Australia

To my wonderful partner, Deborah, who advised, supported and encouraged me at every turn and without whom I could never have finished.

.

When All the Leaves Have Fallen, the second and final book in
the *Chronicles of the Ilaroi* series, continues the story which
began in Book One: *As Fire is to Gold*.

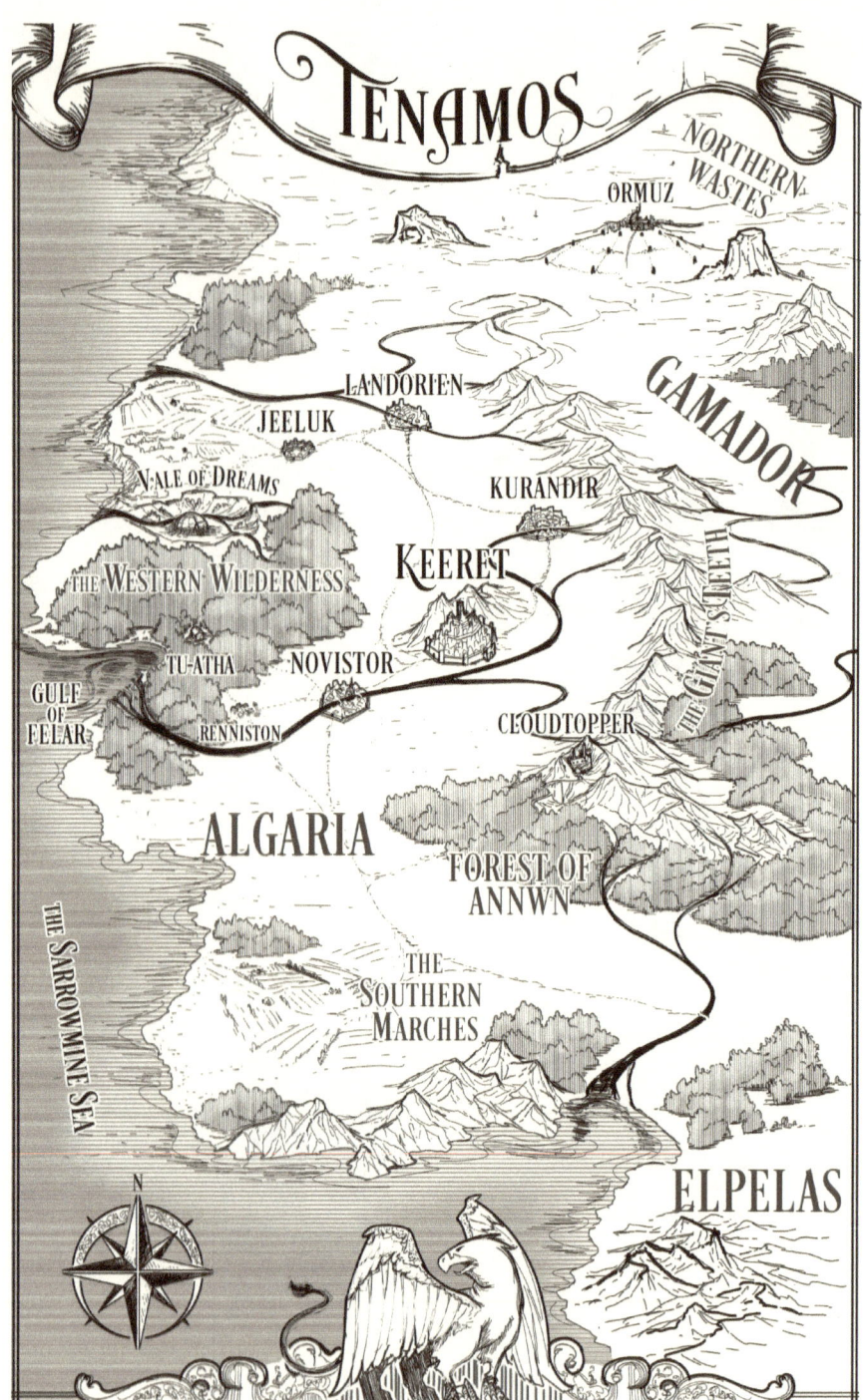

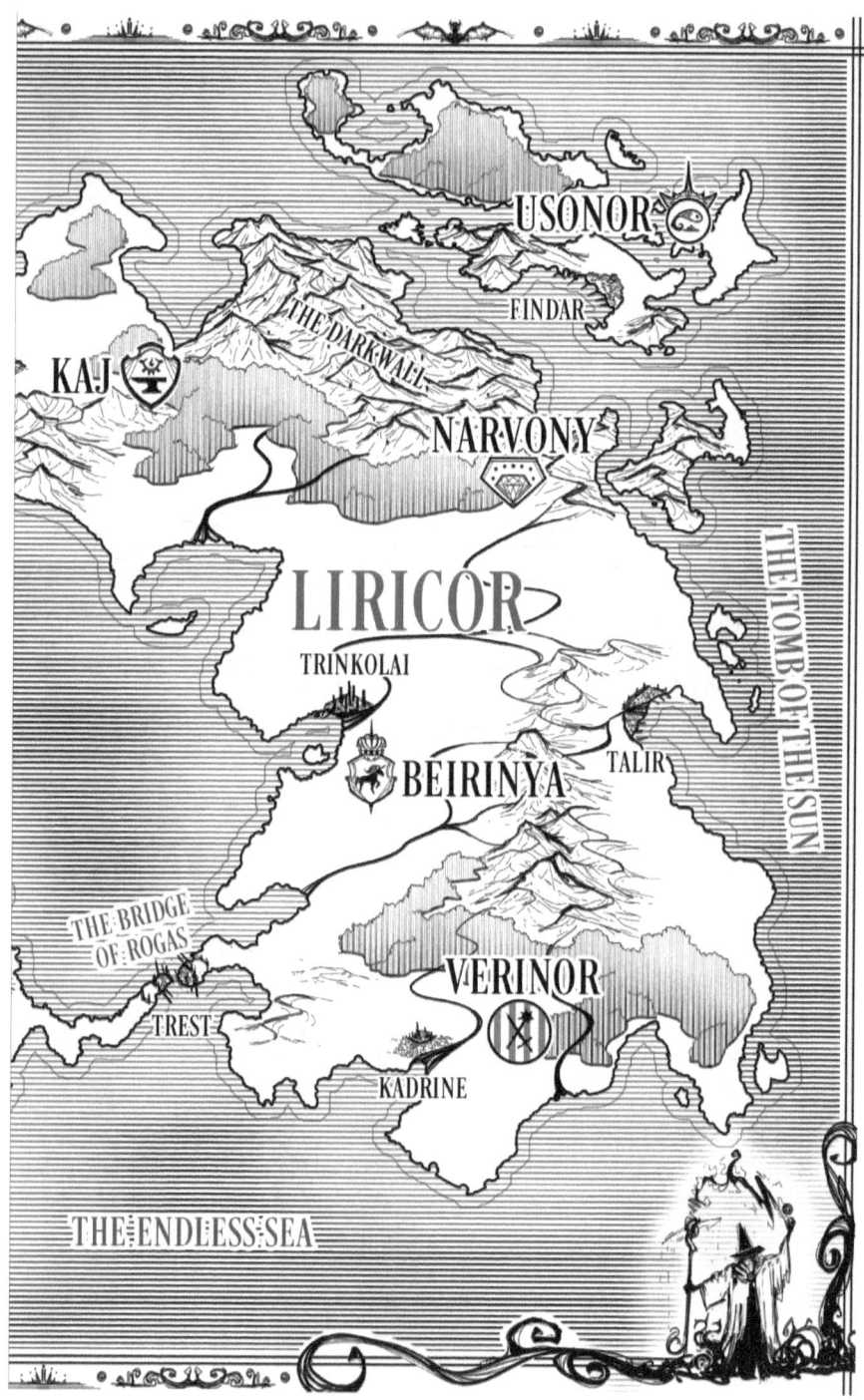

CHAPTER 1

The forest outside the small hut was unusually quiet for a Spring day. It is as if, thought Kell, the whole of Ilythia is holding its breath in dread anticipation of what unspeakable crime Golkar will descend to next. He knew, of course, it was his mood that had engendered such a dark thought, just as he knew that any attempt to shake off his depression would be pointless.

His hopes lay in tatters. He could see no way now to stop Golkar from running rampant with whatever mad plan he had hatched. It had been three days since Tarak had passed and still Kell mourned the loss of his colleague as if it had just happened.

He had known of it the instant it occurred. Kell couldn't explain how, or why. It was an event without precedent, so he could liken it to no previous experience. But he knew, nonetheless, and without a shadow of a doubt. Suddenly, and without any warning, he had sensed that Tarak was gone, either dead or forced in some way to leave Ilythia. It didn't matter which, the result was the same. His colleague was no longer a living force within this plane of existence. Kell was on his own, and he sensed that now, he alone was the last bulwark that stood between Golkar and his total dominion of Ilythia.

That had to be what the madman wanted, why no longer mattered, and it seemed as if it would only be a matter of time before he achieved his goal. If Tarak could be disposed of so quickly, then what hope did Kell have? Whether it was Golkar or his ally who had disposed of his fellow

Guardian seemed equally inconsequential now. Kell knew that he hadn't the faintest idea how to oppose either of them.

At least he wouldn't just sit and wait for them to come to him. He owed it to the people of Ilythia to not go down without a fight. The vows he had taken couldn't be denied simply because he himself was in mortal danger. If anything, he was needed now more than ever. He had thought long and hard about what he should now do and had made his decision.

His first concern was for Nim. He had told the quickling to meet him and Tarak at the hut and, by his reckoning, his friend was overdue. Kell knew there was no reason to be overly concerned at this stage, however. Although he'd expected to see Nim the previous evening, any one of a thousand things could have delayed him given the distance he had been asked to cover. Unfortunately, Kell couldn't afford to wait much longer. If the quickling didn't show up soon he would have to go without him, as much as it would pain him to do so.

They had agreed on a way the wizard could leave a message if he did need to leave without his aide, so that wouldn't be a problem, but he would rather not go without knowing his friend was safe. He had already lost Tarak without being able to lift a finger in his defence and what he was about to do would soon imperil another. To lose Nim as well would be too much to bear.

But he also knew he couldn't afford to tarry. The loss of Tarak had made him realise that to sit and wait would only allow Golkar to keep the initiative he had already seized. For all Kell knew, Nim's failure to show up when expected might be a sign that he too had fallen victim to either Golkar or his helpers. Kell could wait, but not for long. If he was to do anything to hinder his renegade colleague then he would have to start becoming unpredictable. Remaining idle wouldn't achieve that.

It only took him a short time to prepare to leave the hut. He would need to move quickly and stealthily to achieve his goal, and that meant travelling lightly. Hastily gathering his few precious supplies together, he picked out the essential items and discarded the rest. Then, once he had packed and was secure in the knowledge that he was ready to move at a moment's notice, he spent the remainder of the day combing through his books again, searching for something to help him against his fellow wizard, all the while keeping one eye on the pathway down which he hoped to see Nim appear.

The books that drew most of his attention were his oldest and most precious ones. He had kept copies of his notes from his time as a student under the tutelage of Tanis and something told him that if anything could help him it would come from there. Although Kell had no recollection of the mage mentioning such an eventuality, his mentor must have considered what might happen if the Guardians ever fell out with one another. Given that it had been several centuries since he had left, Kell felt that if he scoured through his old notes he might find something there that he hadn't understood the importance of at the time he'd recorded them.

And so it was that he spent his day. To no avail, however. Although he hadn't looked at these records in many a year, and although they brought back many pleasant memories of those early years, ultimately he found himself no closer to an answer than when he had begun. The closest he came were some oblique references Tanis had made to the existence of other worlds.

The Ilaroi, it seems, had not always been here. They had come to Ilythia from some other world, for what reason Tanis either didn't know or chose not to reveal.

Tanis had talked of what Kell at the time had believed to be no more than a theory, that there were, in fact, many other worlds that existed, separate in time and space from Ilythia, not just the one that had been the Ilaroi's original home. He had suggested that it might be possible to either establish or locate intersection points where a crossover between such worlds was feasible.

When pressed on the point, however, he had emphasised that the concept was nothing more than speculation and he had moved on to another subject. At the time, Kell had thought it just an idle idea he hadn't been interested in pursuing. Now, with Norvig's news, he wondered if interaction between such worlds might indeed be possible. After all, the Ilaroi had done it, or at least had claimed to.

Admittedly, they were gods, or the closest things to gods that Ilythia had ever seen, not counting mythical beings such as Zar, the 'god' the sligs were convinced look down upon them. Nonetheless, the Ilaroi's feat proved that it was possible. Even if that were so, however, how Golkar could have achieved such a thing remained unknown.

As the day wore on, his concern for Nim mounted and he began to more seriously consider the prospect that he too had fallen victim to

Golkar. Then, just before dusk, with his hopes fading as fast as the setting sun, the quickling turned up.

Their meeting was a joyous one, with both obviously relieved to find the other safe. For the first night in many days they both ate heartily and Kell found his spirits lifting. Throwing off the lethargy that had dogged him following the loss of Tarak, he allowed himself to hope that he might yet prevail over his colleague. He knew now what he had to do.

He couldn't hope to resist his colleague alone. It was time to call on his own unexpected ally. As hard a choice as that was, it had to be done. Everyone would be at risk should Golkar achieve his aim of becoming the sole living Guardian. Better to imperil yet another of his friends in this deadly game than to allow that to happen. Whatever the cost, Golkar had to be defeated.

In contrast to Kell's new-found sense of purpose, however, Nim took the news of Tarak's demise very hard. Although he knew Kell well enough to know the wizard wouldn't have spoken of it had he not been certain, he found the news hard to reconcile with what he had recently seen. It was only a matter of days since he had left Tarak in the Vale and he'd been sure the herb-master had intended to join them in Annwn as quickly as he was able. He told Kell he had expected to find the two engrossed in plans to combat their colleague. He could only assume that Tarak had unexpectedly run into either Golkar or his mysterious human champion somewhere between the Vale and Annwn.

Most of all, Nim's heart went out to Jekira. Having seen her love for Tarak grow over the years, it saddened the quickling that something so pure could be brought to such an abrupt and unnecessary end, for no other reason than to feed one man's desire for power. Kell could only agree.

At least they had the comfort of knowing that Jekira herself would be safe, for the moment at least. Nim told Kell of Tarak's plan to send her off to her family in Keerêt before he himself departed from the Vale. If he had been true to his word, then by now she should have reached the city. Of all places in Ilythia, there she would be safest. The city was all but impregnable and Nim had seen that work had begun to strengthen its already formidable defences.

For his part, Kell was heartened to hear of the Algarian reaction to his message. He knew how important it was that they know they couldn't count on the aid of the Guardians in what would most likely now become a full-scale war with the sligs. He was pleased to hear of the preparations that Elissa had immediately initiated. Kell knew that she was as fine a leader as Algaria had seen in many generations. For the first time in days, he went to sleep with hope in his heart once more.

The next morning, they were up early and away before the dawn. Nim obviously relished the opportunity to be riding for a change. He might be fleet of foot, but even he needed to rest after the enormous distance he'd had to cover in the past week.

"Are you sure you're ready for this?" he asked Kell as their horses plodded along the forest track silently in the dim light.

"Mmmm. What?" Kell had been leagues away. He'd been thinking back to the time before he had become a Guardian, to the very day in fact that his mentor, Tanis, had taken him as a young lad back to Ral Partha to begin his training. They had ridden right through the night on that occasion. Tanis had been like that. Day and night had meant little to him. It was as if he had operated on some different timescale to the rest of Ilythia.

Kell remembered how on that night the great mage had been so close, barely speaking a word, while he himself had been brim full of excitement, overflowing with anticipation and wonder. In particular, he remembered the next morning, when they had ridden through the forested foothills with the fresh face of dawn just beginning to soften the gloom of the eastern sky at their backs.

He had grown up on the streets of a large town and had never seen a forest like that before that day. Since then he had come to love that time, that brief, and to him magical, interval that separated the night from the day, the pre-dawn, with its soft light, its stillness and its tranquillity. The forest was never quieter than it was then. That's where he had been, remembering another morning long ago, when Nim's voice had disturbed his thoughts.

"I'm sorry," said Nim. "I didn't mean to disturb you."

"It's all right, my friend," replied Kell, smiling softly and sitting up straighter in the saddle in an attempt to shake off his reverie. "I was thinking of happier times. Let it be Mishra's will that we see some more of those when this is over. What was it you said?"

"I asked you if you're sure you're ready for this?"

"Sure? No. I'm not sure. But a better question would be, 'Is there a better option than this at this point in time?' The answer to that, I think, is also no."

"If this is the pep talk," replied Nim sardonically, "then I'm not feeling very inspired. You were supposed to say, 'Of course I'm sure. If I was Golkar, I'd be quaking in my boots right now.'" The quickling's grin betrayed his good humour, though Kell had no need of such signs. He knew his friend well enough to suspect he would still be quipping jokes though the very jaws of death were about to close around him.

"No, my friend," he answered, turning his mind back more fully to the task at hand. "Like all courses, this is a dangerous one. I must do what I can, though, to take the initiative back from Golkar. He must be kept busy trying to deal with me. While he's doing that, the Algarians and the sligs will be left to sort themselves out, without a Guardian tipping the odds for either side.

"If I run from him, that will simply leave him free to go where he pleases when he pleases. The odds are already heavily in his favour without handing him that advantage as well. And if I go to aid the Algarians, then he will simply side with the sligs. Such a war would be a bloody one and my instincts tell me he would still win out in the end. No. I must put him off balance, and keep him so. I must do the unexpected. If he's unsure of me, then he will have to neutralise me before he can deal with his other affairs."

"But can the Algarians withhold the sligs on their own?"

Kell winced, then drew in his breath. "Frankly, I don't know, Nim," he eventually replied. "But I do know that they must. And I also know that I'll need to do more than just put Golkar off balance. In the end, I must find a way to defeat him."

The look of concern on Nim's face made it clear he still wasn't altogether comfortable with Kell's plan.

"I'm decided upon it, Nim," the wizard continued, forestalling any chance for his friend to voice an objection. "So don't try to dissuade me. It's my task now to prod the hornet's nest. I have some tricks up my sleeve that even you don't know of. Once we reach the edge of Annwn we must part. You must go to warn your own people, and the elves as well. Even if we achieve nothing else, it's our duty to ensure that they are warned of the danger ahead. I don't believe Golkar, or the sligs for that matter, will stop if they succeed in defeating the Algarians. Golkar's actions alone suggest some grander plan than that."

"I know better than to argue with you once your mind is set," replied the quickling. "And I can't deny I'll be glad to know my people are forewarned. But prodding a hornet's nest is a dangerous game. The trick is to get close enough without getting stung yourself. I still don't see how you can do that, get near enough, that is. You've been very circumspect about all this. Golkar will surely know as soon as you enter his valley."

Kell smiled. "That's what he thinks, as well. Imagine his surprise when he finds that I can turn up on his doorstep without his knowing it. That will take the wind out of his sails, rest assured. As for the rest? He needs to know that he's in for a fight. I have to declare my hand at some time and now is that time. As I said, Golkar is not the only one with allies."

~~~

Mardur slipped back into her tent as quietly as she could, heaving a sigh of relief as the flap closed behind her. The interior might have been warm and stuffy compared to the cool evening breeze blowing outside, but its closeness offered Mardur a welcome sense of security. Although she felt sure no one had seen her return to the camp, she worried each night that this time she might be caught. She could never forget that the line she walked was a dangerous one.

As she slipped out of her clothes she wondered if the lad was being as cautious as she was. She had done all she could to impress on him the importance of discretion and she hoped that she had succeeded. If any of the others found out what they were up, to it could mean death for both of them. There was always someone seeking to improve their lot at the expense of others and there were few if any in the slig camp who would balk at using such knowledge in their own interests.

Although the risks were high, Mardur knew that it was a chance she had to take. It would have been one thing to strike out on her own and hope to be taken in by another tribe while they were still within sight of the land she was familiar with. With the tribe now deep within Algarian territory, that was no longer an option. Besides, she had to believe there was still a way out of her predicament. Her plan was a good one after all. Norag was in his prime. If his seed wouldn't give her the child she needed then no one's would.

By the Horns of Rika, she mused, the lad was passionate. Holding her clothes up to her face, she inhaled deeply, smiling contentedly as the strong smells flooded her senses. Well, thought Mardur, enough of that. This wasn't supposed to be about pleasure. It was about survival.

The following day, Mardur went about her usual business around the campsite, doing the chores that normally filled her days, tending her babe, washing their clothes at the waterhole, caring for the older members of the tribe, those whose family were either dead or off with the warriors. Somehow, she managed to pretend that life was still normal when in reality fear and worry had become her constant companions.

Gratefully, Norag had the sense to keep his distance while the others were around. It wasn't so easy to avoid Varna, however. It was the usual practice for the women to work in groups, helping each other with the chores and chatting idly to pass the time, and Varna and Drait were both members of the small group of women Mardur commonly worked with.

Thankfully, Drait gave no indication she was aware of Mardur's late-night trysts with her son. If she did know what was going on, she either didn't mind or she wasn't prepared to interfere. Mardur thought it more likely she was unaware. Given the older woman's experience, if she had even the slightest inkling as to what was going on she wouldn't stand by while Norag played such a dangerous game.

Dealing with Varna was another matter. It took some effort on Mardur's part to conceal the bitter hatred she felt for that one. To her mind, it was only that young fool's stupidity which had forced her into the precarious predicament she now found herself in. If Varna hadn't prompted Larnük to reveal everything to Hrothgar, Mardur would have had time to think of some other way of resolving her problems. Instead, she'd been forced to act before she was ready.

Mardur vowed that she would get her revenge on the youngster. For the moment, however, she would bide her time and continue to act as if nothing was wrong. It was essential that she do nothing to draw attention to herself.

Despite the drudgery of the women's tasks, excitement was high in the camp. Their tents were pitched less than a score of leagues to the rear of the slig forces and word of progress with the assault on the Algarians kept trickling back to them. It seemed that everything was proceeding much as they had expected. Evidence of their success could be seen in the small numbers of wounded warriors who had returned to the camp.

Despite their successes, however, they hadn't moved as far into Algarian territory as they had hoped. They should have been much deeper into the border province by now and nobody Mardur talked to seemed to know what was hindering the advance. Nor had there been any news of Hrothgar or his hunt.

Then, unexpectedly, just after midday, Grartok himself, along with a small escort of warriors, returned to the camp. The concern that rippled through the women dissipated just as quickly as it had arisen when it became known the First Warrior was simply seeking a replacement for his mount. It seems his horse had gone lame following a minor mishap that morning. Grartok always kept a small supply of mounts in reserve and he had returned to the camp to choose a replacement. The horse he was now riding was borrowed. Apparently, the lame mount had been put to death on the spot. It had failed the First Warrior, a fatal mistake.

Mardur realised that this was her chance. Although Hrothgar still hadn't returned, he couldn't be far away by now. While the First Warrior was choosing a new mount, Mardur quickly threaded her way through the camp, making a beeline for the tent that was always kept in readiness for the First Warrior. It was there that he found her a short while later.

"What's this?" demanded Grartok, as he drew back the cover to his tent and saw Mardur seated within. She was looking up at him expectantly with a soft glow on her face. "Did you miss me that much, woman?" I didn't come all this way just to bed you, you know."

Despite his dismissive tone, Mardur could sense he was pleased to find her waiting for him. "I thought you would want to know straight away," she replied, fighting to maintain her calm as her heart pounded within her breast. As she spoke, she placed one hand on her lower abdomen, gently patting it as she did so.

She waited while Grartok stared at her hand against her belly. She could see the look of confusion on his face slowly changing as the import of what she had said and what she was doing slowly sank in. When he raised his eyes to her face once more, she locked on to him with her own gaze. With the barest hint of a smile on her face, she spoke again, seductively this time, her soft voice barely a whisper. "I have something in my belly, First Warrior. Something you put there. I am with child, your child."

Mardur fought to conceal her nervousness as she spoke. She had done it now. The die was cast and where it would take her Zar only knew.

For a moment Grartok stood there in the doorway of the tent, speechless, looking from her face to her abdomen and back again. His chest heaved with obvious excitement. Then, suddenly, and unexpectedly, he threw himself down upon Mardur, knocking her backward with the force of his body as he did so. His mouth went to hers, kissing her fiercely as one hand groped under her shift for her breast. To Mardur's surprise, she felt herself responding to his unexpected ardour. This was like Norag, full of untamed passion and desire. It excited something within her she hadn't known had been there. She had obviously spent too much time with that monster, Hrothgar.

What followed was frantic, for both of them. When Grartok was done, he rose and began to rearrange his clothing. The lover became the warrior once more.

"Move your belongings in here woman," he said to her gruffly once he had regained his composure. "You're my tent-woman now."

"What about Hrothgar?" queried Mardur, maintaining a submissive tone despite the exhilaration she was feeling.

"What about him?" sneered Grartok dismissively. "I am First Warrior. I take what I want."

"He'll be angered if he returns and finds that I've moved from his tent, especially when he hears where I've gone. I fear him."

"Mmmm. You're right. It'd be like the dog to do something rash, too. I'll leave a guard. Don't worry. Grartok protects what is his. Forget about Hrothgar. He's nothing to you now."

"Yes First Warrior."

With that Grartok turned and left. Mardur allowed herself a smile. It couldn't have gone better for her. She wasn't out of trouble yet, but another important hurdle had been crossed. The gods were smiling on her, she could see that now. Surely they wouldn't desert her after she had come this far. Now, if they could just help her to get pregnant, then she would be truly safe.

She could fake it for a while, but not for long. No matter. Certainly, now that she had spoken to Grartok, the sands of time were running, but she had also bought herself a bit of breathing space, and some much-needed protection from Hrothgar. Everything now depended on Norag.

Mardur hoped that the youngster was as fertile as he was eager.

~~~

"It doesn't look very impressive," snorted the slig leader as he looked down on the walled town nestled on the floor of the valley below the two riders. Despite the lengthening shadows as the sun slipped inexorably towards the horizon, their position on the crest of the ridge gave them an excellent view of both the valley and the town that it harboured. "They didn't even have the sense to fortify this ridge," Grartok continued, his eyes still assessing what he could make out of Kurandir's defences. Shifting casually in his saddle, he turned to look at the warrior next to him.

Brorgar swallowed in an attempt to moisten his parched throat as the First Warrior's gaze fell upon him. Although his throat was dry, his armour seemed clammy and uncomfortable and he knew that his brow was beaded with perspiration. For the moment, he was safe. The First Warrior was in a good mood. If he hadn't been, Brorgar's head would already have been lying in the dust at Grartok's feet rather than still atop the broad shoulders of the hunt leader to whom it belonged. How long this mood would last was another thing.

Although Brorgar could see that luck was on his side for the moment, he knew that his position was a tenuous one. He prayed to Zar he would somehow make it through this interview with the foremost warrior of the Sagath tribe with his head and shoulders still connected to each other. Unconsciously he twisted his neck, rubbing it absently with one hand as he did so. He wondered if the First Warrior was toying with him, like a desert scratcher playing with its prey before it moves in for the kill.

"They fight like sligs, not like Algarians, First Warrior," he explained to Grartok, forcing the words from his dry throat and trying to sound as composed as he could. "I've thrown everything I've got at them and they still haven't cracked. It must be some élite garrison."

"Elite garrison!" scoffed Grartok with a sudden roar that startled the hunt leader. "I don't think so, Brorgar. Just a pack of dogs that aren't ready to die yet more likely. You've had two days. Take the town by sunset tomorrow or I'll replace you."

Brorgar winced as he nodded silently, unable to induce his vocal cords to produce a reply. He knew exactly what 'replace' meant.

"Now," continued Grartok, as if they had just been discussing the weather, "how about some of that corn liquor you said you liberated? You can help me celebrate, Brorgar. I've just learnt that I've sired the next leader of the slig nation."

As Grartok wheeled his horse away from the ridge, Brorgar allowed himself a momentary glance skywards. Zar was known to be capricious but he sensed that the god must have smiled on him this day. He knew he would do well not to waste this chance to redeem himself. Gods didn't bestow those kinds of favours more than once in a lifetime.

"Grartok is a great leader."

Brorgar pulled his eyes away from the flickering flames and looked up at the retreating back of the slig leader as he made his way off into the darkness, in the direction of the horse corral. "Yes," he grunted to the warrior seated beside him, his voice devoid of any emotion. "He'll lead the Sagath to greatness before he's done."

Rudnak nodded thoughtfully in response, then turned to look at Brorgar as Grartok disappeared from view. If the look of awe on the young warrior's face wasn't a clear enough indication of the impression the slig leader had made on him, the words he spoke next confirmed his adoration of their leader. "It's an honour to serve him."

"Mmmm," grunted Brorgar unconvincingly, turning his eyes back to the pitted metal in his gnarled hands and running the whetstone across the face of his blade once more. "It's not one I'll have for much longer if we don't take that accursed town when the sun rises."

"Aieee, but they fight like demons, don't they?" The mention of battle brought a sense of excitement back to Rudnak's voice. "I didn't think I would ever say it. I thought they were all soft. But these ones, they are truly warriors, and they fight with courage and skill. They are fitting opponents for us. It would be an honour to die fighting the likes of them."

Brorgar looked up at Rudnak through slitted eyes. Nothing seemed to diminish the youngster's enthusiasm, not even the carnage they had both witnessed a few hours earlier. "That's all very well, Rudnak," he replied after a brief pause, "but I'd like to see the end of this war. I too want to die with honour, but not just yet, thank you."

Brorgar knew that Rudnak was young. Time would change him. The hunt leader also knew that honour meant nothing when you were lying in the hot dust with your blood pooling around you and your life slowly ebbing away as the battle raged above you. That kind of death was all very well for campfire stories on winter nights, but Brorgar had found the older he got the more jealously he clung to life. Like all sligs, it was important to him that his prowess in battle be seen and acknowledged by all; but he also had a fine tent-woman and a strapping young son and he wanted to see them both again one day. A lot of warriors would die on both sides before that could happen.

At first, Rudnak offered no response to his comment. He sat there silently, gazing into the crackling fire, apparently uncertain as to how he should respond. Then, suddenly, he broke the silence.

"I too want this war to end. But my blade has tasted Algarian blood and it thirsts for more. It won't let me return home until it has sated its needs. Isn't that the true way for a slig warrior?" As Rudnak finished speaking he looked across at his hunt leader. The blank look on his face hid whatever concerns had been left unvoiced.

Brorgar was no fool, however. He knew what the unspoken words were. *Why don't you feel this way too, hunt leader?* Rudnak was thinking.

Well, let Rudnak think what he wants, he thought as he continued to stroke his blade with the whetstone. He could sense the turmoil in his young companion's mind and he knew that he would be wondering now if his hunt leader had gone soft, or if he had lost his nerve following the setback at the gates. Like most of the young warriors in Brorgar's hunt, Rudnak had never seen battle before and his notions of war were naive and simplistic.

That was Brorgar's problem. His hunt had never been blooded in battle prior to this assault on Kurandir. Apart from some minor raids and the unopposed sweep across the Algarian eastern frontier that had brought them here, Brorgar was the only one in the whole hunt who had any real experience of note. He knew that for many of his warriors their idealistic concepts of war would be shattered before the current campaign was over. Brorgar also knew that he would be lucky if he didn't pay for their inexperience with his life.

"No matter," said Brorgar, brushing aside his fears for the moment, "your blade's need won't go unquenched." He would never guide his hunt to victory if they lost their faith in his ability to lead them. "We have them now," he said, trying to sound positive. "With the gates open our next assault should finish them."

His words belied what he really thought of their situation. They had battered their way into the town only hours earlier that day, in the final assault before night had fallen. With their deadly crossbows keeping all but the foolhardiest of the Algarians away from the parapets, a small group of warriors had borne the ram they had fashioned right up to the walls and commenced to batter away at the huge wooden gates. It had taken some time and they had lost a number of warriors, but eventually, the timbers had begun to crack and splinter and finally they had won their way through. With a huge roar, they had rushed in through the breach, hurling their war cries and brandishing their weapons with deadly intent, ready to slaughter their opponents to the last man, only to find the cursed Algarians had laid a trap and were there waiting for them.

The defenders had built a huge wall made up of wagons piled one on top of another around the open square the gates led into. They had perched archers atop the ring of wagons and on the surrounding rooftops and as soon as the square had filled with sligs they had rained arrows down on the 'killing field' they had created below. The hunt had lost a great many warriors in the confusion that followed, until eventually they had broken and fled.

It had been a sight that Brorgar was unaccustomed too, that of slig warriors routed in battle, unable to get at their foe and falling over one another in their desperation to escape from the deadly hail of arrows that was raining down on them from above. Thank Zar that Grartok didn't hear of that.

Despite the debacle, Brorgar's experience told him the wrecking of the gates should mean that the end was now in sight for the defenders of Kurandir. Their last tactic had taken the sligs by surprise, but Brorgar wouldn't allow himself to underestimate either their wiliness or their courage again. The gates were irreparable and with the walls breached the next assault should be the final one. Brorgar knew that it had to be. His own life depended on it.

CHAPTER 2

The door to Tu-atha stood closed. Kell had a clear view of it from across the small clearing that surrounded the entryway. From there, he could easily make out the wooden beams and thin metal bands of the large door that gave entry to Golkar's manse. He stared down at the construction intently, as if he might somehow see through it and into his colleague's abode. His mount moved nervously beneath him. The surrounding forest was unnaturally quiet.

"Steady, Thyfur," Kell crooned softly to the beast beneath him. "He's there, I sense it now. Soon he will sense me as well. It's time I removed the masking spell."

In an instant, Kell was aware of his companion's reply. Silently he cursed himself. It was hard to get used to telepathic communication when he hadn't used it for so long. Thyfur's message was curt and to the point. *I long to be at the brute, mage.* The deep rumble that emerged from the beast's throat conveyed some sense of the mood that accompanied the thought.

The wizard resisted the urge to stroke the flanks of his mount. He had always found it hard to accept that the creature could feel anything through its metal plumage. Although, like any other winged beast, its feathers rippled and moved as it shifted its weight from one clawed talon to another, even after all this time, Kell's mind still resisted the knowledge that the gryphon responded to tactile contact like any normal creature of flesh and blood.

For normal it certainly was not. None, not even Kell, knew the tale of where the creatures had come from, though few that had seen them doubted their genesis was elsewhere than in Ilythia. One look at the beasts was enough to confirm their alien origins.

The creature was huge, for a start. From his position astride its neck, Kell looked down on the door from at least double its height, if not more. Its wingspan was equally awesome. In flight, the gryphon would spread its immense wings like those of the great eagles its upper body so closely resembled. From tip to tip, when fully extended, they covered a distance of more than a score of paces. It was its appearance, however, more than its size, which made it such a daunting sight.

Its head and wings closely resembled those of an eagle, albeit a huge one at that. Its hooked beak, given its size, was an intimidating weapon in its own right and the steely eyes that glared out from beneath the tufted feathers of its brow gave it a look that was both cold and menacing. The feathers themselves were equally off-putting. Metallic in nature, yet strangely flexible nonetheless, they dully reflected the bright sunlight of the cool forest morning. Similar plumage adorned the rest of the creature's upper body. Although its wings were folded at the moment, tucked back along the length of its massive body, razor-sharp talons could be seen, if one looked closely enough, nestling beneath the feathers of its forequarters.

In utter contrast, its lower body was akin to that of a lion or some such similar beast of the earth. Tawny fur covered its powerful, muscular hindquarters. Its talons gripped the forest floor tightly, carving deep wounds in the grassy surface upon which it stood. Thyfur, for that was its name, was clearly a formidable being.

Kell had tamed the beast long, long ago. Circumstances had led him to take a leading role in rearing it from the time it had been barely a chick; not an easy task and one he doubted any human had ever attempted before. He'd had no choice, really. Having been forced to slay its mother he couldn't bring himself to leave her chick to die as well.

It had pained him to take the life of such a magnificent creature and he had only done so because his hand had been forced. Gryphons were rarely seen in either Tenamos or Liricor and seldom had any contact with the other sentient inhabitants of the land. They lived long lives, longer, Kell knew, than those of him or his colleagues. The passing of such a beast was, therefore, a singular event in the history of the land.

The beast in question, only the second he had ever encountered, had for some unknown reason turned its obdurate rage on the elves of the Great Forest, Elpelas, that hugged the southern coastline of Tenamos, and had been systematically destroying their woodland dwellings when their elders had called on Kell for assistance. He had responded as was his duty and had attempted to reason with the creature.

The gryphon was sentient and as such Kell had been able to establish a mind link with it, akin to normal speech but communicating directly, mind to mind, without the use of language as such, a little-used skill he and his fellow Guardians had been taught by Tanis. It had been to no avail, however. The gryphon had seemed determined to personally rid Ilythia of every elf it could find and it quickly turned its fury on him when he made some passive attempts to dissuade it from the ruinous course it had chosen. Whether its blind rage was caused by illness or by some real or imagined transgression by the elves was never established. In the end, he had no choice but to try to kill it. The battle that had ensued had been the toughest Kell had ever endured and he had barely escaped with his life.

The creature had been all but impervious to the effects of magic. In battle, it attacked with a swiftness unsurpassed by any other creature and with a battle-lust that fuelled its murderous intent but did nothing to blunt its amazing tactical acuity. Kell had been lucky in the end to stumble on the one spell that seemed to draw a response from the beast, a muted response but one that had slowed the gryphon just long enough to ensure its defeat.

It was after the battle, when Kell had sought out its lair, that he had found its one offspring. It was only a fledgling, even if it was already the size of a large lion, and in his guilt, he had taken pity on the poor thing. He had named it Thyfur, and had raised it and cared for it, even though the task kept him from returning to Cloudtopper for some time. He took the opportunity to strengthen his acquaintance with the elves, and it was at that time that he had first met and befriended their near neighbours, the quicklings, although his friendship with Nim came much later.

Thyfur had grown rapidly and, with no parent to guide it or tutor it, had quickly bonded with its foster parent, Kell. Over time it had become a fierce and loyal companion, a true friend, and Mishra knows, thought Kell, how few of those the Guardians had. 'Mage' it called him, though it knew his name well enough. The creature was almost as strong in intellect as it was in body. It was the first being other than his colleagues he had ever considered an equal.

Eventually, as is the way of things in nature, the beast had outgrown its need for the wizard and they had parted. Though the leave-taking had been a sorrowful one, Kell knew that he had neglected his responsibilities as a Guardian for too long and that Thyfur, like all creatures that move from adolescence to adulthood, needed to see what he could achieve on his own. The beast also longed to search for others of his own kind.

The bonds of closeness and friendship remained strong, however, and the mind link the Guardian and the gryphon had established enabled them to maintain contact, even over the longest of distances. Few though such contacts were over the centuries that had passed since then, each knew he could call on the other in direst need, though neither had needed to do so in all of the years since that time, until now.

What had drawn Thyfur's mother to Tenamos remained a mystery to Kell. The gryphons' normal haunts, he later learnt from Thyfur, lay far out on the very edges of the world, among the wild creatures that roamed far from the shores of the two largest land masses. Theirs were lands that Kell knew little of and the gryphon seemed reluctant to enlighten him further.

Rarely did Thyfur make the long passage across the seas to Tenamos and it had been more than half a century since the two friends had last renewed their acquaintance. Kell was grateful his friend had so readily agreed to his recent request for help.

The wizard knew he was exposing Thyfur to great risk by drawing him into the contest between the Guardians. He also knew, however, that should Golkar overcome the last of his colleagues and become the sole Guardian of Ilythia, the wizard's madness would then be unfettered and all the creatures of this world, no matter where they resided, would be at risk. All this he had explained to Thyfur. The gryphon clearly understood what was at stake and had agreed to stand with him. Indeed, instinctively, it quickly formed an intense hatred for Golkar. It was the nature of gryphons to be like that, fiercely loyal in friendship, deadly and murderous to their foes.

An enemy of thine is an enemy of mine, mage, the beast had said to Kell. *I would no more stand by while your life was in peril than would you should I be in danger.*

And so Kell waited for Golkar. Neither of his fellow Guardians had ever known of the existence of Thyfur. Certainly, Kell knew that they would have known something at least of the gryphons. They may each even have had their own experiences with these and other creatures which Kell himself knew little or nothing about. But this friendship would come as a shock. Thyfur was an incomparable ally. Golkar had sought the aid of another; now he would see that Kell did not stand alone either. *Let us see what will come of this*, thought Kell. *Let us see now how far Golkar's strength has grown.*

~~~

The thud of booted feet on the staircase below them signalled to Dain and Bardor that the trap they had set for the sligs was ready to be sprung. They had heard the thick, guttural voices of the warriors as they had argued in the room below and now the heavy steps on the wooden planks of the staircase indicated that their search of the ground floor had been completed. As anticipated, they intended to search the upper rooms of the dwelling as well. It had taken no genius of foresight to predict this. Their pattern of clearing the town house by house was now well established.

As he pressed his body against the cool stone of the wall beside the stairwell, Dain wondered who was the hunter here and who was the quarry. He and Bardor might have laid the ambush but it remained to be seen if they could pull it off, and they were the ones with no other means of escape, not the sligs. If anything went other than as intended, he knew how quickly the tables would be turned and the hunter would become the prey.

At least they were evenly matched. From the voices they had heard, and now from the footsteps, it seemed that there were only two of the beasts in the house. Though the sligs were trained warriors, accustomed to battle, this form of street fighting was hardly their preferred mode of combat. The Algarians would also have the advantage of surprise.

The warriors were ascending the stairs slowly, their leisurely approach probably more the product of apathy than it was of caution. They didn't appear to be taking the prospect of encountering anyone very seriously at all and were making little if any attempt to conceal their presence in the house. From the creak of the floorboards under their steps, the two Algarians could follow their progress up the staircase with some precision.

Dain held his breath as the thud on the steps indicated their opponents were approaching the arched entryway to the upper floor. Gripping his weapon tightly, he found that the warmth of the sword hilt against his skin did nothing to appease his nervousness. Looking across at Bardor, he could see his companion was in no better state than he was. The bow he held, though drawn and with an arrow nocked and ready to fire, shook in the cooper's hands. Dain wasn't concerned.

He had learnt to appreciate the nervousness that preceded a fight, knowing the adrenalin rush it produced would be sorely needed once battle was joined. He also knew that his friend would not let him down. They had been fighting side by side since the first day of the slig assault. Dain knew his man well. At this moment, there was no one he would rather have at his side.

Opening his mouth to draw in a lung-full of oxygen, Dain prepared to act. As the third last step creaked under the weight of the slig warrior, Dain swung into the open archway, plunging his sword with all his might towards the startled warrior that appeared in the entryway. As he swung, he sensed Bardor moving to guard his exposed shoulder.

Like the true warrior he was, the surprised slig somehow managed to bring his own blade up to parry the one that suddenly appeared in front of him, but to no avail. It all happened too quickly for him to achieve anything more than a glancing blow that turned Dain's thrust slightly up and to the right, protecting the slig's abdomen but only at the expense of other more vital organs. As Dain recognised the all too familiar sickening feeling of his blade plunging deep into flesh, he pushed down with every ounce of his strength, burying the sword even deeper still and toppling the slig backwards with the combined effect of his weight and the force of his thrust. With no chance to arrest his own forward motion, Dain found himself caught up in the tumble of bodies careering back down the staircase the sligs had just ascended. As he fell, he desperately tried to maintain control of his descent, glimpsing for one brief moment in the tumble of arms and legs the second slig who had obviously been unable to retain his own footing as his companion hurtled back on to him so unexpectedly. Within moments, the melee of bodies reached the bottom of the staircase.

As the bodies thudded into the floorboards at the foot of the staircase, Dain quickly rolled to his side, ignoring the stabbing pain in his knee and fumbling for the knife in his belt as he did so. He had let go of his sword as soon as the fall had commenced, knowing there was nothing to be gained in trying to hold on to it. It would do more good right where it was, buried deep within the chest of the leading warrior.

Scrambling to his feet and knowing his opponents would be frantically trying to do the same, Dain was relieved to see an arrow thud into the chest of the second of the sligs, just as he was about to regain his footing. As he teetered, still on his knees, a second arrow punched into his neck. With a sickening gurgle, the slig slumped back on to the floorboards, twisting awkwardly and scrabbling vainly to staunch the sudden flow of blood from the wound in his throat.

As planned, Bardor had followed the tumble of bodies down the staircase and had taken advantage of the confusion to inflict further damage on their opponents before they had a chance to recover. Incredibly, despite his injuries, the slig struggled to rise again, brandishing his axe in one hand as he did so. The arrow protruding from either side of his neck lent a macabre air to the scene that, for the briefest of moments, stunned the two Algarians. Realising that to hesitate was to die, Dain forced himself into motion again, flinging his body at the warrior with reckless indifference to their disparity in size and weight.

It was like running into a stone wall. Dain wondered who took the most damage from his lunge, him or the slig. He didn't waste any time thinking about it, though. His aim was to get close enough to use his blade before the slig could get his axe up in position to swing it, and use it he did. While he grappled for the slig's weapon arm with one hand, he used the other with murderous efficiency, plunging his knife time and time again into the beast's scaly neck until finally it ceased to struggle and he felt the body slump lifelessly beneath him.

As he lay there, panting for breath and wondering what wounds if any he had taken himself in the scramble, he hoped the sudden silence meant that the battle was over and that his and his companion's luck had held yet again.

He couldn't attribute their success to anything more than that. In the past few days, he had come to learn at least one thing about combat. Survival depended as much if not more on good fortune as it did on skill. A twist here, a missed step there, any one of a thousand small and seemingly inconsequential things could determine the eventual outcome of a contest when it came to armed conflict.

Turning his head, Dain watched as Bardor knelt over the body of the other warrior and plunged his knife into his stomach. He knew the cooper wasn't acting in anger; nor was he finishing the slig off. The brute was clearly as dead as his companion was. Bardor was simply retrieving the two arrows that were sticking out from the warrior's tunic, just inches away from where Dain had buried his sword. The bolts were precious and their supply was dwindling at an alarming rate. Any opportunity to retrieve them couldn't be ignored.

Dain turned his head away as his friend pulled the arrows free and wiped them clean on the slig's tunic. So much killing, he thought, so much blood, and they had all become inured to it so quickly. Could he ever return to a normal life, even if he did somehow survive this war? Would these scenes return to haunt him long after the war was over? Kurandir stank of death and he had contributed to that stench as much as any of those who had fought here.

Taking the hand his companion offered, Dain pulled himself to his feet, the twinge in his knee as he did so reminding him of the knock he had taken in the wild descent of the staircase. "Let's go," called Bardor with his eye on the door as Dain retrieved his own weapon from the corpse beside them. "There's bound to be others close behind them."

They quickly made their way to the back of the house, Bardor in the lead and Dain struggling to keep up behind him. Now they were moving, he was finding it hard to walk freely on his injured knee. It felt like he'd sprained a muscle or a tendon and it was all he could do to hobble along and try to ignore the sharp pains that were spearing through his leg each time he placed any weight on the joint. Thankfully, they halted for a moment while Bardor peered out through the partially open door into the empty lane beyond.

Once the cooper was satisfied the way was clear, he darted down the lane and into the open door of another house, oblivious to the injury impeding his companion's capacity to keep up. He knew where they were going. They had chosen the building they were heading for earlier as the most likely spot for their next ambush.

With a quick glance up and down the lane, Dain hobbled after his companion. As he made his way down the thoroughfare, he couldn't resist a furtive glance back over his shoulder. The emptiness of the streets unnerved him even more than the abandoned houses. Not a soul could be seen. Even the rats seemed to have deserted Kurandir. What right did he have to be moving about as if he owned the place?

As soon as he reached their destination, he darted through the open doorway Bardor had disappeared into only moments earlier. The house that he entered, though equally as deserted as the rest, seemed almost warm and inviting after the unnatural silence of the streets.

"It's clear," said Bardor, coming back from a quick inspection of the rest of the house. "What took you so long?"

"I twisted something in my knee on that damned staircase," grunted Dain, bending and rubbing the joint with his hand. It was sore to the touch and he grimaced with pain as he gently swivelled his leg, trying to see precisely which movement produced a painful response. "This is a young man's game. It's not for the likes of me."

"It's not a game that I care to play any more, either."

For the first time, Dain noticed the look of exhaustion on his companion's face. It reminded him of how drained of energy he himself felt. He knew that it wasn't physical exertion that was doing it. It was stress, the continual stress of looking over their shoulders, of hand-to-hand fighting where only one of the two combatants could come out alive, of killing and cutting into flesh.

"We've been lucky today," Bardor continued. "How much longer that can hold, I don't know. If the worst we come out of it with is a sprained knee, it'll be a miracle."

Dain nodded. Bardor was right. They were swimming against the tide and they both knew it. All of the Algarians here in Kurandir, if there were any of the others still alive, knew it. They just had to keep going and forget about everything else, forget about tomorrow, forget about their loved ones, forget about their chances of surviving. There would be time enough for that when the job was done. Right here, right now, that's all that mattered.

Turning his mind back to their task, Dain took in the room they were in. The kitchen provided an ideal spot for their next ambush. It had a small servery that opened into the front room and through which Bardor could cover anyone trying to enter from the front of the house. The back door through which they had entered opened onto the alley, which itself provided a number of opportunities for a swift escape. If the alley itself was blocked then an internal staircase led to the roof. From there they could move quickly without impediment and be streets away before any pursuit got near them.

Dain took a gulp of water from the jug they had left on the table when they had reconnoitred the house earlier, then moved to his assigned position, watching the alley from the rear door. He was tired, and hungry. He longed to stretch out and have a good rest, maybe even a little nap. It was mid-afternoon and they had been at it all day.

As they had expected, the sligs had attacked just before dawn. They had tried to hold them at the gates but that hadn't lasted long. Since then it had been hand-to-hand fighting, with the sligs having to clear the way street by street, and at times, house by house.

Captain Sulyok and what remained of his Rangers had drilled their little band of farmers and townspeople in the tactics of street fighting as thoroughly as time permitted in preparation for this very eventuality. He had warned them that once the walls were breached there would be no way they could stop the sligs from entering the town. All they could hope for then was to make the inevitable slig advance as drawn out and bloody an affair as they could.

Sulyok had told them the sligs liked open battlefields and had little or no experience of the type of fighting which would be required once they got inside of Kurandir. Usually, that was when a battle ended. Once the walls were breached, the defenders of a town usually surrendered, or they tried to fight their way out through the enemy lines. Sulyok said surrender wasn't a viable option when the enemy were the sligs.

But if, he claimed, rather than try to fight their way out, the Algarians defended the town and forced the sligs to fight for every street, almost for every house, then the trained warriors would be out of their natural element and the odds would be evened up considerably. He didn't think they could win the battle, but he did think they could hold the sligs up for days, precious days that would help the rest of their countrymen.

The sligs had entered through the merchant's quarter, that part of the town nearest the main gates. The goal was to slow their advance through that section. Once that was lost, it was every man for himself. The best chance then would be to slip out over the walls after dark and try to evade the slig patrols. At least some of them should be able to make it back to wherever it was the defensive line was now being formed. Captain Sulyok was insistent that one was being formed. They all knew they had to believe that. If not, then what was the point of their stand?

And so they had been at it like that all day. Dain and Bardor had no idea how anyone else was going any more. The last time they had seen any

24

of their companions had been over an hour earlier. They had been too busy looking after themselves since then. Sulyok's tactic seemed to be working, though. They were retreating into the town with each house they abandoned, but at a cost the sligs wouldn't have anticipated. And they hadn't retreated far despite almost a day of fighting.

The sligs no longer knew what to expect, an empty house, booby traps, or some Algarians lying in ambush. They were confused and had no answer to the hit and run tactics the Algarians were employing. They had also found that their own tactic, brute force applied in large numbers at any weak point, simply couldn't be applied under these conditions. Nevertheless, they were progressing, and Dain and Bardor both knew that many of the men they had talked and shared a meal with the night before would be dead by now.

A movement at the corner of the alleyway pulled Dain's attention back to the job at hand. "Hssst," he whispered to Bardor. "Could be sligs in the alleyway."

Bardor stayed where he was for the moment. Dain knew that he was waiting on his word. If he said 'go', they would both make a run for it, to the rooftop would be his choice, and, as the lookout, it was his call.

Cautiously Dain edged out of the doorway again, just far enough to see if anything was coming down the alley. His stomach flipped over as he spied three slig warriors running right down the middle of the alleyway, straight towards him, with their murderous axes at the ready.

In one movement he turned and shouted out the word he knew that Bardor was dreading. "Go. Go. Go." As they scrambled for the staircase, they heard the front door of the house crash open. The thump of booted feet on the floorboards of the front room indicated that they were caught in a pincer. Somehow the sligs had located them and they were coming at them from both entrances at once.

The staircase was their only hope. A small flight of stairs led to the second storey and from there a smaller set led through a trap door to the roof. The trap door was open, or at least it should be. They had left it that way for just this eventuality.

Dain reached the stairs first. He was closer than Bardor and somehow he managed to ignore the pain in his knee for the moment. The cooper was only a heartbeat behind him. As Dain reached the top of the first staircase, he turned to help his companion. Just at that moment, the first of the slig warriors reached the foot of the staircase. It was the only portion of the room Dain could see from his position at the top of the stairs.

Before he could yell out a warning, the slig in front grabbed a hold of Bardor's leg and with one powerful tug yanked him bodily back down into the room. Dain saw the look of shock on his friend's face as his upward motion was swiftly reversed. His feeble attempt to arrest his descent by grabbing hold of the railing was to no avail. The prodigious strength of the slig was too great to resist.

As Dain drew his sword and prepared to go to his companion's aid, he saw that he was already too late. The room below was filling with sligs. As Bardor hit the floor at the bottom of the stairs, a scaly hand grabbed hold of his hair and cruelly jerked back his head. Just as quickly, the swinging blade of an axe sliced into the cooper's throat, decapitating him in one vicious stroke and spraying blood all over the wall and the lower stairs of the staircase. Everything seemed to slow down. Bardor's body slumped to the floor, blood pumping from the neck and onto the boots of the warrior that stood beside it. The head, which had fallen in a lazy arc from the shoulders, offering up a fleeting glimpse of the shocked grimace on its frozen features as it turned, thudded sickeningly to the floor beside the body. As Dain looked down, unable to avert his gaze, rooted to the spot as if his feet had turned to stone, a slig warrior stepped into the opening.

Dain blanched as the brute turned his cruel face upwards, spying him standing there, waiting, at the top of the stairs. For a few brief moments their eyes locked, then the slig threw back his head and opened his mouth. The roar from his throat sent a shudder racing down Dain's backbone. It was the roar of a beast that has sighted its prey and is ready to spring. The axe the beast held in his gnarled hand was dripping with blood. Dain looked down at the creature, wanting to move but unable to do so. He watched in horror as the slig lifted one foot and slowly began to ascend the staircase.

CHAPTER 3

Try as she might, Sara found that she couldn't form a clear mental picture of what might lie beyond the wilderness. It was as if the continuous canopy of the forest was acting as some kind of barrier to her imagination, like a stone wall rather than the cluster of leaves and branches it actually was, suppressing all but the vaguest impressions of what might lie outside of her current field of view. Even with her eyes closed, all she could picture was bark, branch and leaf, or combinations thereof, which wasn't surprising given her experience in Ilythia thus far. From the day she had first arrived in the place, other than the term in her cell and their brief stay in the cave, she had seen little else than endless trees.

And so, that morning, when she and Rayne emerged from a thick clump of underbrush to suddenly find clear sky above and open fields in front of them, her first thought was that she had fallen asleep and was dreaming of home. The change of scenery was so abrupt and so unexpected she couldn't believe it was really there.

Only a few strides behind them lay the towering beech trees she'd become so familiar with. In front of them, as far as the eye could see, lay rolling hills, dotted with trees and traversed, in a reassuring display of imposed order, with hedgerows, stone walls and wooden fences. Behind them lay pristine wilderness, all but untouched and unspoiled, with barely a hint of the existence of humanity. In front of them lay cleared pastures and tilled fields, unmistakable signs of habitation and the impact of sentient life.

Only a short distance away, a small flock of black-nosed sheep stood idly cropping a grassy slope, mute testimony to the dramatic change of environment the two travellers had suddenly experienced.

Despite the evidence before her, Sara found it difficult to accept what she saw. Looking around from her position astride Nell, she blinked once or twice, quite purposefully, wondering if it might all disappear when she re-opened her eyes. But it didn't. It wasn't a dream. Her heart soared as the realisation struck home. They had made it. They were finally out of the interminable wilderness.

Sara felt a surge of hope well up from deep within her. If this, something she despaired they would never achieve, was possible, what more might they now accomplish? Could she dare to hope they might yet find their way through to the other Guardians, she wondered. Maybe there was even a way home. At the very least, they weren't done for yet. The fat lady still hadn't sung!

"So, what do you think?" asked Rayne, interrupting her thoughts.

With some reluctance, Sara drew her eyes away from the panorama before them. She smiled as she noticed that Rayne, though he had broken the silence, was still staring at the open fields in front of them. From the look on his face, he seemed just as enraptured by the sudden change as she was.

Turning her own eyes back to the scene ahead of them, Sara found herself reminded of a painting she had once seen in a book, an old master's portrait of an idyllic rural scene. She half expected a pair of centaurs to come trotting over the nearest hill while they stood there gaping.

"My God, Rayne," she finally managed to reply. "It's glorious, it's . . . I don't know, it's just wonderful. Words seem inadequate to describe it."

Josef had told her she had not yet seen the real beauty of Ilythia but she hadn't appreciated the full significance of his words at the time. Neither their circumstances nor their surroundings had been conducive to her giving his statement much credence. Now she understood at least a little of what he had meant. If this was a taste of what lay beyond the wilderness, then she couldn't wait to see more.

"There're sheep here, too," she continued, gushing excitedly at the sight of something so comfortingly familiar. "Real sheep, just like at home."

"Well, where else did you think we'd get wool from?" asked Rayne with a chuckle. "From birds maybe, great big woolly ones that fly into the barn once a year and wait patiently for the farmers to shear them."

"Stop it," cried Sara, turning her head away in mock indignation. "You don't have to make fun of me. You might have got it from llamas . . . or alpacas."

"From what? Alpackers? What in the name of Martan's teeth is an alpacker?"

"Never mind. Suffice to say that where I come from you can get wool from things other than sheep, smarty-pants. Not from birds, though. I can't say I'd fancy the idea of being a shepherd under those circumstances. I'd certainly want a very broad-brimmed hat." Sara's broad grin showed she was enjoying the mood that had come over them.

"Now you are being silly," laughed Rayne. "Anyone would think you were happy. Come on." With that, he gave Ned a gentle nudge in the ribs and moved out into the sunshine, away from the shade of the trees. Sara was only too happy to follow along in his wake.

As they ambled their horses down the gentle slope, she sensed a lightness in her heart the likes of which she had not felt in many a day. The day was a glorious one. From the warmth of the morning sun that beat down from a cloudless sky, Sara guessed that spring had almost run its course. If the weather in this land was anything like at home, they would probably be in for a long hot summer.

Looking about her, she could see that the lush green grass of the hillside was dotted with what seemed to be thousands of wildflowers over and among which flittered a delightful parade of brightly coloured butterflies and what seemed to be endless battalions of bees. The low hum that drifted up from the latter into the warm morning air seemed to bewitch the senses into a mesmerising indolence. After the continual tension of the last few weeks, Sara was only too willing to submerge her thoughts in this uncharacteristic peacefulness. It wasn't long before she found her thoughts drifting.

The slope they crossed could easily have belonged in the hills that surrounded her own hometown. It all seemed so reassuringly familiar. On lazy summer days like this, she and Gemma would often go riding together, and for one brief moment, she thought it was so. The gentle clip-clop of the horses' hooves, the soft summer breeze on her face, she had been here so often before.

It didn't last long, though. Her mount wasn't right. Dear Nell, as sweet as she was, could never be mistaken for Freya. Her colouring was wrong for a start. Shaking off her reverie, Sara lifted her head and considered the broad shoulders of her riding companion as he swayed back and forth on the horse in front of her. It wasn't just Nell that was out of place, she realised. Rayne, cherished friend though he was, could never be mistaken for Gemma.

Cherished friend? Is that what he's become, she thought? They'd come a long way since that night in the tent. Their first kiss! She still remembered it. But what should she call what had grown between them since? How should she label him now?

Boyfriend? No. It was more than that. Lover, then? No, not that either, she wasn't ready for that. Though . . . why not? she wondered. What they felt for each other was love, she was sure of that. They seemed so close now, as if they were bound to each other, as if they had known each other for years rather than weeks. Everything about him seemed so right to her. And she knew that he felt something for her, too. She could see it in his eyes, and in the need they seemed to share, the need to be close, physically, that is, to be constantly touching each other in some small way, be it a hug, a gentle caress, a brief touch of their hands, or a soft kiss.

She thought of his kisses. They were those of a lover, of that she was sure, as was his touch. When they lay down together at night and he held her in his arms with his firm body pressed up against hers, there were times then when she longed to tell him, what? Not to stop? That his kisses weren't enough any more? That when he turned her face to his and gazed down into her eyes, that she felt a desire for him then that was so powerful it threatened to consume her?

She didn't dare tell him those thoughts. It was all too daunting, too confusing, too frightening. Who knew what would happen if Rayne knew the feelings that stirred within her? She had never known a boy like him, never felt this way before, didn't know what to do, didn't dare break the spell that held them together. It had all happened too quickly, leaving her no time at all to fathom it out. She wasn't sure where one went from here and there was no one to ask, no friend to confide in. She dared not take the wrong step now, not with so much at stake.

Was it always like this, she wondered? Did all lovers feel this way? Was he going through the same torment? Should she ask him if that was what he wanted? And what would she do if his answer was yes?

The question sobered her. It wasn't the first time she had arrived at that point and she still wasn't ready to go there. With a slight pang of regret, she wrenched her thoughts back to the present. Best not to dream too much, she thought, of home, or anything else for that matter. No good would come of it. *"Que sera, sera,"* as her mother was so fond of saying. "What will be, will be."

With a gentle squeeze from her knees, she urged Nell forward. They had fallen slightly behind and that wouldn't do. Best to press on and get where they were going. *That was her best chance for happiness now*, thought Sara. They had a job to do and it wasn't just their own survival that depended on their getting it done.

They continued slowly down the hill and when they encountered a worn path they turned and followed it for a while. Eventually, they struck a road of sorts. It was definitely a track for vehicles; the two ruts for wagon wheels were ample proof of that, though from the way the ridge between the ruts was overgrown with weeds it seemed unlikely too many carts had come this way for some time. They followed it nonetheless. It headed eastwards and that was the direction they were taking, away from the wilderness, away from pursuit, away from Tug and away from the sligs.

Sara knew a little of the land that they had entered. Josef had told them that once they were clear of the wilderness it would be less than six or seven day's ride to their goal, to the Forest of Annwn and the two Guardians, to her only real chance of finding her way home, to the only hope now of stopping Golkar.

She remembered that he'd told them of the narrow swathe of farmland that ran between the wilderness and Annwn. To the northeast, he had said, the rolling hills flowed out into the broad sweeping plains that constituted the heartland of the Algarian nation. Far away east, across those plains, lay the Giant's Teeth, a jagged mountain range that ran almost the length of Tenamos. To the south lay Kardonia and the Southern Marches. The isthmus of land in between held the most southerly of the Algarian provinces. The river that ran through its midst ran right down to the Gulf of Felar and out into the Sarrowmine Sea, names that meant nothing to Sara, exotic though they were. Rayne had told her that he had heard that country comprised some of the richest farming land in all of Tenamos. The little she had seen thus far confirmed what he had heard.

They followed the road they found for some time, noting with reassurance the increasing signs of habitation as they moved further and further away from the forest's edge. The track they followed soon joined another more worn path and then, not long after that, to Sara's great delight, they spied a man.

He was standing in a field some distance from the road and seemed to be watching them closely, as if intent on ascertaining what two strangers were up to riding so brazenly across his land. Sara waved to him. It seemed the polite thing to do and she longed for a friendly voice after all they had been through. To her chagrin, the farmer ignored them, not even deigning to acknowledge such a simple attempt at communication with a nod of his head.

"The natives are friendly, aren't they?" she muttered to Rayne, who was peering back intently at the farmer.

Rayne hesitated a moment, then let out a raucous laugh that rocked him back on his saddle. "Why, it's a bird-chaser!" he cried. "No wonder he didn't wave back. He's full of grass."

"A bird-chaser? Oh," cried Sara, her consternation turning into a smile as she suddenly realised what he meant. "You mean a scarecrow. We call them scarecrows. I've never seen a real one. I guess we won't get much conversation out of him." Although she was disappointed, she took the sighting as a good sign. People made scarecrows. In fact, farmers made them. She doubted if sligs did, nor draghar for that matter.

Her disappointment didn't last long. They didn't go much further before they encountered a real farmer, and there could be no doubting that this was no scarecrow. For one thing, he didn't stand still. In fact, he was coming their way. Better yet, he was herding a flock of sheep along the dusty road directly towards them.

As the animals neared them, Sara and Rayne halted their mounts and both sat quietly, drinking in the rural simplicity of the scene. The little black-nosed sheep swept forward without missing a beat and were soon swarming around their horses. Like a swift-flowing stream that encounters some immovable object, the little bundles of dirty wool swept around them, combining once more as they passed with a fluidity that suggested the obstacles had been forgotten as quickly as they had been dealt with. The old farmer strolled along behind them, idly waving his crook at an occasional straggler while his ebullient work dog ran frantically back and forth, nipping at the heels of the sheep as if his next meal depended on his keeping every single one of them in strict formation.

As the farmer passed, he tipped his hat to them. "Mornin," he mumbled in a quaint rustic accent with barely a glance in their direction before his attention was drawn back to his charges. "Git along there, you boys," Sara heard him call out in a thick voice as he passed. "Git 'em, Scratch, git 'em," he called out to the dog, cackling in delight as it rounded up a pair of sheep that had taken advantage of his momentary distraction to make a bid for freedom through a gap in the stone wall that ran along beside the road. Before Sara realised that she had missed her chance to strike up a conversation, they were gone, the swirling dust and bleating of the sheep as they receded into the distance their only legacy.

And so the morning went. A young lad rode along with them for a league or two and finally, they were able to appease their burning desire for information. He was only twelve, but he seemed well informed for his age. All was not as peaceful as it seemed. Although they were safe here, he told them, the most easterly of the Algarian provinces had gone up in flames only a week or so earlier following a major slig offensive the likes of which hadn't been seen in many a year.

"Me dad's gone away to help the Rangers," he told them quite proudly, puffing out his chest as he did so. "Me mum cried, but dad said he'd be back soon enough. He said the Rangers'll put things right as quick as you can blow out a candle."

"I'm sure they will," responded Rayne in a confident voice, though both he and Sara knew what Josef claimed would be the outcome of the war that was now beginning.

"I'm the man of the house now," said the boy proudly, puffing out his chest even further still and trying to look as earnest as he could. "I told me mum we gotta prepare for the worst. Just in case, mind you." Then he added in a conspirational aside, "Me dad said that would keep me mum busy and stop her from worrying too much about him."

"I think that's very wise," said Rayne with a straight face. "Maybe you should have a few essential things packed and ready to go, in case you have to leave in a hurry. Your mum could work out what you could take."

"Yes," said the boy thoughtfully, rubbing his chin as he did so. Sara wondered if he were mimicking a habit of his father's. "That's not a bad idea."

"How far is it to the nearest town from here?" asked Rayne after a few moments. "And what's it like?"

"Renniston's not far. It's about an hour from here. They've a blacksmith there. And a store."

"Is it very big?" asked Rayne. "Does it have an inn?"

"Oh yes, it's quite big. It don't have an inn, but old lady Farrarson has a room she lets to travellers."

"What's the biggest town hereabouts, then?"

"Novistor," he answered without hesitation. "Me dad went there once. It's huge. There's a big wall around it, and a mill, and shops, lots of shops me dad told me. One of them sells nothing but sweets."

The conversation continued on in this vein but revealed little else in the way of useful information. When the boy turned aside from their trail for his neighbour's farm, the two travellers continued on, alone once more. About midday, they reached Renniston. It wasn't at all what Sara had expected.

The picture she had formed in her mind when the boy had mentioned it was one of a small village full of white-washed, stone cottages with thatched roofs, and flower beds all around the walls and spilling over from window boxes below quaint little curtained windows. That was what she expected. It wasn't what she found.

Renniston was small, that much was right at least. Rather than stone, however, the walls of the houses seemed to have been made from large, roughly shaped blocks of what looked to Sara like a dried mix of mud and straw. Most had indeed been painted, though whitewash seemed not to have been favoured. Brown was the colour of choice. For curtains, simple rough sheets of material served adequately, if not attractively. Most hung limply, obscuring any view of the interiors of the dwellings. The roofs were indeed thatched, but not in the tight and orderly way Sara had seen in pictures at home. The layer of soil that had been sprinkled over the reed thatching came as a shock to her. She had no idea what purpose it served and could only guess at the dirt that must seep down through the thatching, particularly when it rained. The whole affair seemed very rough and ready, though she guessed it must be effective. Presumably, no one would want to live in a house that leaked water through the roof.

Bundles of flowers hung from the overhang of the roofs of many of the houses. They were most likely herbs, thought Sara. Tied in bunches and hanging upside down in the morning sun, they seemed to cluster around the doorways in particular. At one house, a pair of muddied boots sat beside the front door. A ginger cat could be seen on the windowsill of another, sitting and watching them lazily as they passed on by. One house had a wooden frame attached to a side wall from which hung strips of cloth. From the low trough which had been placed beneath the material and in which could be seen a thin layer of coloured water, Sara guessed it was cloth that had recently been dyed.

She was particularly intrigued by the small recess which could be seen in the wall to the left-hand side of the door of each of the houses. A small squat figurine could be spied within and below this invariably hung a short string of garlic. Though she could see that the figures were gaily painted, Sara had no idea what they represented or what purpose they might serve. In answer to her query, Rayne said simply that they were 'the Protectors of the Hearth', as if that explained everything. Sara wasn't even sure what a hearth was, let alone why or how it could be protected.

The whole town comprised only a dozen or so of these dwellings clustered around a slightly larger building that appeared as if it might be a general goods store of some kind, judging by the paraphernalia that was stacked along the wall bordering the road. A blacksmith's workshop could be seen under a lean-to attached to one side of the building. Two horses were tied to a post near the entrance to the workshop, and the forge, which was visible to them as they passed, was cold and silent. Sara wondered if, like the boy's father, the blacksmith had gone east to the war.

Despite, or perhaps because of, its lack of ostentation, Sara sensed that the town's inhabitants were hard-working people who led simple but honest lives. The few people they saw as they passed through the hamlet, though showing little inclination to stop and talk, greeted them with smiles and friendly looks and seemed relatively unperturbed at the sight of strangers. Sara found it hard to believe that only the night before she and Rayne had slept uneasily, wondering if they might awake to find slig warriors standing over them with blades drawn. The thought of sligs appearing here in this peaceful little hamlet seemed inconceivable.

After watering their horses at the trough outside the blacksmith's, Rayne suggested they push on to the next town. Though the village was pleasant enough, they had no need to stop. He said he wanted to put as much distance as he could between them and the wilderness while the weather was fine. It was with some regret that Sara agreed. She felt safe in the village and hoped it was only a taste of what they could expect to find now that they had left the forest.

Beyond Renniston, the countryside was much as they had seen that morning, rolling hills and tilled fields, broken by the occasional stream. The locals they encountered were invariably women, children or old men. Though they too were friendly enough, like the villagers, few had much to say.

As far as Sara could see, everybody seemed to be busy with something, either going somewhere or keen to get whatever it was they were doing done before . . . before what? Before the slig storm descended upon them? Probably not, she thought. They wouldn't be expecting matters to reach that sort of pass. They hadn't the advantage, or was it the misfortune, of the prescience Josef had shared with her and Rayne. Nor the awesome responsibility that went with it, thought Sara ruefully.

Not far from Renniston, they broke their journey beside the road, where a stone bridge spanned a babbling brook. Stretching out on the thick carpet of grass that ran right down to the water's edge, they ate a quiet meal, greedily soaking up the serenity of the surrounds, both guessing there would be days ahead when they would wish themselves back where they were now. They chatted together happily and for once no mention was made of what lay behind them.

Sara sensed that Rayne's hopes had lifted as well. He talked of what lay ahead, of the route they should take, of the Algarian people and their preparation for the war that was coming and of how that might make their task easier. The confusion, he said, should aid them. No one would have the time or the inclination to bother with two travellers making their way across the province. Five or six days, he thought hopefully, should see them in Annwn.

After a short rest, they moved on. They covered a good many leagues that day and finally, as the shadows began to lengthen, the town walls of Novistor loomed up in the distance. The road had by this time become quite busy.

They had found that the deeper they travelled into the province the more willing to chat the people they met seemed to be. By the time that Novistor came into view, Sara was not only becoming accustomed to their thick accents. She was beginning to feel quite relaxed in their presence.

At first, she sat back quietly and let Rayne do most of their talking. She had already met many more people in this one day than she had encountered in the whole of the previous few weeks. Although she found that daunting initially, as the afternoon wore on she began to relax. They were just people after all, much like Rayne and herself. Most appeared friendly and as she warmed to them she found their mannerisms and sayings both quaint and intriguing. Eventually, without realising it was happening, she began to venture into the conversations herself, cautiously at first, and then with increasing confidence as the afternoon progressed.

Most of the talk was of the slig assault, though few knew much of its progress, only that it seemed to be the biggest offensive in living memory and that much was being done to prepare for what few believed likely, that the fighting should spread this far.

Most of the traffic they met was headed, like them, for Novistor. Those that were prepared to heed the warnings saw it as the most likely place of refuge. Apparently, its walls and its size offered protection the smaller towns and villages could not.

Despite what they had heard, when the town did loom up in the distance, they were both greatly surprised. This was certainly a town, not a village, and its huge stone walls along with the towering buildings that rose behind them could be seen from some distance away. The traffic seemed to jam up as they made their approach and by the time Sara and Rayne arrived at the gates it was almost dusk.

They were held up there by a small squad of Rangers who were examining all who sought to enter or leave the town. A small queue had formed but it was moving forward quite briskly. The Rangers were clearly going about their duties with some efficiency and those waiting seemed patient and in good humour. Finally, when the wagon in front of them passed in under the arch of the gate, it was Sara and Rayne's turn to be questioned.

"What business would you in Novistor?" asked one of the guards of Rayne, who had edged Ned slightly forward of Nell.

"We seek lodging for the night," answered Rayne. "Can you recommend a decent inn? This is our first visit to Novistor."

"The province is under martial law," declared the guard in a haughty tone, ignoring Rayne's question. "Are you planning to stay in Novistor?"

"No. We're passing through. We should be on our way again on the morrow."

"You've the sound of Marcher," said the guard, relaxing a little. While he spoke, one of his companions moved along side of Ned and gave Rayne and his gear a good looking over. "Where are you making for and on what business?" continued the first guard as this was happening.

"My sister and I are on our way to see our uncle," replied Rayne, without a moment's hesitation. "He has a smallholding on the bounds of Annwn. Our father passed away not two months back and we bear the ill news to his brother."

Sara felt herself blinking at the natural ease with which the lie rolled off Rayne's tongue. They hadn't discussed what they might say in such a situation so either he had amazingly quick wits or he had previously thought through what he might say if questioned. If it was the latter, then he had done so without mentioning it to her.

It hadn't occurred to Sara that the truth might be best kept to themselves. Who knows, it suddenly dawned on her, what reaction they would get if they said they were searching for one of the Guardians. Certainly, it would draw more attention than they needed at the moment, especially if anyone was still looking for them.

That prospect seemed to have diminished considerably now. In the wilderness they had been alone and their trail had been an easy one to follow. Here they were but two among thousands and the further they travelled the harder they would be to find. Still, she couldn't say that she wasn't grateful for Rayne's continuing caution. If they could just get themselves within this town without attracting too much attention, she guessed that pursuit would become virtually impossible.

"Mmmm," said the guard, scratching the rough stubble on his chin and looking up at Rayne's face with a brief but piercing look.

Although Sara could feel her own stomach doing somersaults, she sensed that Rayne was in control of the situation. She felt sure that if she were questioned her anxiety alone would betray them. Talking to their fellow travellers along the road was one thing; standing up to an interrogation by the town guards was another entirely. Ignoring her pounding heart, she somehow managed to glance around at the activity going on around the gate, trying desperately to look calm and relaxed as she did so. Though her eyes swept the surrounds, her ears were tuned to the exchange between Rayne and the guard. For a few moments there was silence, then the guard spoke again.

"Next."

Sara breathed a sigh of relief. She had worked herself up over nothing. The guards had no reason to stop them. They were no different from all of the others, just two travellers busily trying to get from one place to another. She sensed Ned moving forward from beside her. As his hooves began to clatter on the wooden planks of the bridge that spanned the small culvert that surrounded the walls, she urged Nell to follow.

Beyond the bridge lay the huge arch of the gateway and as they passed under it Sara found herself looking up in wonder. The engineering feat that had enabled the Algarians to lift the huge stone blocks into place seemed to her in direct contrast to the simple dwellings of Renniston, with their thatched roofs weighted down by soil and muck. Pulling her gaze back down to street level as the gates passed behind them, she felt a momentary feeling of panic. They had entered Novistor and all of a sudden there were people everywhere.

It seemed to take them hours to find a decent inn and by then it had long since fallen dark. Fortunately, the streets of Novistor, or at least the ones they travelled, were both adequately lit and well frequented. Lamps had been hung up at every junction and interior lights from dwellings or businesses lit most of the rest of the way. Of greater comfort was the presence of townspeople out and about in the cool of the evening, though it seemed to Sara her dad's advice when she and her family had travelled to a large city back home applied equally well here. "Stick to the main roads where everyone else is," he had said, "and don't go nosing around back-streets where no one's about." Even the locals seemed to steer clear of the dark little lanes and alleys that branched off from the better-lit thoroughfares Rayne kept them to.

Sara was of no use at all to Rayne in the search for an inn. She spent the first half hour or so 'rubber-necking' as she would have called it at home. So much so that when she finally did begin to tire of the 'sights' she hadn't the slightest idea how they had got to where they were or how far they had come from the gate. At first, however, she bombarded Rayne with an endless stream of questions.

"What's a cooper?" she asked. "Who's St. Terac?" "What's a reeve?" "What does a wheel-wright do?" "What's a farrier?" "Is two shillings a lot of money?"

When she sensed he was tiring of that, she kept her peace and contented herself with taking it all in. And there was much to take in: the man who was rolling a large barrel down the middle of the street; the two men in bright red robes who chanted in harmony as they slowly made their way along the wooden boards that constituted the sidewalk; the young woman with the strange, little, feathered cap and the heavily smocked skirt who looked for all the world as if she had just won the lottery as she strutted along by herself, smiling broadly at everyone who looked her way; the little girl who skipped along holding her father's hand and humming a tune that Sara could have sworn was 'Twinkle, twinkle, little star'; and much more besides.

When she saw two more young women enter a building arm in arm with their beaus, she couldn't help but comment to Rayne on their outfits. "I like those cute little hats with the tall feathers," she remarked chirpily. "They seem to be all the rage here."

"They're harlots," responded Rayne with a slightly embarrassed look. "The tall feather marks them as harlots."

"Oh."

After that, she kept quiet again. She did think it a shame though that such a cute fashion should be reserved only for prostitutes.

The inn they finally settled on was the third they had tried. Though the previous two had rooms on offer, Rayne had chosen on both occasions to keep looking. The first, he said, was a rough place that was unfit for either of them to stay in unless they were incredibly desperate, which they weren't yet. The 'Archer and the Boar' it was called, though Rayne said neither its name nor the fine painting that hung over its door, of a hunter about to shoot an arrow at a wild boar from behind a tree, were any indication of the quality of the establishment itself. From the wild sounds coming from the downstairs room, Sara sensed that he was right and she was only too glad to give the place a wide berth. It seemed to her that the inn was on the verge of a riot.

The second, grandly named 'The King's Knight' despite the somewhat shabby appearance of its exterior, was one Rayne said he might have considered if he had been by himself. He declared he had no intention however of asking Sara to stay there, regardless of her earlier pronouncement that anything with a soft bed would be fine by her.

Once more she tended to agree. She didn't like the surreptitious glances she received from a number of the drinkers in the downstairs bar when they went in to discuss prices with the innkeeper, a wiry little man with a mottled face and a nervous tic in one cheek. They both felt unnerved by the distinct lull in the level of background noise that began with their entry and continued right up to their exit some minutes later.

The third inn looked much more homely and even its name sounded warm and inviting. 'The Spreading Fig' the sign declared from beneath an artist's rendition of a large tree that seemed to loom over a two-storied house that clearly represented the inn itself, though if there really was such a tree Sara could see no sign of it in the dark of the night.

As soon as they entered the building, they both realised they had found a place for the night. The downstairs room, though crowded and smoky, exhibited none of the boisterousness of the previous two establishments. Nor did their entry draw more than the occasional glance from a few of the patrons. The vibrant chatter of the place, interspersed with occasional laughter and the clinking of glasses, seemed not to miss a beat as they made their way from the door to the bar through a sea of red-faced though good-humoured strangers.

When Rayne asked the middle-aged woman behind the counter for a room for him and his sister, the 'oh yes' she gave them with a glance towards Sara suggested she wasn't at all taken in by his story. If she did wonder what their real status was, though, it seemed not to bother her much. She couldn't have been friendlier it seemed to Sara, who warmed to her right from the start.

"Call me Mrs Forrodeer," she said with a broad grin once Rayne had negotiated a price. "Anything you want you just let me know and I'll see what I can do." With that, she called for one of the serving girls to show them to their room.

In response to her summons, a young girl bobbed up from out of the crowd with her arms full of empty beer tankards. She looked barely thirteen if she was a day to Sara, but was handling the tankards as if she had been doing it all of her life. Once she had safely deposited her load on the broad wooden top of the bar, she turned to the two travellers and gave them a small curtsy.

"Take these two good folk up to chamber number six, Alys, there's a good girl," directed Mrs Forrodeer.

"Yes, Miss. Follow me, please," replied the girl in a bright voice.

The girl then proceeded to lead them across the room and up the staircase that hugged its rear wall. From the top of the stairs, a corridor led them past a number of doors to their own room, a small chamber with two beds, a dressing table, two chairs and a small window that looked out over the courtyard at the rear of the inn. Through the window Sara could make out the twisting branches of a large tree, the fig, she concluded, that the inn was named for.

While Rayne went off to make arrangements for the stabling of the horses and for their gear to be brought upstairs, Sara took a seat in a corner of the room and watched as the girl put fresh covering on the two single beds. The soft beds looked very inviting after the weeks she had spent sleeping on the hard ground.

Before the girl was done, Mrs Forrodeer turned up. She was carrying two large, earthen pitchers, one with hot water, she announced, and one with cold. Both were placed on the small dressing table between the beds.

"Hurry up there now, Alys," whispered Mrs Forrodeer in a quick aside to the girl before she turned to speak with Sara. "Now, young miss," she said, fixing Sara with a matronly glare. "If you and your . . . brother . . . are hungry I've some soup still warm. I've some lovely fresh bread to go with it, too, baked this very afternoon by my own hand. We've a small room off the scullery where you can eat in private if you've a mind. And if you don't mind me saying, it'd do you the world of good. You do look a bit pale. You aren't with child are you, my dear?"

Sara felt herself blush furiously at the woman's question. She knew Mrs Forrodeer was scrutinising her intently, waiting to cast judgement on her response, and out of a corner of her eye she could see the young servant girl discreetly watching her while pretending to busy herself with the beds. "No," she replied, a little tremulously. "We've been on the road for some time and I'm, I'm just very tired. I think some soup would be most welcome, though, thank you very much. I'm sure Rayne will agree too."

"That's good then. You're far too young for that sort of business. I'm sorry if I was direct, my dear, but there's no use hiding such things. Some girls in that sort of situation try to and it doesn't do anyone no good. Your young man looks like a nice enough young boy, but I'm the Queen if he's your brother. That's all right by me though, dear. You just make sure he looks after you. There. I've said my piece and that's the end of it. Don't mind me, my dear. I'm always sticking my nose in where it don't belong. I don't mean anything by it. Just wanted to make sure you were all right. Once you've settled in you come down and see me or one of my girls if you've a mind to. A good supper's what you need." With that, the old lady bustled away, leaving Sara alone with the serving girl once more.

"Will that be all, Miss?" asked the girl in a small voice once Mrs Forrodeer had left.

Sara, who had been staring out the window when she had spoken, thinking about the ease with which the woman had seen through Rayne's story, looked up in surprise to see the girl standing beside the open door waiting for her answer.

"Ummmm. Yes. No, wait." Rayne had given her several coins earlier in the afternoon. He had said it might be useful for her to have some money on her now they were among other people. She had slipped them into the pocket of her breeches and hadn't thought of them again till now.

"Is it the custom for me to give you a coin for making up the room?"

"If it pleases you, Miss," answered the girl, blushing slightly and keeping her eyes fixed firmly on the floor at her feet as she spoke.

Sara reached into her pocket and drew forth the coins. Looking down at the small collection of copper and silver pieces in her hand, she realised she had no idea of their worth. Rayne had said something to her about them but she hadn't been paying attention. Not wanting to insult the girl, she took two of the small silver ones and dropped them into her outstretched hand; the coppers seemed to be too small to be worth much at all.

The small gasp from the girl and the widening of her eyes signalled instantly to Sara that she had given her too much. "Why thank you Miss," gasped Alys, clutching her hand tightly around her windfall. "Thank you sooo much, Miss." With that, she gave a little curtsy and turned and rushed out of the room.

When Rayne returned a short while later, Sara saw no need to bother him with her mistake; it was no big deal after all. She did make a mental note, however, to find out from him as soon as possible some idea of the value of things here in Ilythia. For all she knew, she had given the girl a month's wages with those two coins.

She also didn't mention Mrs Forrodeer's suggestion that she might be pregnant, though she did apprise him of her offer of supper. As neither of them had eaten since their lunch by the bridge, they quickly washed the dust and grime from their face and hands and headed back downstairs in search of the scullery. They were both heartily sick of travel rations and the prospect of a cooked meal was too good a one to refuse.

When they reached the bottom of the staircase they began to cast their eyes around in search of either Mrs Forrodeer or the way to the scullery. The mass of people in the common room hadn't lessened while they had been upstairs. If anything, it was even more crowded now than it had been when they had arrived, and they could see no sign of either her or her staff among the press of people. Sara was wondering how a small inn could manage to attract so many customers when it suddenly dawned on her. There was no television here, no movie theatres, no malls. This was probably it as far as 'nightlife' went in Novistor. If you didn't go to the local inn, then you probably stayed at home.

Sara could feel her apprehension rising as the two of them began to make their way through the throng of people between the staircase and the bar. The close proximity of so many strangers in such a small space after all of the time they had spent virtually alone in the wilderness unsettled her so much she was about to suggest to Rayne they go without their supper. Just at that moment, Alys suddenly appeared, popping out from between a group of men right in front of them with an infectious grin on her face that instantly dispersed Sara's anxiety.

"This way please . . . Miss, Sir," she said, leading them through the crowd to the other side of the common room. It was as if the Red Sea had parted in front of them, thought Sara. As Alys led the way, a path seemed to open up before her. A gentle nudge, an 'excuse me, Sir', or a slight push with the shoulder was all that was needed and they were through and out the other side before they could blink. The door she then opened led them into a small but thankfully quiet room.

Seating them at one end of a long refectory table, Alys disappeared through another door, allowing them a brief glimpse of the scullery beyond. A few minutes later and she was back with two large bowls of the promised 'home-cooked' soup. While they fell to their meal with a gusto borne of days on end with not enough to eat, she kept darting in and out, attending to their needs, bringing fresh bread to go with the soup and a large tankard of ale for each of them, and generally ensuring that they had all that they wanted.

The soup itself was not only still warm, as Mrs Forrodeer had promised, but delicious. Sara had no idea what it was, and what's more, she didn't care. It was hearty and tasty and it went down easily, as did the soft chunks of warm, fresh bread, dripping with butter. By the time they were finished, Sara, for the first time in weeks, felt as if she'd eaten enough.

"I think I've had an elegant sufficiency," she said to Rayne, leaning back in her chair with her hand on her stomach. "In fact, any more would be a superfluity." It was a favourite bit of nonsense her family was fond of and it drew the reaction she expected.

"You're what?"

"I'm full," said Sara with a smile, resisting the urge to burp.

While Alys cleared their plates away, Rayne finished his ale. Sara had only sipped at hers. Though she found the taste enticing, it was stronger than the wine she was occasionally allowed at home.

As they rose to leave, Alys' head popped around the doorway. Seeing that they were done, she was about to withdraw when Rayne called her back. Taking some coppers from his pocket he dropped them into the hand she tentatively placed before him. Alys looked up at him with a look of shock on her face.

It was all Sara could do to stop herself from laughing. If they kept on like this the girl would end up owning the place. When Alys looked from Rayne to her, Sara gave her a broad smile and a wink which drew the deepest blush to the young girl's cheeks. Once again, she curtsied awkwardly to them both and then disappeared through the door behind them as fast as she could.

"Feeling generous are we?" asked Sara, suppressing her mirth with some difficulty.

"I felt it was the least I could do given the fuss she made over our supper," replied Rayne. "I think I might have overdone it with two coppers, though. That's probably more than she earns in several days here."

"How many coppers is a silver piece worth?"

"Twenty."

"Oh dear," exclaimed Sara.

"Yes, that's a lot of money here. Look after those few I gave you, we may need them before long."

Sara turned away and pretended to fuss with her handkerchief. "Mmmm. Okay."

CHAPTER 4

Rayne awoke from his sleep with a start. He felt sure he had heard a noise.

The room was dark, but as he opened his eyes he became aware that someone was lying on the bed next to him. Correction. They weren't on the bed. They were in the bed. It was Sara, and she was curled up against him, fast asleep. She hadn't been there when they had turned down the lamp; she'd been in her own bed on the other side of the room. She must have slipped in beside him after he had fallen asleep.

Before he could absorb that thought, he heard the noise that had awoken him again. Someone was knocking somewhere. In fact, now that he was getting some sense of where he was, it sounded like they were knocking on the door to their room.

"Miss, Sir," he heard a female voice call out in a loud whisper that cut through the still, night air. "Wake up."

Rayne glanced at the window. It was still dark outside. Why would anyone want to wake them in the middle of the night? As he sat up in bed, either his movement or the sounds from the door disturbed Sara. She began to stir beside him, rolling over on to her back at first, then mumbling something unintelligible as she began to waken. Rayne was fully alert now and his eyes had adjusted to the darkness of the room. Leaning closer to Sara, he whispered into her ear.

"Sara, wake up. It's me, Rayne. There's someone at the door. Don't make a sound."

The sound of knocking again brought Sara fully awake. "Miss, Sir," came the insistent female voice from the other side of the door.

"What? . . . What?" Sara sat bolt upright in the bed.

"It's okay. I'm here," whispered Rayne, taking hold of her arm to calm her. "Someone's at the door. Grab your knife while I found out who it is."

Slipping out of the bed, Rayne crept over to the window. He had left his gear beside a chair next to the window and he could see his sword leaning against the wall beside it. Picking it up, he drew the blade from its sheath and took a deep breath. His heart was racing, but somehow he felt more secure with the weapon in his hand. As he began to move towards the door, a glance over one shoulder told him that Sara had also found her blade. She was fully awake now too, seated on the edge of the bed and bending down to put her shoes on while still keeping one eye on both him and the door. She had her knife in one hand as she slipped her shoes on with the other. As their eyes met, he smiled grimly, not knowing whether he was trying to reassure her or himself.

"Miss."

The insistent female voice from the other side of the door sounded even more frantic than it had before. "Who is it?" Rayne replied. His own voice was a bare whisper, matching that of the person beyond the door.

"It's Alys, Sir. It's important. You and Miss have to get out of here. Quickly." Alys' voice was urgent, almost frantic, but Rayne could hear relief there as well, even through the closed door between them. Relief that she had finally woken them, he guessed. But was this a trick? Why would they have to get up in the middle of the night?

Gripping his sword tightly, Rayne opened the door. He felt the breath rush out of him at the sight of the young maid, alone, with a lamp in her hand. He'd had visions of a band of burly men, or worse still, sligs, armed to the teeth, standing behind her. But it was only Alys. She was alone, but clearly frightened, looking up at him with wide eyes, then turning quickly to look back down the corridor, before facing him once again.

"What's wrong?" he asked her. "What do you mean, we have to 'get out'?"

"Sir," began Alys, trying to peer around him as she did so. Spying Sara, she nearly broke down, clutching her hand to her chest and gasping back a sob. "Oh, Miss," she gushed. "There are soldiers coming here. You've got to get out, quickly. They're going to arrest you, you and the Master both."

Taking Alys' arm, Rayne quickly drew her into the room, closing the door behind her after a quick glance down the corridor. "Arrest us?" he asked, turning her to face him. "What for? At this time of the day, I mean night. Alys, it's the middle of the night. How do you know, anyway?" The girl's claim didn't make any sense. No one knew they were here, and soldiers were the least of their trouble. It wasn't soldiers he feared, it was sligs, or Tug and his henchmen.

Turning away from Rayne, Alys directed her reply to Sara. She spoke quickly and excitedly, with a clear note of panic in her voice. "It's true, Miss. I was at the baker's just now, picking up the loaves for the morning meal. That's my job, Miss. I have to go down there at three bells every morning. There were soldiers there, Miss, four of them." Alys was wringing her hands as she spoke.

"They were standing around, eating bread and talking. I heard one of them say, Miss. He said they shouldn't be wasting their time getting up at three bells to arrest two runaways, even if one was the daughter of one of the Guardian's servants. He said 'good luck to the young fella', Miss. He said Rayne sounded like a Marcher name and Marcher folk were okay by him, even if they did run off with a bit of skirt. Begging your pardon, Miss, but that's what he said. Then the big one asked Master Wainscott where The Fig Tree Inn was, Miss. I came straight back here fast as I could when I heard that, Miss. Please hurry, Miss. They'll arrest you if they find you here." By the time Alys finished, she was almost distraught, looking from Sara to Rayne and back again and wiping tears from her eyes.

"It's okay, Alys," replied Sara in a soothing voice. She took the young girl's hand in an attempt to calm her as she spoke. "It's not your fault, and you did right to warn us. You must go now or you'll be in trouble too. We'll be all right." Letting go of Alys' hand, she began stuffing her gear into her pack with little apparent thought for how it went in. Rayne could tell from the edge to her voice that she thought they would be anything but 'all right'. Silently, he agreed.

He saw no choice but to follow Sara's lead. Unlike her, he had no soothing words for the girl, however. "We'll never have time, Sara," he blurted out as he rushed back and forth, grabbing clothes and other items which had been left around the room. "We've got to saddle the horses. They must be almost here by now."

"If you hurry, Sir," interrupted Alys, "you can make it." She'd made no attempt to leave when they began packing. "You must. I ran back as hard as I could, Sir. And I took a shortcut. I told Jakeb to saddle your horses, Sir, and to take them down to the tallow maker's. That's two streets away from here. I can show you how to get there, but we must go now." With that, Alys took hold of Sara's arm and began to pull her towards the doorway.

"You're a good girl, Alys, and a good friend," responded Sara, slinging her pack over her shoulder as she followed her out the door. "C'mon Rayne, she's right. Let's go."

Rayne's mind raced as they both rushed out of the room in the young girl's wake. Thank the stars he'd been over-generous with the two coppers he had given her the previous night, he thought. He could only assume the risk she was taking to help them was her way of repaying that munificence.

They were both winded by the time they reached the tallow maker's shop. Alys had taken them down the stairs and out the back door and the three of them had run through the back alleys until they had reached the shop. It had been hard going, running like that with their packs on their back, and Alys had to keep stopping every now and then so they could catch up. She set a fast pace, nonetheless, and they were both relieved when they rounded a corner to find a young lad holding their horses' reins.

"I can't thank you enough for what you've done for us, Alys," gasped Sara between breaths, as Rayne strapped their gear to the back of the horses. "And you too, Jakeb," she said, acknowledging the lad. "Thank you both."

As Sara moved to embrace Alys, Rayne's thoughts were on their next move. "What's the quickest way to the gate?" he asked Jakeb.

"That-a-way, Sir," the boy answered, pointing back over Rayne's shoulder. "But the gates won't be open for some time yet, Sir."

Rayne felt his hopes fall at the youngster's words. The look on Sara's face told him she hadn't thought that far ahead yet either. "What's wrong?" she asked. "Can't we just go there and be first out as soon as they open."

"By that time they'll know we've flown the coop," he replied despondently. "The first thing the soldiers'll do will be to warn the guards at the gates. That's what I'd do, and I'm not even a Ranger. We're trapped." Though he was holding on to the pommel of Ned's saddle, his head was slumped forward and he kicked angrily at the dirt as he spoke. He had no idea what to do. They had to move from where they were, and quickly, but he hadn't the faintest idea where they should go. He had been asleep no more than ten minutes ago and had made no plans for this sort of eventuality.

"He's right, Miss," said Jakeb. "You shouldn't go to the gate."

"But we have to," cried Sara. "What else are we to do? We can't stay here."

"C'mon," said Rayne, trying to calm Sara now she had realised the dilemma they were in. Waiting here was going to get them caught for sure. "They haven't got us yet. We'll find somewhere quiet to lay low for a while, and then we'll find a way to get out without the guards knowing, maybe tonight. There must be a way out of a big town like this without the guards knowing."

Rayne hoped that Sara didn't know him well enough by now to see he didn't really believe what he was saying. They didn't even know how to get to the gate, let alone find somewhere they might hide in the town. Their prospects were dim, to say the least, and no amount of encouraging words was going to change that.

"There are other ways out, Miss," piped up Alys. "Plenty of them. But you can't stay here like this, Miss. The guards must be at the inn by now. They'll start looking for you once they see you've gone."

"She's right, Sara," urged Rayne, as he climbed up onto Ned's back. "We must go, now."

With a final clasp of the maid's hand, Sara silently mounted Nell. As she took a hold of the rein to turn her mount, Alys grabbed a hold of her leg.

"I've got it, Miss. I know where you can go," she cried out excitedly. "My brother will know where to hide you."

Sara turned to look at Rayne, and the silent nod he gave her brought a smile to her face. It was clear to him they had little chance of evading the Rangers without someone to help them. The girl's offer was all they had. They had no choice but to take it. He pushed the fear that they might end up bringing trouble down on Alys' head as well to one side. He couldn't let Sara get caught.

"Thank you, Alys," said Sara, reaching down and clasping the young maid's hand. "Once again we owe you our gratitude. How can we find your brother?"

"I'll take you there, Miss. Here, Jakeb, help me get up behind." In a moment, Alys had clambered up behind Sara and they were away.

With the young girl directing their progress, they made good speed. Rayne tried to maintain some sense of where they were going but he soon realised that it was impossible; he had no real point of reference to start from. They had travelled from the gate to the inn the evening before largely in darkness, and the wild flight from the inn to the tallow maker's shop had only served to further disorient what little sense he had of where they were in the town. There was nothing for it now but to trust their guide.

At first, his thoughts wandered through the implications of this new crisis that had been so unexpectedly thrust upon them, just when they were beginning to think they had finally won clear of pursuit. From what Alys had overheard the guards saying, it was clear someone had concocted a story about them that had set the Algarian Rangers on their trail.

For a few moments, Rayne considered if there could be any truth behind what they had said. Was Sara, in fact, really just the runaway daughter of one of the Guardian's servants? That would certainly explain a lot that had happened. But no, he chided himself, he refused to believe that Sara had lied to him. He didn't sense any duplicity in the girl at all; quite the opposite in fact. And why would Tug and his men have tried to kill them both if that was the case? And what about the sligs, why would they be after them?

He quickly pushed the notion aside, berating himself as he did so for even considering such an idea. No, the story was an invention, put about by Tug perhaps, or even Golkar, to enlist the aid of the authorities in tracking them down. This was a dangerous turn of events. Until now, it had been sligs and draghar that had been after them. With the Rangers pursuing them as well, they were surely doomed. Though he felt his own hopes rapidly sinking, Rayne realised that he couldn't let Sara know how slim he thought their chances now were. He couldn't bear to think of what that would do to her.

At least there was no sign of pursuit from the guards as yet, he thought, taking a deep breath and trying to find something positive to latch on to. They seemed to have managed to give them the slip for the moment, and each step their horses took was increasing what had already become a healthy distance between themselves and the inn.

Looking about, he could see their surroundings were gradually changing. The area around the inn had abounded with artisan's shops. From the increasing number of warehouses and stores they were now passing, Rayne guessed that Alys was leading them into the commercial quarter of Novistor. While most of the establishments were closed at this early hour, in a few, the day's activities had already begun. The commercial warehouses, in particular, were a hive of activity. Around these, carters and hauliers were busy loading their wagons for the longer trips to be made as soon as the gates were opened. The runners, he could see, had already begun their local hauls.

Rayne knew from stories his father had told him that the job of the latter was to carry small loads to the local businesses, either on their back, if it was a sack of meal or grain, or on small carts, if the load was a little larger. His father had told him that theirs was a gruelling task. Only the desperate took on this work, and they didn't last long. The burn out rate was appalling.

The first rays of the rising sun were only just now beginning to soften the morning sky and yet the runners would have been about their business for some time already. For most, the signal that their work for the day was done wouldn't come until the evening bell that heralded the closing of the gates and the lighting of the lamps. Whatever errand they were on then would be their last, though they would be up and at it again before sunrise on the morrow. And all this for a pittance a day. Labour was cheap, and for those who thought the work too demanding for such little recompense, there were many more ready to take their place. Life was tough, no less so here in the big towns than out on the Marches.

It was to a lane at the rear of one of these big warehouses that Alys eventually led them. The two large wooden doors that fronted the lane were open and a wagon could be seen jutting out slightly into the lane itself. Four more wagons were lined up outside, waiting their turn. A small gang of men were loading large crates on to the first wagon under the direction of a small, balding man with a barking voice. When Alys left them at the entrance and disappeared inside the building, neither the workers nor the overseer paid Rayne or Sara any heed. The men simply continued about their task with an efficiency obviously borne of years of experience. Very few words passed between them; it seemed that the task they were about was one with which they were all familiar. Looking up, Rayne could see a name, 'Johnson and Haddir, Long Haulage Contractors', written in large, fading, red letters above the big double doors.

"Maybe we can get out with some of these wagons," whispered Sara to Rayne after they had been watching for a few moments.

Rayne nodded slowly. "Maybe," he replied. "Though we'll still need horses. I'm sure it can be done. The question is whether we can find someone to show us how."

It didn't take long for Alys to return, and when she did she motioned for them to follow her into the warehouse and to bring their horses with them. They quickly did as she said, finding that the building was much bigger than they had imagined it to be from the outside. As their eyes adjusted to the darkness of the interior, they could see that the structure comprised a wide central avenue on either side of which were stacked all manner of paraphernalia, most of it in crates and barrels stacked higgledy-piggledy around the sides of the warehouse. Here and there, ladders ascended, disappearing through small trapdoors to an apparent upper level. Alys led them to a row of stalls at the rear of the building where she helped them to tether and unsaddle Nell and Ned.

"My brother will help you, Miss," she assured Sara, as she helped her to dismount.

"Thank God," replied Sara. "I don't know what we would have done without your help, Alys. I'm not sure we deserve it. I do know that I can't thank you enough, though."

"It's fine, Miss," replied the girl as a blush began to cover her face. "Good people have to help good people. That's what Mrs Forrodeer always says. I knew Jon would help. He's the best brother a girl could have. He'll look after your horses too, Miss. He's a marker here. He said he's got a spot where you can spend the day, no questions asked. He also knows someone who can get you both out of the city after sundown. I'll come back and bring you something to eat when I can later in the day."

"You've been too kind to us," replied Sara. "I really am worried about your safety. Will you be all right back at the inn? Do you think there'll be any trouble for you there over this?"

"Oh no, Miss. Mrs Forrodeer will make a big fuss when she hears what's happened. She got all weepy talking about you last night. Said you and the Master reminded her of herself and Mr Forrodeer. Said she eloped too when she was your age."

Rayne saw Sara smile at the girl's comment. "We haven't eloped, Alys," she responded. "Nothing as romantic as that." Then, leaning conspiratorially towards the girl, she spoke in a softer voice, though not so soft that Rayne couldn't hear what she said. "Though if I was going to elope, Rayne's just the sort of man I'd want to elope with."

He felt himself blush as Sara turned and gave him a grin and a wink. Alys looked at him too, and then turned back to Sara with a matching grin when she saw him blushing. When the two girls both giggled together, he thought his face must be turning scarlet.

Luckily, Alys' brother turned up before he could be put through any further embarrassment. Once Alys had introduced them, she rushed off, anxious to get back to the inn. Jon then asked them to follow him, saying he would show them where they could spend the day well away from prying eyes. Within a few moments, they found themselves clambering up a wooden ladder which led to the upper level.

The loft was both dusty and dark but somehow reassuring in its isolation. Jon led them to a quiet spot, hidden from view by some old wooden chests in the unlikely event that anyone did venture up there. He assured them that, though he had taken this precaution, it was really quite unnecessary. No one other than him ever came up to the upper level any more and they could wait out the day there in total safety. He also told them he would be back once it was dark with someone who could help them to get out of the town. With that, he left them.

True to her word, Alys returned in the middle of the day with a small basket of food, a few pieces of bread, some cheese and some fruit. Jon accompanied her.

Rayne was glad to see her, and he could see that Sara was too. It was the only human contact the two fugitives had had all day and their wait had been a long and a worrying one, despite Jon's assurances. Rayne didn't feel at all secure knowing their safety now lay entirely in the hands of strangers.

At least he trusted Alys. Thank Mishra for her, he thought. Without her help, who knows where they would be. Caught, that much was for sure, though what the Rangers would do with them if they did catch up with them was much less clear. Of course, he and Sara would deny whatever story Tug and his men must have concocted. Rayne knew enough about how things went in Ilythia, however, to know that their word would count for little against that of a servant of Golkar. He remembered how sceptical he himself had been when Sara had first told him what had happened to her. It was only when Tug and his men had tried to kill them at the falls that he had truly believed a Guardian could do such a thing.

He knew they had no choice now but to put their trust in Alys' brother as well. It seemed that choices were something they had long since relinquished a right to. Events just seemed to sweep them along, like a stream in flood. Once more, they would just have to go with the flow and see where their fate took them.

While Rayne and Sara ate, Jon explained that he had a friend who could show them a way out of the town without their being questioned by the Rangers. It would cost them a few silvers, but the route, he assured them, was relatively safe.

It seemed that, although the main gate was closed at night, it was always attended by two guards. Jon's friend, Kip, knew from experience that the two guards who had that shift at the moment were eminently bribeable. Kip had acted as a go-between for such deals a number of times and apparently he had agreed to lead them to the gate and to help them transact the deal. He would return with Jon later that evening, once the town was quiet and bedded down for the night. And so they were left to wait again.

Neither of them slept during the course of the afternoon; they just sat together in the darkness of the loft, holding hands and exchanging the occasional few words. The sun set and still they waited. It was so dark in the loft that Rayne could no longer see Sara, even when she crawled over to him and lay down with her head in his lap. He could smell her wonderfully distinctive odour, however. That and the silky feeling of her hair as he ran his hands through it more than made up for his loss of sight.

They stayed like that for some time. When Rayne eventually removed his hand, Sara spoke for the first time in hours. "Please don't stop," she said. "I like that."

And so they waited, chatting infrequently, quiet as field mice the rest of the time, both lost in their own thoughts. Finally, when Rayne was beginning to wonder if they had been forgotten altogether, Jon returned. As soon as Rayne saw the flicker of lantern light and heard Jon's soft whistle, he helped Sara up and they set about getting their few belongings together.

Rayne's joints were stiff from hours of inactivity and he could see in the soft light of the lantern that Sara was in no better condition than he was. They knew they had to get going, however. After a few quick stretches, they slung their gear over their shoulders and scampered after Jon as he led the way to the ladder.

Downstairs, they were pleased to find Alys waiting to farewell them. What a friend she had turned out to be, thought Rayne with wonder. Mrs Forrodeer had sent some fresh fruit and bread for them, as well as two pieces of game pie, straight from her own oven. The latter were hastily devoured while the other items were stowed in their packs for later. Then, after a tearful farewell between Sara and Alys, they were on their way.

Their new companion, Kip, took the lead. He was a slender lad, very similar in build and height to Rayne, though a year or two younger. Rayne noticed that the boy even had his hair tied back in a ponytail in a similar fashion to his own. That, however, was where the similarity ended.

Where Rayne was nervous and unsure of himself in the narrow streets of the town, the boy was street-smart in a way that Rayne could never dream to be. Right from the moment he had been introduced to them, Rayne had seen that if the lad lacked anything, it wasn't confidence. Even the way he had stood as he had been introduced, with his thumbs hooked into his belt and his head cocked to one side as he silently appraised them, had bespoken a confidence Rayne could only envy.

But Rayne had been decidedly unimpressed at the way he had flirted tentatively with Sara. Even the obvious rebuff she had given him hadn't fazed him, though it had brought a smile to Rayne's face.

Like him or not, though, he was now their guide, and all their hopes rested on his abilities. Despite his quirkiness, he gave every impression of knowing exactly what he was doing. Rayne hoped his over-abundant self-confidence was well founded and not just a façade.

They travelled by foot at first. Kip led the way, followed by Sara with Nell in tow and Rayne and Ned bringing up the rear. The lad kept them close to the buildings, hugging the shadows in the dim light of the night sky. Though it was a cloudless night, the moon hadn't risen. The stars were their only source of light, but it was enough, in fact, it was ideal; too much light would only have hindered their progress. Their goal was to make their way to the gate with the minimum of fuss and attention, and so they stuck to the laneways, crossing the bigger streets only when they had to.

Rayne was tense from the moment they set out. On more than one occasion he had to force his muscles to relax, only to find moments later that he had tightened up yet again. The narrow streets made him nervous and he felt completely disoriented in what was to him an alien environment. They had been through tighter spots in the wilderness, but he had always felt in control there. Here, he was totally dependent on the skills of others. He had never had to do that before.

As he was bringing up the rear, he was constantly looking over his shoulder, checking to make sure that they weren't being followed. At the same time, he was on the alert for any unusual sounds. The darkness provided them with welcome cover, but the fact that they were alone on the streets made the noise of their passing seem intolerably loud to him. To add to this, the town itself was unnaturally quiet. In the forest, there was always some noise, even in the dead of night. Here, there was nothing; nothing at all except the sound of their steps. All he could do was keep his ears and eyes open. Kip was their guide and he gave every appearance of being relaxed and in control of the situation.

Despite Rayne's concerns, all went well. A few stray cats and one rat were their only companions. Eventually, they were obliged to follow one of the major thoroughfares for a short way. Kip said that they couldn't cover the whole of the route to the gate without at least some brief usage of the major by-ways. In a few stretches, they would just have to do so and hope not to be seen. This particular street seemed safe enough to Rayne. They waited for a short while in the shadows of the alley they had been following, and then, when they were satisfied that all was quiet, they ventured out into the wider way.

Rayne could feel his apprehension rising. In the forest, this would be the equivalent, he guessed, of crossing an open clearing or a stream. He couldn't help reaching up involuntarily to feel his arm as he remembered the stream they had crossed in the wilderness and the encounter with the sligs that had followed. There was no pain there any longer, but the thought was a dark one and he tried to suppress it, pushing it back into the recesses of his mind from where it had sprung. That kind of memory was not going to do them any good here.

His trepidation soon proved warranted, however. They hadn't gone far down this particular concourse when, of all the things they could have encountered, a troop of some dozen or so Rangers appeared out of a side way, only some forty or fifty paces away, and began to march right down the middle of the street. They were heading straight towards them.

Luckily, the three fugitives were still hugging the shadows close to the buildings and they quickly flattened themselves against the wooden wall beside them. Sara turned to look at Rayne and her unspoken message was as clear as if she had shouted it. 'What will we do?' the look of panic on her face said to him. She was obviously ready to take flight at the slightest sign from him. To his surprise, whatever he was feeling himself, the look he gave her seemed to reassure her.

When he looked beyond her to their guide, however, he had to struggle to keep a rein on his own nerves. The desperate look on Kip's face as his head darted back and forth, obviously looking for a means of escape from the jam they were in, confirmed what he had already feared. Unless they did something soon, they would be seen within a matter of minutes.

Before Rayne's thoughts could go any further, Kip turned to them both and signalled with a wave of his hand for them to stay put. Once he was satisfied his message had been understood, he slowly ambled out into the middle of the street, heading straight towards the Rangers with his head down and his hands in his pockets, as if he wasn't even aware they were there. Rayne motioned for Sara to stay put. As they edged back even further into the shadow of the building beside them, his eyes remained fixed on Kip and the approaching Rangers.

The youngster sauntered down the deserted street until he was no more than ten or fifteen paces away from the Rangers, then looked up, as if in surprise, and suddenly turned and bolted down a side alley Rayne hadn't even realised was there. Without a moment's hesitation, the Rangers, to a man, took off in hot pursuit, with cries of "Halt" and "Come back here you." Within a few moments the whole lot of them, Kip included, had disappeared from sight, the cries of the soldiers barely audible now as they receded into the distance. Rayne looked at Sara and saw that she was just as stunned at this sudden turn of events as he was.

"What do we do now?" she whispered.

At first, he was at a loss for words. He had no idea where they were, let alone what direction the gate was in, or how to negotiate a way through it once they got there. As to what they should do next. He had been happy to let Kip be their guide and hadn't even considered an eventuality like this.

"I . . . I guess . . . I guess we should try and backtrack to the warehouse. I don't know whether I'm sure of how to find our way back there, but I do know we'd have no chance of finding the gate without Kip. We'd just wander around until eventually we were caught by someone. Oh, Sara. I think I've got us into a very bad situation here."

Rayne could feel himself beginning to tremble. His worst fears were materialising before his very eyes. He was out of his element here and Sara was counting on him to get them out of trouble. Yet again he was letting her down. Only, this time, they were really in a mess. And Josef wasn't around to pull them out of this hole.

"It's okay, Rayne," soothed Sara, moving alongside him and placing her hand on his. "You didn't get us into this situation. If anyone's to blame, I am. If it weren't for me you'd be sitting safe and warm somewhere; not out here in a jam with me. I think you're right. We should try and go back. There's nothing else we can do. If we work together, we might be able to remember the way."

"Okay." Rayne knew he had to get a grip on himself. Sara's calmer tone of voice had made him realise he was on the verge of making an even bigger fool of himself than he already felt. He could sense that she was worried too, but that she was masking her feelings in an attempt to help him to calm down. That's what he should have been doing for her. What would his father think of him now?

"Okay," he repeated. "Let's get back into the alleyway. We'll be seen if we stay here."

Just as they began to move out of the shadows, back in the direction of the alley they had come from, they heard a sound. It came from the alley Kip and the Rangers had disappeared down. Before they had a chance to react, a person came running out of the alley and into the street. Instinctively, Rayne's hand went for his sword, but he had no more than half drawn it from its scabbard when he saw that the person was none other than Kip. He was breathing hard, but he had a broad grin on his face as he came to a halt in front of them.

"I gave 'em the slip," he said with a wink. "There's not many can catch me at the best of times, 'specially not in the dark. Let's get out of here, quickly."

As he turned and headed back along the route they had been following before their encounter with the Rangers, Rayne and Sara quickly moved to follow his lead. Kip led them at a cracking pace now, walking so fast they almost had to run to keep up with him. Neither of them complained. Rayne, for one, saw the lad in a different light now. Whatever failings he might have, he certainly had some nerve. Besides, they didn't have time for recriminations or debates. It was clear that they had to get as far away from where they had encountered the Rangers as possible, and as quickly as they could.

Despite the pace, Rayne now made a very conscious effort to try and take notice of the route they were following. Whenever they took a change in direction, he looked around for some distinguishing feature that might remind him where they had been should they have to retrace their steps. Better late than never, he thought. Although this wouldn't guarantee their ability to find their way back without Kip, it would at least give them some chance. He needn't have bothered, as it turned out, though. They made the remaining distance to the gate without a further encounter, unless you counted two dogs and one snoring drunk, the latter blissfully asleep propped up against the side of a building.

When they finally turned a corner to find the gate only a few paces away, Sara stopped and turned around. Though she was smiling, Rayne could see the tears in her eyes as she walked back to where he was. As she approached him, he reached out and drew her into his open arms.

"It's all right, we made it," he whispered, as she hugged him to her tightly. He could feel his own emotions welling up within his own breast. The whole journey from the warehouse to the gate had felt like walking a tightrope.

A discreet cough from Kip interrupted their brief moment together. "I need ten silvers for the guard," he informed Rayne, almost apologetically. "That's the usual fee."

Rayne was in no mood to haggle over price; he assumed that Kip knew his business. Though ten silvers was a lot of money, what they were doing wouldn't be without some risk to the guards as well. They would also know that anyone desperate enough to seek to leave the town in this manner would undoubtedly be more than willing to pay for the privilege.

Kip put out his hand to take the silvers that Rayne counted out from his purse. After slipping them into the pocket of his breeches, he told them to wait in the shadow of a nearby building.

With a quick look back in the direction they had come from, he turned and crossed the street, heading for the door of a small wooden building which was butted up against the wall, just to the left of the big gates themselves. Rayne guessed that this must be the guardhouse. Though the wooden shutter on the small window facing the street was closed, thin strips of light could still be seen between small cracks in the woodwork. Someone was awake inside.

He watched as Kip tapped three times on the door. A moment later, the door opened, spilling light out into the street. After a brief exchange with the occupant of the building, Kip entered and the door closed behind him.

Rayne and Sara waited nervously in the cold night air. Rayne guessed that this was a critical point. Kip hadn't said whether he had already struck an agreement with the guards or whether the 'deal' was to be transacted on the spot. Everything he had said had led Rayne to believe the latter to be the case, however. He wondered what Kip would do if the usual guards weren't on duty. What if they weren't interested in any 'deal' and suddenly came rushing out to arrest them? The shiver that ran down his back then wasn't just from the cool night air.

He had barely begun to turn his mind to thoughts of some rough plan for a quick escape should they need it, when the door of the guardhouse opened and Kip came out followed by the two guards. "C'mon," he whispered across to Rayne and Sara. "Hurry up. They're going to open it up." As he spoke, the two guards walked over to the gate. Taking hold of a handle beside the large beams that formed the frame of the entryway, they began to work the mechanism which raised the iron grille which barred the gateway.

Sara and Rayne looked about nervously, concerned at the noise the mechanism made in the quiet of the night. It seemed inconceivable that half the surrounding area wouldn't hear what was going on. Perhaps whoever lived within earshot of the gates was used to such goings on, thought Rayne. Or maybe they simply knew better than to interfere with what was none of their business.

The task was soon completed, however, and with the gate finally open Rayne and Sara took their leave of Kip, thanking him for his help and asking him to pass on their thanks to Jakeb and Alys. Rayne gave Sara a helping hand up onto Nell and then quickly mounted Ned. As he turned his mount around, towards the gateway, a voice suddenly rang out through the darkness.

"Halt right there, you two. You're under arrest. Don't give us any trouble now."

Looking around, Rayne was dismayed to see a half dozen or so Rangers blocking the street behind them. Any thoughts of escape quickly evaporated as he turned his head back to the gates themselves. Several more Rangers had appeared from outside the walls and were blocking the open gateway. A number of them had bows drawn with arrows ready to shoot.

They were trapped, trapped and caught.

CHAPTER 5

Looking down at the sleeping girl beside him, Thom couldn't help but wonder how she would fare once the war was over. Once it was over! Would it ever be over?

In the course of their journey, he had considered all of the different courses the war might take and had resolved very early on in the piece to focus only on the most positive of all possible outcomes, the eventual Algarian victory he was certain would roll the sligs right back to their ancestral grounds. He had to believe that. How else could he deal with the horrors they had seen over the last few days?

Together, he and Jinny had seen sights which would unnerve the most battle-hardened veteran. To accept that this might continue, that it was more than just the devastating impact of a surprise initial onslaught, that what they had seen here might soon be repeated right across the whole of Algaria, that was just too ghastly a thought to contemplate. No, as far as he was concerned it wasn't a matter of if but of how long it would take before the Algarians rallied and completely reversed the current situation.

So how would Jinny fare then, once the war was over and things returned to normal? Her father was dead; that much seemed certain. Her mother was also gone, lost to fever some two years ago now, and Thom had never heard of any brothers or sisters. What few other relatives she did have were likely to have fallen with the rest of the unfortunate souls at Brand's Ford.

She would be a war orphan, that's what she would be. Thom would have to look after her, if she would have him. Together they could build a new life together. His da would help them, and his ma. His parents would both be all right, of course. They had got out in time, not like some. Most likely they were sitting out the fighting quietly in Kurandir right now, taking it easy for a change after all the hard work getting that crop in.

The truth be known, his da had been working too hard for far too long now anyway. He needed a rest. He had talked of making the trip to Kurandir many times over the years, but somehow he had just never got around to it. Well, now he had.

Kurandir. He and Jinny should be there by morning. It wasn't far now, though it had taken them much longer than he had thought it would to get there. He hadn't counted on how many sligs there would be. What's more, rather than thinning out as he had thought they would the closer he got to Kurandir, the opposite seemed to be the case. He couldn't figure what that meant. Maybe, he thought, with sudden insight, maybe the Rangers were massing there for the big Algarian assault. That would explain this build-up of slig forces. That would be very good news, and something to see.

But what of his parents? The Rangers wouldn't want a whole bunch of refugees filling up the town if they were regrouping there. Most likely, the civilians would have to be sent further west. His parents may have just had to keep going until they were well out of harm's way.

Thom let out a deep sigh. Though he longed to reach the protective walls of Kurandir, he had hoped to be reunited there with his da as well. Well, 'no use thatching the roof till the walls are up', as his da would say. One thing at a time. First, let's just get there, he thought, and then we'll see what's going on.

The dwindling light told Thom that it would soon be time to wake Jinny. As soon as the sun set for the day, they needed to be on their way again. Travelling by night wasn't easy, especially with no moon to light their way, and he meant to get as early a start as he could. With luck, this should be their last leg. Tomorrow night he hoped they would be sleeping safe and sound with the Queen's Rangers on lookout duty instead of he or Jinny.

Jinny. Just the thought of her made him smile. Gently he reached down and brushed back a lock of hair that had fallen across his companion's forehead. "It's time to wake up, Jinny," he whispered, leaning down close to her.

Though the spot they had chosen to spend the daylight hours in was well concealed, Thom had grown accustomed to caution. The little hollow they had crept into, with its surrounding thicket of bushes, provided the two essential qualities they had learnt to covet, concealment from prying eyes and shade from the sun. Some small animal, a bush hog, or a nerricoot, or something very similar to that in size, had probably spent the day cursing them for stealing its bed. Or maybe it would return when night fell to reclaim its home. No matter, for now, it was theirs and they were glad to have it.

Jinny sat up with a start. Like Thom, she had slept lightly over the past few days and it took only the slightest of noises to bring her fully awake.

"Is everything okay?" she whispered, placing one hand on his arm as she twisted her head back and forth, scanning the surrounding area, alert to the prospect of danger.

Thom's heart went out to his friend. If her tone did little to conceal her fear, the wild look in her eyes certainly confirmed it.

"We're safe," he answered her softly. Lifting her arm, he placed his hand in hers and gave it a gentle squeeze. "We must be moving on soon. The sun's almost set. There's time enough for a quick bite to eat, and some water, and then we better get going. We can be in Kurandir before the sun rises if we get a wriggle on tonight."

"Oh. I got such a fright just then." Jinny turned to face Thom as she spoke. Her wide eyes glistened in the soft light of the dusk. "I was having a bad dream, a very bad dream."

"It's okay," said Thom soothingly. He could see she was on the verge of tears. Reaching out, he drew her into his arms and held her slender body against his chest.

"I dreamt we were back at that farm we saw last night," she sobbed, releasing her hold on her emotions as she clung to him tightly. "We turned over the body of that man we found there and . . . and it . . . it was my pa. His eyes were open . . . but he was dead Thom. He was dead."

With that, Jinny burst into tears, releasing all the emotion she had been struggling to contain. Her body jerked violently against his as she buried her face in the crook of his shoulder. Thom held her tightly to him, stroking the back of her head and speaking to her softly, trying to soothe her with calm words.

"It's all right Jinny. It was only a dream. Your da would want you to be strong now. You know that. We're going to be all right. Wherever your da is, whether he's safe somewhere or whether Mishra has called him we don't know, but he'd want you to make him proud. I'll look after you now. It'll be okay."

His words seemed to have the desired effect. Sitting back again, Jinny wiped her eyes with her sleeve and took in a few deep breaths. Thom placed a hand under her chin and gently lifted her downcast face till she looked him in the eye once more. "You okay?" he asked as she used the back of her palm to wipe back another tear that had trickled from the corner of her eye. Jinny nodded, and then managed to force the briefest of smiles in response.

"Thank you," she said after a few moments. "I'm sorry. It was so real. I was so scared."

"I know. I have those dreams too. It's best not to think of things like that right now. C'mon, let's eat."

Jinny was only too happy to accept the small pieces of dried meat and the bread that Thom had laid out beside them. The bread was stale, but she knew that it and the meat were all that were on offer. Their supply of food had run right down, so much so that they had only enough left for one more small meal. Water wasn't a problem; they had found plenty of opportunities to fill up their flasks along the way. Food, though, was scarce. What little had been left behind by the departing Algarians had invariably been looted by the sligs. It was a good thing they would be in Kurandir on the morrow, thought Thom. As if eluding the sligs wasn't enough of a problem by itself.

They ate their meal in silence, and when they were done they rose from their resting spot and moved on. Though it was tempting to stay where they were and sleep right through the coming night, they both knew what had to be done. Somehow they found the energy for a final effort and for the first few hours they made good progress. The knowledge that they were getting closer to their goal seemed to lighten their step.

To Thom's surprise, it was some time before they saw more sligs. The course that he led them steered clear of the small hamlets and farmhouses that dotted the area they were traversing. He wanted to spare Jinny any further distress if he could. She had seen enough corpses in the last few days to last her a lifetime, they both had, and, if anything, the sight was only getting harder and harder to bear. The bodies they found in and around the deserted houses now were invariably bloated from days of exposure to the elements. Too often, the corpses had been mutilated as well. Many of the victims had clearly been tortured before they'd been killed. Thom knew that some of the images he and Jinny had seen would stay with them for the rest of their lives. The fact that they were avoiding the farmhouses had the added benefit of keeping them clear of the spots most likely to be frequented by the invaders. Their very caution, however, was what eventually led to them becoming careless.

It must have been close to midnight by Thom's reckoning, and he had decided he would call a halt for a short rest once they cleared the small ridge they were ascending. They had nearly reached the crest, and Thom had turned to look back and confirm his bearings, when it happened. His eyes scanned the slope behind them, searching for the old rotted tree he had been using as a landmark during their ascent.

"We'll rest soon," he whispered to Jinny as she passed him by. She had been trudging along in his wake for most of the evening and obviously wanted to get the climb over and done with before she stopped for a breather. A few moments later, just as his eyes caught sight of the blackened stump of the tree he'd been searching for, Jinny's scream pierced through the night air. Instinctively turning his head in the direction of her voice, Thom was nearly bowled over as the girl came bolting back down the hill towards him.

"Sligs. Run." she shouted as she sprinted past him, back in the direction they had come from. The look on her face was one of sheer terror. Even in the dark of the night, Thom could see the outline of the huge warrior that was scrambling down the hillside in hot pursuit. He wasn't far behind her, perhaps a dozen paces, no more.

It all happened so quickly. Before he could think, Jinny had passed him and he had quickly turned and sprinted after her. "Run Thom," she gasped as she flew down the hill, as if he needed any encouragement. The roar from the warrior behind him told him that death was only paces behind him. He felt something touch his back and the fear that gripped him then gave him the strength to surge forward. He ran as he had never run before in his life. As fast as he ran though, Jinny was outstripping him.

There was no time to think; it was all he could do just to make sure that he didn't lose his footing in the dark. The cracking of twigs and branches from behind told him the warrior wasn't far in his wake, but he didn't dare break his stride to look back. The only thought he had seemed to repeat itself over and over again in his head. *Don't fall*, it said. *I mustn't fall. Jinny, please, please, please, don't fall. Just run.*

And run she did, like the wind. And so did he. After a while, he didn't know how long, he began to tire. They had almost reached the bottom of the ridge and his breathing was becoming labored, but still he dare not stop. Somehow, he willed himself to keep going. A quick glance over his shoulder was of no help. He was running too hard to get a proper look and he dare not stop or slow down long enough to see whether they were gaining or losing their desperate race. At any moment he feared the slig might reach out and grab him, or its cold blade would cleave into his back.

Jinny had actually drawn some distance ahead of him and it was only when she stumbled that he finally began to catch up to her. She regained her footing quickly, but it was enough to allow him to close the gap. She was obviously tiring too. The trees were thinning out and soon there would be a fence to negotiate. He remembered them clambering over it some time earlier. Eventually, he knew he had to slow enough to risk a look over his shoulder, and he did so. There was no sign of the slig. He kept running anyway.

"I think we might have lost him," he gasped to Jinny as he drew level with her. Their pace had slowed considerably now, though neither was prepared to stop as yet. They kept going like that for some time, gradually slowing down, and looking back for the slig frequently. There was still no sign of the creature. Thom began to think the beast might have given up the chase. Finally, they had to stop. They had almost reached the point of exhaustion.

They stood for a while, gasping and wheezing, bent from the waist with their hands braced against their thighs, both desperately trying to replace the oxygen they had just so flagrantly consumed. Neither of them could take their eyes away from where they had come from. The slig was back there somewhere and they both knew it. Perhaps he had given up the chase. They had certainly flown like the wind, but maybe he was still out there looking for them. Maybe he had just slowed to get his breath as well.

"Let's go," said Thom. He was still gasping for air but he dare not stay where they were. Jinny was in no better condition than he was, but they both knew the danger of standing still. They took a right angle turn from the course they had been following before they had seen the slig. There was no going back, but they couldn't follow the line they had been taking either. They moved along in silence and at as quick a pace as they could manage, stopping frequently to listen for sounds of pursuit. Thom knew that his heart was still racing. He was tired, and he longed to lie down on the ground, but they had to keep going. Jinny couldn't be in any better shape than he was.

He couldn't credit what a close call they had just had. They had put a foot in the very jaws of death and somehow managed to escape. Just how many close encounters could they hope to survive? Surely their luck would run out at some point soon.

It must have been hours before they finally halted for a proper rest. They saw no further sign of the slig, or of any other sligs for that matter. They were both totally exhausted, and when they stopped, they just lay down on the ground, right where they were. Thom's legs were aching. He heard Jinny's voice from beside him as he stretched his aching limbs.

"Wh . . . what'll w . . . we do, Thom?" She could barely speak. Though she must have been as tired as he was, the sound of fear in her voice was unmistakable. She was still scared out of her wits.

"We've lost him now. I'm sure of it," he replied. "I know that was too close for comfort, Jinny, but we got away. No one could have caught you the way you flew down that hill. It was all I could do to keep up with you."

"You . . . you've got to promise me, Thom. Promise me you won't let them catch us."

Thom rolled over and took a hold of Jinny's arm. Looking into her eyes and in the most solemn voice he could manage, he responded to her request, knowing as he did so he had no way of ensuring he could deliver.

"I promise, Jinny. I won't let them catch us. I'm sorry. I made a big mistake back there. I should have been much more careful. They aren't going to get us, Jinny. They aren't."

That seemed to quieten her. She said nothing for a few moments, and when she spoke again it was in the barest of a whisper. "Hold me, Thom. Hold on to me, please. I'm so scared."

The dawn had already arrived by the time they made their final approach to Kurandir. Though their mad race from the slig warrior had been their only sighting of the enemy throughout the course of the night, that encounter had been enough to ensure they had proceeded with the utmost caution from that point on.

Thom had wanted them in Kurandir before the sun had risen, but that was no longer possible. Though they could see as far east as the Giant's Teeth from their vantage point atop the plateau, the fiery orb hadn't yet shown its face above the horizon. It could only be moments away from doing so, however, and the land was awash with the soft glow of the impending dawn.

He and Jinny weren't that far behind schedule after all. Once they reached the edge of the escarpment, Kurandir would be but a few leagues to the west. They should have a clear view of it from that vantage point and the trip down to the gates wouldn't take them long from there.

It was time to move forward once more. They had waited and watched for a while but had seen no sign of the sligs anywhere on the plateau. Thom was glad to find it so on two counts: as well as ensuring their own safety, he knew it meant that the invaders were not attacking Kurandir. If any such attack had occurred, then they had either pulled out or been forced back from the town.

Thom had heard enough about military strategy to know that if an assault had been underway, the plateau, and the escarpment in particular, with its commanding view of the valley that harboured Kurandir, would be a vital strategic point. It would have been crawling with sligs. The fact that it wasn't was a clear indication Kurandir was not only still safely in the hands of the Rangers, but it was under no immediate threat of assault. It was possible the sligs had simply passed it by, but Thom preferred to believe they had suffered a defeat here.

Moving out from their hiding place, the two weary travellers slowly made their way westward, towards the edge of the escarpment. Though every indication was that they were no longer in any danger, they stuck to their routine, moving slowly, from cover to cover, keeping low to the ground to ensure that their silhouettes didn't show up on the horizon. As they moved forward, Thom began to feel the first twinges of doubt.

Over the last few hours, the glow in the western sky had helped guide them to their goal. Thom guessed that the glow was sourced in the fires of the Algarian troops that would be billeted in and around Kurandir. Now, for the first time, he saw the plumes of smoke that were drifting up into the cool morning air from the valley ahead of them. It seemed more than he would have expected for just the cooking fires of the troops.

Slowly they approached the edge of the escarpment. The last few paces led them to a rocky ledge. As they crawled across the cool stone surface, something told Thom to maintain his caution and he motioned for Jinny to keep her head down. Together, they edged themselves up to the precipice and peered over the edge.

Thom could do nothing to choke back the cry he unwittingly released as he saw what lay before them. There lay Kurandir, nestled in the floor of the valley, just as he had expected. All of his hopes and all of his expectations were dashed, however, in that one moment, as he looked down on the town to which his parents had fled. No army lay encamped around its perimeter. No gleam of metal shone from the helms of the defenders as they manned the walls, alert to the prospect of attack. No flag fluttered proudly from atop its battlements.

Kurandir was a smoking ruin. It had been all but burnt to the ground. Even from this distance, he could recognise the bodies of both Algarians and sligs that littered the ground around its shattered walls. Not a living soul was to be seen in the whole of the valley. Black plumes of smoke drifted lazily up from the remains of the many fires that had all but burnt themselves out. Kurandir had fallen. The invaders had sacked it and moved on.

~~~

A loud rumble pealed across the valley, battering Kell's eardrums as it passed. Desperately the wizard fought to maintain his seat as the gryphon beneath him struggled to maintain both height and airspeed in the aftermath of the lightning bolt's passage. It wasn't enough to avoid being struck by the bolts themselves, for the buffeting that followed was equally as dangerous. More than once already, the winged beast and his rider had barely avoided being dashed against the rocky crags along the eastern side of the valley by the treacherous aftermath of a bolt's passage.

Somehow, Thyfur rode out the buffeting from this latest missile. *How much longer can we last like this?* wondered Kell. It was all he could do not to raise a hand to the searing pain that arced across his scalp. The burn was hellishly painful, and he knew from the red streaks that smeared his arm where he had brushed his cheek that blood was running freely down the side of his face as well. Though Kell couldn't be certain of the exact extent of the beast's wounds from where he sat, he could tell that Thyfur was faring little better than he was.

That his renegade colleague had their measure now was obvious to the Guardian. That Thyfur was tiring rapidly was equally certain. The gryphon's wounds were beginning to take their toll. The battle, which had started out so well for Kell and his comrade, had now turned decisively in Golkar's favour. With a wrench of despair, Kell realised there was no choice but to beat a retreat before his adversary finished them.

As quickly as the decision was made, Kell signalled his intention to Thyfur. The gryphon responded within a heartbeat, acknowledging Kell's thought and wheeling suddenly, and with amazing adroitness given the current state of his health, to his right and upwards. From the speed of his response, Kell guessed that Thyfur had been anticipating his decision. Within the space of a few moments, they were up and over the crest of the crags and out of direct sight of Golkar.

With a few beats of his mighty wings, Thyfur swept down into the adjoining valley and turned to follow its course. They headed east, away from Tu-atha, to safety. Kell knew that each stroke of the great wings came at great cost to his mount's remaining strength. He also knew that the gryphon would make better speed if he expended the energy now to climb in one ever-expanding spiral high up into the sky where he could find and harness the great thermals on which he could glide for leagues with barely a flap of its wings. He understood his friend's need to put a considerable distance between themselves and Golkar before he did so, however. Any attempt at such a maneuver here, this close to their opponent's abode, would only expose them to further assault from Golkar's awesome range of weaponry, not least from the deadly lightning bolts which had finally turned the battle against them.

Looking back over his shoulder, Kell could see no sign of pursuit. Not that he expected to tell much just by looking; it had been an instinctive act more than anything else. Tentatively, he used his other senses to scan the area for the telltale signs that only a creature of power would produce. It was a risky move. If Golkar or any ally of his was in pursuit, the scan would nullify Kell's ability to mask his own presence. He had to do it nonetheless. He needed to know if Golkar meant to continue the battle.

Kell knew that neither he nor Thyfur was in any state to continue. The critical question was whether Golkar realised how close he had come to destroying them. If he did, he would certainly act to finish them now before they had a chance to recover. Kell breathed a sigh of relief. He could sense nothing.

Using the mind link, he sent out a simple message to Thyfur, *To Ormuz*. Yes, to Ormuz, he thought to himself, but whence from there? Their bolthole in the Northern Wastes was the only logical choice after the debacle they had just endured. But what then?

As he clung to the great beast's neck, Kell wrestled with his thoughts. He chided himself for his choices. What had he been thinking to drag Thyfur into this mess? And why risk all, as he just had at Tu-atha? His foolishness had almost handed Golkar the victory he sought, and on a silver platter to boot. Why, the madman hadn't even had to go looking for him. Like a fool, Kell had simply knocked on his door, just like Tarak had done before him. The result had been perilously close to the same as that which must have befallen his colleague.

At first, Golkar had been visibly shaken by their presence. The fact that Kell could appear unheralded at his door had clearly unnerved him. For him to be accompanied by a mature gryphon, a fearsome creature at the height of its power, had clearly also been more than he had bargained for. It was only a momentary lapse, however. He had grown in power much more than Kell had guessed and the conciliatory tone he had initially adopted had merely gained him the time he had needed to prepare for the vicious onslaught that quickly followed.

Without warning, Golkar had initiated a furious assault on the pair of them, bringing to bear an impressive array of offensive spells that had put Kell immediately onto the backfoot. He wasn't to be so easily overcome, however. He had also prepared for this battle. Though it had been a close thing, Kell had somehow managed to weather that early storm. The incredible speed and agility of the gryphon had then come into its own.

It had been Golkar who had been hard pressed then, desperately erecting barriers to fend off both the physical and magical attacks which had rained down on him, allowing him precious little time to continue the offensive he had started. At one point, he had staggered under the weight of the dual assault, and Kell had thought that the battle was his. Golkar's defensive shield had been weakened for an instant as he had attempted to regain the offensive and Thyfur's deadly claw had sliced through.

Though the opening in his shield wall had been repaired in a twinkling of the eye, the damage had been done. The gryphon's claw had struck home, rending flesh and tearing sinew as it sliced through Golkar's shoulder like a knife through goat's curd. For Kell, it seemed that time had stood still. Golkar had stumbled to one knee, with one hand clutching his gaping wound.

An uneasy silence had fallen across the field of battle. The gryphon has settled to the ground a safe distance away from the stricken Guardian and Kell had watched from his position astride the beast, debating whether to call for his foe's surrender or to end it then and there. While he deliberated, Golkar had dug deep into his reserves. In a moment, he was up again and the battle resumed. The chance had been lost. Kell wondered now if the fate of all of Ilythia had hinged on that one moment.

He knew that Golkar would never have hesitated had it been his opponent who had been so exposed. He would have pressed the advantage relentlessly. He would have driven him down until there wasn't a breath left in him. He would have killed Kell without a moment's hesitation.

But not Kell. He had hesitated. What had he thought at that moment? Was it compassion or foolish hope? Or was it simply blind stupidity that had fuelled his vacillation? It didn't matter now.

Golkar had regained the initiative from that point and he had never relinquished it. When he had unleashed those infernal lightning bolts, Kell had known that the battle was lost, though he had been reluctant at first to acknowledge it. They were like nothing he had ever experienced before, drawing on some unnatural source of power that was out of Kell's reckoning. Even then, if he had broken off the fight at that point he would still have achieved what he had initially sought to do. Golkar would have won that round, but it would have been a hollow victory. Kell would have escaped unscathed and Golkar would have been left to lick his wounds and wonder at the closeness of the contest.

Instead, Kell had fought on, unwilling to acknowledge the recklessness of his lapse and allowing Golkar to clearly establish his supremacy. Though the latter had been wounded in the encounter, in the end, it had been Kell and Thyfur who had barely escaped with their lives. They had thrown everything they had at the fiend, and still he had rebuffed them. What choices were left to them now?

Kell continued to torture himself, going over and over the battle and cursing himself for his missed opportunities, until his friend finally interrupted his mental self-flagellation.

Despair is the cloak of the lost, mage, came a clear thought from Thyfur as they made their way eastward. *You said that the goal was to unsettle him, if for no other reason than to draw his thoughts away from the Algarians. We achieved that. We wounded him into the bargain. He bested us, but he knows not the extent of his victory. He has not followed us. Whatever his plans were, they are now awry. Take heart, mage, all is not lost.*

Kell smiled grimly. *You are right, as always, friend Thyfur. We have bought some time. We did achieve our goals, though at great cost to ourselves. My fear is that the battle may well have been our last real chance to defeat him.*

You are wounded, as am I, replied Thyfur. *And you are not used to battle. We will find better counsel after we have rested.*

Yes, thought Kell, *after rest.* The throbbing in his head was muddling his thoughts. *I must rest,* he thought, as he clung tightly to Thyfur's neck. *Then perhaps I'll know what to do.*

CHAPTER 6

The commanding officer's cane rapped against the vellum map around which the small group of officers had clustered. Fintan couldn't resist his usual bit of theatrics, even though the gravity of the occasion was such that he had no need for props to secure his men's attention. It was a habit of his, one he had picked up from old Greshel back at the academy. He saw no reason to drop it now. Neither he nor his classmates had ever dared interrupt Greshel when he had the floor, and that was the way Fintan wanted it to be for him as well. 'Mark my words,' old Greshel used to say, and Fintan always had. He expected the same respect now from the men serving under him.

Fintan scanned the faces of his officers, and what he saw pleased him. They were excited, nervous, apprehensive; some were even scared. The tension in the room was palpable. Whenever he paused, as he did now, an unearthly silence descended upon the room, only to be broken when he commenced speaking again. Fintan was gratified at the way his audience collectively held its breath, hanging on his every word. He had trained them well.

"It is here we can expect them to strike," stressed Fintan, continuing with his speech. "The sligs've done little to conceal their troop movements. They're obviously massing for an attack on Landorion. My analysis of the scouts' reports is that we have three, possibly four days, before they launch their assault."

He paused to draw in his breath and let what he had said sink in. This was what he had been waiting for. All those years at the academy would pay off now, for all of them. For him, it would not be before time. Maybe now, finally, he would get the recognition that was his due.

Fintan's mind inevitably went back to his final year at the academy. How many times had he gone over that dark period in his life? His father had been so bitterly disappointed at his results; not for himself, he said, but for the family, for the Hayachek name. Theirs was a long and proud tradition of exceptional military achievement; they weren't accustomed to mediocrity.

Mediocrity. Fintan despised the word. His father's word, not his. It was the way the old man said it that really wounded, the deep sense of revilement that came out with the syllables, as if it was a placard that Fintan should wear around his neck, as if he had some kind of disease. 'Watch out for the leper,' it might as well have said. Then his posting to what everyone thought was a backwater up here in the northernmost reaches of the empire had only served to deepen the old man's shame, leaving Fintan no choice but to put a brave face on it.

The empire needed good men everywhere, not just in the heartland, he had said defiantly to those who would listen, though not to his father. Give him time, he had said. He knew he was destined for great things. His chance would come. He would cover the family's name in glory, just like his forebears, he was certain of it. In the end, he had been glad to go, glad to be out of Keerêt and away from the stinging rebukes of his father.

That was six years ago. Six long years that had all but drained his ardour. Oh yes, thought Fintan, he'd had more than his own share of doubts, there was no use denying it. At first, he had hoped that the posting would only be a temporary one. Surely his father's analysis of his performance had been overly harsh. A man with his skills would obviously be needed elsewhere and someone high up would realise that soon enough. But they hadn't, and the long-looked-for recall to a more favourable situation was now long overdue. How could he hope to prove his worth if they wouldn't even give him a chance?

But now, all his doubts were gone, evaporated, as quick as a summer morn's fog. Such fogs were ever the harbinger of a beautiful, warm, cloudless day; and so this would prove to be, he was sure. His true destiny now lay before him. Mishra had heeded his call. He could feel it deep within him, right down in his soul. She was calling to him, calling him to arms. Why, the fate of the empire might very well hinge on what happened here under his command. This would be *his* hour. He was as certain of it as he was that the sun would set in the west. This was the moment his whole career had been leading up to.

Fintan could feel the adrenaline coursing throughout his system, fuelling his self-assurance. He felt more alive than he had done for years. Unconsciously, he clenched his left hand, feeling the muscles of his upper arm flex in response. By Mishra, he would show these sligs what they were dealing with. These were no farmers he led. These were highly trained Rangers in the prime of their lives. Fintan gazed at the map before him, picturing the troop movements he would order, the units which would need to be moved, defences that had to be strengthened, until a discreet cough from one of his men brought him out of his reverie.

Quickly dismissing a momentary feeling of embarrassment, Fintan slid easily back into the persona of the experienced commanding officer, straightening his back and glaring fiercely at the man who had coughed. Dravid, of course. He was a weak link that one. Have to watch him, thought Fintan. A bit too uppity for his own good is that one.

Fintan had every reason to be confident. He knew there would be no debate when he issued his orders. His officers were raw and inexperienced. The 'old man' they called him. He couldn't suppress the flicker of a smile that crossed his face at the thought. The 'old man'! Why, he was no more than a decade older than the youngest of them. It was a mark of respect though; he could see that. They looked to him for leadership and guidance, and never more so than now.

They were watching him now as he began to speak again. Some nodded in agreement, others he could see shuffled from one foot to the other, nervously sneaking glances at their comrades, trying to gauge their reactions to his orders without revealing their own anxiety.

"We must concentrate our forces to defend Landorion. That is where this issue will be decided. The recruitment and training of the farmers will continue, of course. Gemir and Telpor, you will continue with that task. We will give the semblance of strength along the length of the frontier to mask our plans, but Landorion is where we will focus our efforts. We will move at night. We don't want them knowing we're on to their plans until it is too late for them to change them. We won't make the same mistake they have."

Fintan paused and smiled reassuringly at his men. "Never underestimate your opponent," he confided, allowing his voice to soften and lose some of its formality. "Remember that, if you remember nothing else. The sligs are vicious fighters. This will be a tough fight. Don't expect anything less. But remember, we have the advantage now. Our scouts have given us that, let's not waste it."

Fintan knew they would heed his advice. They respected him. His family history was well known. Their confidence in him was absolute and that was how he liked it to be. A firm but fair leader, aloof perhaps, but with just a touch of tactical brilliance. That was how he saw himself, and he didn't doubt for a moment that his men shared that view.

"Your written orders are there on the table. Let's be at them men, and may Mishra guide your path. Dismissed."

Almost as one, the small group of officers came to attention and saluted their commanding officer, clicking their heels together in unison as they did so. The formalities done with, they silently filed out of the room, each taking the small envelope labelled with his name as they exited by the only door.

Fintan stood with his back to his officers as they left. He paid no attention to their chattering as they went. His thoughts were already elsewhere. As he gazed through the window of his office at the compound beyond, he considered the words of his own commanding officer. The message had come in by Imperial Messenger a little less than a week ago now. No written orders these, that was too risky. The Imperial Messengers were trained to repeat their messages word for word, no matter how long or complex. The Marshal's message had been neither. It was typically brief and to the point.

"Look to your frontier, Commander," he had ordered. "If the sligs attempt to open a second front then they must be held. Prepare your defences and use your scouts. Let reconnaissance be your foremost strategy."

The orders had been followed to the letter. While the garrisons had been put on high alert, Fintan had put all available scouts into the field. Their reports were back in now, and they all told the same story. The sligs were massing in the mountains here in the north, as had rightly been anticipated by the high command. The enemy's goal was clear, Landorion, an obvious choice and fortunately the first that Fintan had moved to strengthen. There was still much more work to be done, but Fintan was confident he and his men could hold it.

Landorion was strategically situated, guarding as it did the only passable ford on the whole of the northern reach of the Balan River. The Balan, a broad, swiftly flowing river for most of its length, formed a natural line of defence here in the northern provinces. Though it was bridged in two places, Fintan knew that his men could bring the bridges down quite easily, and he had already dispatched a brigade to do so. The sligs would know that as well. That left the ford at Landorion as the only viable spot for the sligs to bring horsemen across the river in great numbers. The small garrison town on the eastern side of the ford was ideally situated to deter any such attempt.

That was where Fintan would hold them. That was where he would earn the respect that was his due.

~~~

Grartok held the large pewter bowl high above his head and slowly tilted it forward, allowing the liquid within to spill out in a long, scarlet stream, straight into the open cavity of his waiting mouth. As the warriors around him began to chant their encouragement, the slig leader gulped greedily at the seemingly endless stream of liquid, feeling it sliding, hot and potent, down his throat and deep into his belly. A cheer went up around the campfire as he flung the empty bowl into the crackling flames.

Throwing back his head once more, Grartok let out a mighty howl which quickly became a deafening roar as his voice was joined by those of his companions, each emptying his lungs and casting his voice skywards in honour of Zar, the great God of Battles. The bloodcurdling clamour sped out into the night air like some maddened beast in search of its prey.

Here and there some small animal, nocturnal in habit, heard the cry and stopped whatever it had been doing, looked up and sniffed the air, seeking the danger the commotion presaged, or flattened itself to the ground in instinctual response. Rodents frantically sought for their burrows. Birds screeched in panic as they wheeled desperately away from the source of such a deathly din.

One by one, each warrior finished his cry and fell silent. Grartok, the first to begin, was also the last to be done. The night fell stonily silent. Not a living thing dared to stir till Grartok's guttural laugh broke the silence once more. "Let the Algarians hear that and shake under their beds." The image drew a similar response from his companions.

Grartok felt good. The First Warrior of the Sagath could feel the potency of the fluid he had just consumed flowing throughout his body as his companions returned to their feasting. Idly he glanced across at the body of the Algarian ranger that lay just beyond the circle of seated warriors, sprawled on its back, its limbs twisted crudely, its chest ripped open to expose the organs within. There was no greater pleasure, thought Grartok, than to drink the blood that's just been squeezed from the still-beating heart of your enemy.

He also knew that such a drink was said to be the most powerful of aphrodisiacs. Pity in some ways, he thought, that Mardur is bearing such precious cargo. If she weren't, he'd have her and the rest of the baggage train much closer to the front than they were. Still, he thought, they're not so far away that a visit wouldn't be possible on the morrow. Things were going well enough for his army to do without him for a day.

Grartok was pleased with the progress of the campaign. Brorgar had finally taken Kurandir and the Sagath were now advancing steadily across Algaria with little hindrance from their foe. Having taken one stand and lost it, the Algarians seemed incapable of rousing the heart to resist the invaders' progress further. More importantly, though, not one of the Guardians had made any attempt to intervene.

Though it was some time since Grartok had spoken with Golkar, the wizard had obviously been successful in diverting the attention of the other Guardians from the slig offensive. But what of Norvig, and Hrothgar? Had they found the human girl-child that Golkar sought? Surely they must have completed that mission by now, mused Golkar; they'd had ample time to complete such a simple task. And what of Kell and Tarak? How had the Master of Cloudtopper taken Norvig's news, wondered Grartok. Surely that would have unsettled even him. Were the wizards at each other's throats yet? Was that why there'd been no intervention from the Guardians?

Grartok knew that these were events about which he could do nothing but wait and see. In the meantime, he meant to press the advantage he had been given for all it was worth. The Algarians were floundering now; their forces were in complete disarray. A little more pressure from the Sagath and they would crumble like dried brugon's droppings. The time was ripe for

Nargal to strike. Once their northern frontier collapsed, there would be nothing the Algarians could do to avoid their fate.

Nargal. He was one on whom the First Warrior knew he could count. Better that he was Second Warrior than that treacherous cur Hrothgar. *And where is my pox-ridden brother*, thought Grartok, his anger rising as his thoughts turned to his sibling.

Grartok knew that the time of reckoning had come between him and his overly ambitious brother. As his thoughts turned to Hrothgar, he gave full vent to the malice that simmered within his breast. *When he returns to the tribe, I will remove that sneering head of his and string it from my lance for all to see. Mardur is mine now, and so is the child growing in her belly. As for that bawling spawn of Hrothgar's, I'll see his head dashed against a rock before I listen to its caterwauling one more time.*

~~~

Krarsht knelt beside the stump of the tree, busying himself with the ropes that had been wound around and around its base. He had already recognised the gait of the approaching warrior and knew that his best strategy was to keep his head down and keep working until his hunt leader had passed. He could only hope that his wrath would be directed at someone else this time.

Broag, a harsh leader at the best of times, was rarely in a fouler mood than he was today, and all of the men knew why. The timetable Third Warrior Nargal had set them was a demanding one. Woe betide Krarsht and his companions if the ropes weren't ready when the army arrived for the crossing in the morning.

Krarsht watched surreptitiously as the mud-stained boots carried the hunt leader past him. Broag was headed in the direction of the second of the work groups, which was working but a short distance away. Though it was dark and the hunt leader's back was now to Krarsht, his rasping voice could still be heard as he picked up his stride. Krarsht cringed involuntarily.

"What kind of work is that Grashnir? Those ropes have to hold the weight of many warriors. My camp dog could do a better job than that. Why am I the only hunt leader with prondor's spawn instead of warriors to lead?"

Krarsht shook his head and returned to his own work. He was wet and tired but he knew better than to even think of taking a break. There would be no respite for any of them until they had finished. "Let's check those knots again, Dramcra," he whispered to his companion. "Broag is very close to losing it. Remember what he did last time that happened."

"Yah," his companion grunted in reply as they put their weight against the rope. "Sardoc was a good fighter. The hunt is the weaker for his loss." Dramcra spat on the ground as if to emphasise his disgust. Krarsht knew that Sardoc and Dramcra had been friends. He wouldn't thank Krarsht for reminding him of his comrade's fate.

The knots were strong, as they should be. The tangle of strands they had been working on was easily thicker than a warrior's arm. They had done their work well and even with both of them putting all of their strength into the effort, the ropes wouldn't budge.

"It'll take axe work and plenty of it to bring that undone," said Dramcra, standing up and wiping his ridged brow. Both of them stood there quietly for a while, admiring their handiwork with some satisfaction.

"Well," said Krarsht when he could see his comrade wasn't about to make the first move. "Only one more and then we're done. A flip of the blade to see who takes the ropes across this time?" Krarsht knew that neither of them relished going back into the freezing waters of the river. They had each had a turn already and this would be the last.

"You're on."

"Ever the gambler, hey Dramcra." joked Krarsht as he picked up his axe from its resting spot and spun the haft as he tossed the blade gently into the air. "Call," he cried as the blade reached its highest point in the arc of its flight.

"Horn."

They both stepped forward and peered down at the shiny metal face as the blade fell to the turf with a soft thud.

"Ahhhhh. Claw. How do you do it? May your father's bones rot in Fradnor," Dramcra cursed as he turned and headed towards the water, stripping off his vest as he made his way down to the coils of ropes that lay at the river's edge.

Krarsht watched impassively as his companion looped the ends of four of the coils about his waist and edged his way out into the water, taking a hold of one of the existing ropes as he reached deeper water to keep him from being swept away by the swift-flowing current. Dramcra's strong arms moved him along the course of the rope steadily. Krarsht knew that, though the water was bitterly cold, Dramcra would have little difficulty in quickly reaching the other side.

This crossing was a different one to his first, earlier that evening, before any of the ropes were up. On that occasion, the strong current had swept Dramcra a considerable distance downstream before he had reached the further bank. If he hadn't been as strong a swimmer as he was, he might not have made it at all.

Krarsht had to admire the shrewdness of Nargal's strategy. Though summer had barely arrived, this river was still young and vigorous here in the north; it hadn't yet flowed far from its source in the snow-capped peaks of the Giant's Teeth. Its currents were swift and treacherous and only the foolhardy would spend any more time than was absolutely essential in its icy waters. A warrior in full battle gear would have no chance of crossing it, no matter how strong a swimmer he was. Nargal's plan eliminated these risks.

Third Warrior of the Sagath was Nargal. Only Grartok and Hrothgar stood higher in the tribe's reckoning. Krarsht could see why he was held in such esteem. Like all good plans, this one would catch his opponents flat-footed. The Algarians would be caught unawares and the sweet sound of axes separating heads from bodies would soon echo across the northern plains. Krarsht could almost taste the sweetness of it now. He was proud to be Sagath and he would vie with the rest for the number of heads that would fall to his blade in the coming battles.

Broag had explained it all to his warriors before they had left camp. First, Nargal had bid the outriders keep a close eye on the scouts the Algarians had sent up into the mountains. They made no attempt to capture or kill them. Instead, their every move was closely followed. Everything they were allowed to see was carefully orchestrated to make it appear as if the sligs were intending to unite their scattered forces at one spot, the ford on the great river.

The success of that strategy had now been confirmed by the sligs' own scouts. They reported that the Algarians were quickly moving the majority of their troops to defend the ford. They even seemed to be making some effort to conceal that intent by conducting their troop movements at night; though that only made it easier for the slig scouts to venture far enough into Algarian territory to see what the enemy were up to.

Once Nargal was sure that the Algarians had taken the bait, Broag had been given his orders. While a small force would attack the Algarians at the ford, he and his handpicked group were to secure a spot where the major portion of Nargal's army could cross the river without the use of either bridge or ford. These ropes they were now stringing across the river would be used to secure safe passage for both men and horses across the swiftly flowing river. It would be slower going than using the more traditional crossing points, and they wouldn't be able to get supply wagons across this way, but it would be totally unexpected by the Algarians.

Once on the other side, they would be free to attack the enemy at will. While the majority of the Algarians were being kept busy at the ford, the Sagath would pillage the remainder of the province. Eventually, the Algarian commander would face a difficult choice, stay where he was while the Sagath sent the whole of the province up in flames, or abandon the ford and attempt to bring the invaders to battle. If he chose the latter, as he surely would have to in the end, then the sligs would not only be able to bring their supply wagons across the river by way of the ford but they would be able to choose the field of battle. Nargal had heard of the slig debacle at Kurandir and knew how difficult a task it could be to dislodge defenders from a fortified town.

Yes, Krarsht thought, you have to hand it to the big ones, Nargal, Grartok, Hrothgar, they were great leaders. It was a good time to be a Sagath warrior.

~~~

"Keep ya thieven eyes off it," snarled Dain as he shot a furtive glance over his shoulder. The small canvas bag he clutched in his hand was as good as gold to a starving man and he meant to share it with no one. "Ya got to that bread afore me an ya ain't getting this lot. It's mine."

Withdrawing the contents of the bag, he quickly and feverishly stuffed the small cubes into his mouth, paying no heed to the thin film of green that had formed on their surface. He couldn't see the thieving scumbag who had beaten him to the last cache of food, but he knew he was somewhere close by. Dain knew that he had beaten them this time though.

What a find, he thought, as he savoured the tangy taste. Cheese. How long had it been since he had tasted cheese? How long since he had last tasted anything for that matter? Was it yesterday? Or the day before that?

He couldn't remember.

What he did remember was all the times he had found the sure signs that someone had beaten him to it. They were mocking him, he knew that, leaving tell-tale little signs, like a few stale pieces of bread, gnawed around the edges to make it look like rats had eaten it, or dried and cracked bones, stripped bare of every morsel of meat. Oh yes, they were clever, and they wanted to taunt him, wanted to drive him crazy. But he wouldn't crack. Not him. Not Dain.

As he knelt in the rubble, Dain ruefully passed his hand along his torso, feeling once more the distinct ripple of his ribs just below the surface of his skin. Much more of this and that's all there would be left of him, skin and bones and nothing else. At least today had been one of his better days.

He had been digging through the rubble of what had once been the home of one of the inhabitants of Kurandir, scrabbling among the ruins like a dog searching for a long lost bone, when he had stumbled on treasure. Prising open a metal container that had lain buried beneath a pile of charred timbers and shattered roof tiles, he had found a small canvas bag within. The smell had told him instantly what the contents were and he acted quickly, gobbling down the food before anyone else could beat him to it. This was one cache they wouldn't get before him.

There had been precious little of it, though. Dain's stomach was still grumbling and he knew it wasn't complaining about the quality of its most recent offering. It wanted more, much more. He was ravenously hungry and hoards like this were becoming harder and harder to find. Soon he would have no choice but to venture out of the town and take his chances in the countryside.

That's probably what they want me to think. Get me out of here so there's one less to share with.

Dain didn't relish the prospect. It was a choice he had been actively avoiding. Here in the ruins of Kurandir he was safe. After the sligs had sacked the town they had abandoned it. He could see no reason why they would be likely to return. The countryside might be another matter.

He still remembered the dangerous game of cat and mouse he had played with the sligs while the beasts swarmed through the buildings, plundering everything worth having. From the occasional screams and cries, he knew others had also played, and lost.

Somehow, he had survived, always managing to stay one step ahead of them. Then the cutthroats had torched the town. He had seen out the inferno up to his neck in a sewerage pit. He still stank of the stuff. But at least he was still alive, hungry, weak, tired, but still alive. They hadn't got him yet.

And they won't get me. I'm too quick for them. Too damn quick for the murderous bastards is old Dain.

Sure that he'd seen a flicker of movement out of the corner of one eye, Dain picked up a piece of rubble and flung it violently in that direction. "I'd be fine," he shouted. "I could live 'ere forever if it weren't for you stealin me food, you thieving scum."

Dain knelt for a while, darting quick looks to his left and his right and listening attentively for the faintest sound, waiting for his adversary to betray his presence with a slip of his boot on the rubble. The ruins were silent. He could neither see nor hear anything other than his own laboured breathing. Satisfied that he'd discouraged the thief for now, he rose and scrambled away.

Clever. Very clever.

Dain muttered and cursed to himself as he continued his search. It would be night again soon. He hated the nights.

CHAPTER 7

The bright sun shining down onto Sara's back, welcome though it was, did nothing to lift her spirits; she knew that her fate was sealed. Having recaptured her after such a long and arduous chase, Tug was unlikely to let her escape from his clutches a second time. As the motion of her mount forced her to twist awkwardly in her saddle she couldn't help but grimace. The sharp pain in her side was an ugly reminder of what she could expect if she attempted to make another bid for freedom. The effects of the beating the draghar had given her once they were out of sight of the Rangers still hadn't worn off.

All in all, that wasn't an experience she would like to revisit. For the moment, at least, she couldn't even think about another attempt at escape. The thought of another hiding like the one she had just endured was too horrible to contemplate. Where would it get her, anyway?

Look at the debacle their attempt to escape from Novistor had turned into. Even after that long chase through the wilderness, she and Rayne had still underestimated Tug's determination to catch up with them. Who would have thought that he would follow them right into Novistor, or that he would be so easily able to enlist the support of the Rangers in capturing her?

Sara wondered if Tug and his friends had somehow gotten ahead of them in those few days when they had been holed up in the cave with Josef. Maybe the draghar had been scouring the province for a sign of them for days. After all, with all of the confusion the slig attack had engendered, he and his men wouldn't have attracted much attention. Then again, perhaps they had simply been watching when she and Rayne had entered the town and had followed them all the way to the inn. She, for one, had been so intent on gawking at the marvels of the city she hadn't even considered the prospect of being followed or watched once they were inside of Novistor.

She hadn't really given too much thought to Alys' story either. The young maid had told them that the guards believed her and Rayne to be runaway lovers. That alone should have been enough to alert them. How else could they have got such an idea except from Tug, or someone else in Golkar's employ? Instead, she and Rayne had been too busy with their plans for getting away to think about who might have started such a story, too busy running yet again to contemplate what or who it was they were running from.

Not that they would have been able to do much about it, she realised. Novistor had proven to be one big trap. Once the Rangers had got onto their trail they probably never really stood a chance.

Sara was still coming to grips with just how much the Guardians were revered in Ilythia. The name of Golkar had clearly been all that Tug had needed to gain the cooperation he had wanted. The Rangers had obviously accepted his story at face value. Unfortunately, her and Rayne's actions must then have only seemed to corroborate what he had said, what with their trying to sneak out of the town under the cover of darkness, and her having no credible story of where she had come from to counter that of Tug's.

Poor Rayne, though. She had to fight back the tears at the thought of him. Surely he would be okay now that she was out of the picture. Though she knew from the Rangers that he was on his way to Keerêt, she hoped that the matter would end there. Golkar would surely have no further need to press the issue now that Tug had recaptured her.

She couldn't bring herself to think about the prospect of Rayne languishing in some gaol. Still, it was hard to see how what he had done could be considered more than a minor misdemeanour. Perhaps they would impose some minor penalty and then set him free. Then he could get on with the life she had so selfishly disrupted, assuming there was going to be a life for anyone here in Ilythia once Golkar fulfilled his plan.

Sara just wasn't ready to think about that last bit too much. She knew she would have no chance of keeping her head together if she allowed herself to dwell too deeply on what was to come. It was hard enough coping with her current circumstances without looking ahead.

At least she hadn't had to endure seeing Rayne die defending her from Tug and his henchmen. She hadn't even been sure where they had taken him the night they had been captured at the gates. She had been marched off in one direction and him in another and that had been the last she had seen of him. She could still picture his face now, with its look of concern as he had looked back over his shoulder at her when they had frog-marched him off into the darkness. It was only the kindness of one of the Rangers the next morning that had enabled her to find out he had been sent to Keerêt.

Sara had to blink back the tears that came to her eyes at the memory of their friendship. She had never experienced its like before, and now . . . now it was gone, taken from her before she had been able to fully appreciate its value, like a beautiful, crystal vase that is suddenly knocked to the floor; one minute, an exquisite and valuable piece of craftsmanship, a tribute to its creator and a source of pride and wonder to its owner; the next, nothing more than fragments of broken glass, scattered across a dirty floor.

Of course, her denial of Tug's story had proved useless. The draghar had played his part well and her talk about sligs and conspiracies had only made her own story sound all the more unbelievable. The Rangers were clearly convinced she really was the daughter of one of Golkar's man-servants. Nor did they doubt his assertion that she and Rayne had run off together when her father had forbidden her to see him any more.

Though that was no major crime in itself, Tug had made it clear that Golkar had promised his man he would see to her safe return. He made it sound as if Rayne had taken advantage of her inexperience and induced her to run away against her own better judgement.

Though Sara had howled and screeched and begged and cajoled, none of it had any effect. In the end, though they clearly didn't relish going to such lengths, she had given them little choice but to gag and bind her and put her up on to Nell so that Tug and his cronies could lead her away.

She could see that the senior Ranger had misgivings about the whole affair. He clearly wasn't at all comfortable with the idea of binding her. But she only had herself to blame. And what could he do anyway? To defy the wishes of a Guardian would clearly be a courageous step for anyone, let alone a mere captain of the Rangers.

And so she had been led away to her doom. Tug had been all sweetness and light while the Rangers were around, but soon as they were out of sight he had given her a beating the likes of which she would probably never forget. And he had got the result he wanted. He had cowed her into submission.

She hadn't given a single thought to escape since that night. Tug had told her that if she made even the slightest attempt to disobey him again he would take to her with a knife the next time, said he was just itching for an excuse to pay her back for what she had done to him and Ruz.

Sara had no doubt that if she dared to cross him again he would carry out his threat. Though she had been scared of him from the night she had first met him, he only had to look at her now and she swore her heart stopped beating. She had a horrible feeling he was going to do something very bad to her before he got her back to Golkar. All she could do was try not to give him an excuse.

She had learnt an important lesson that night, one that few people ever came to understand, no matter how long they lived. Courage was a finite resource. One could be brave in the face of adversity, not just once, but many times. Eventually, the drain on your spirit took its toll, however. At some point it simply ran out; the well ran dry. Sara knew she had reached that point that night when Tug had beaten her. She had used up a lifetime's amount of bravery over the last few weeks and, finally, she had exhausted her stock.

So here they were, trudging the long miles back to where her nightmare had started. Having made good speed going back through the farming country she and Rayne had crossed only a few days previously, they weren't far from the wilderness now. The signs of habitation were clearly beginning to diminish and Sara knew that before long they would be back among the towering beech trees again. From the talk she had overheard, she knew that Tug and his men would be glad of that. They were anxious to be clear of Algarian territory. They clearly didn't enjoy explaining themselves over and over again to the people they encountered along the way.

She had to admire the Algarians though. It would only have been natural for no one to want to get involved in her predicament. To her surprise, however, there weren't many that were prepared to watch three men lead a bound girl past them without challenging them. Quite often, it was only the token the Ranger captain had given Tug and his men that finally convinced people their actions were sanctioned by the Rangers themselves. Unfortunately for Sara, or perhaps, fortunately, for she knew that Tug and his men would have dealt ruthlessly with anyone who tried to hinder them, that was enough to silence even the most doubtful.

Turning her head slightly, Sara considered the larger of Tug's two companions. He was riding along beside her at the moment. Though her hands were bound, and Nell herself was being led by a rope attached to Tug's saddle, they kept a close eye on her at all times. This one's task was to ride beside her and make sure that she didn't try anything foolish.

Ter the others called him. Sara had already determined that he was as nasty a piece of business as Tug was. Though he looked like a big, harmless oaf, she knew that his heart was black. She shuddered as she remembered how he had sat opposite her at their camp the previous night. He had taken great delight in telling her in graphic detail just what he would have done to Rayne if he had been able to. She had nearly thrown up she had been so sickened by what he had said.

Apparently, the man Rayne had shot with his bow at the top of the falls had been Ter's brother, and Ter was burning up with frustration at being denied the opportunity to avenge his death. It didn't seem to matter in the slightest that his brother had tried to kill Rayne first. Ter just wanted his chance for revenge.

Luckily, the Rangers had refused to hand Rayne over to them, insisting he would have to answer to an Algarian magistrate for what he had done, albeit one at the capital given Golkar's involvement in the matter. Sara guessed that their reaction would have been the same even if the charge had been murder. If Golkar hadn't been involved, though, it was hard to see how they would even have bothered with arresting him. They would have probably just sent him on his way with a warning of some kind.

Ter was obviously none too happy with all of that. By way of recompense, he seemed to get some sort of sick pleasure out of terrifying Sara. So far, he had not only succeeded in achieving his aim but also in confirming her belief that Rayne was better off where he was. Whatever would happen to him in Keerêt, at least he would live to tell the tale.

What an evil crew they were, thought Sara. She wondered how in the world Golkar could maintain his façade as protector of Ilythia with a gang of cutthroats like these working for him. Maybe it was fear that provided him with the cover he needed, that and his remoteness from the average Ilythian. The Rangers at Novistor were certainly not of a mind to question his authority. Though they had demanded proof that Tug was really what he said he was, when he had shown them the ring with the wizard's crest on it they had accepted its authenticity without question. Sara doubted whether any of them even knew what Golkar's seal looked like. She wouldn't have thought it was the kind of thing many people had ever seen. It didn't matter though; the mere claim that the ring was his token had been enough to silence their doubts.

In any event, by her own admission Tug and his men were what they said they were, representatives of Golkar. She only realised later that she might have fared better if she had protested the whole thing had nothing to do with a Guardian. The Rangers would have been left in a quandary then and might have had to refer the matter up to a higher authority. Maybe someone with more clout would have demanded more proof that she was who they said she was before they would have been willing to hand her over to them. That might have then gained her and Rayne sufficient time to find a way out of their predicament.

Maybe. What good were 'maybes' now, thought Sara. It was over and that was all there was to it. All she could hope for now was a swift and painless death. Sara couldn't stop the tears that flowed down her cheeks at the thought. She had been trying not to think about what was ahead of her. *It's all very fine to be brave*, she thought, *like in all the stories, but I'm scared. I just want all this to never have happened. I want Rayne to be safe. And I want to go home.*

"Quit your blubbering," snarled the man riding beside her. "I can't stand that snivellin. Makes me wanna puke." As if to emphasise his point, he leaned over and spat on the ground between their two horses. Sara could feel her stomach knotting up as the villain turned his attention to her. Just the sound of his voice made her heart race, and she knew that goosebumps were coming up all over the bare skin of her arms.

"Wait till we git you back to Golkar," he continued, almost spitting the words at her. "Then you'll have somethin' to bawl about." His last comment was followed by a wicked laugh. "Aint that right, Rew?" he called out, having a good chuckle to himself. "Golkar'll give her somethin to blubber about, won't he Rew?"

"Reckon he will."

Ter's companion's deadpan response came from somewhere behind Sara. The skinny one didn't seem to get the same pleasure that the bigger one did from baiting her. He had a more sinister side to him, however.

It seemed to Sara that almost every time she had glanced at the man since then she had caught him staring back at her. To her mind, he was far and away the creepiest of the three. 'Watch out for the silent ones', isn't that how the saying goes? Well, whatever thoughts he did have about her he certainly kept them to himself. And a good thing too thought Sara. She had a good idea she would be much better off not knowing what was going on in his sinkhole of a mind.

Glancing around at her surroundings, Sara made a concerted effort to shrug of her depressing thoughts, both of her captors and of the terrible prospects ahead of her. The road they were travelling on, she noticed, was the same one she and Rayne had followed when they had finally broken free of the wilderness. She wondered what had become of the boy whose father had left him in charge of the household while he had gone off to join the war. They weren't far now from where they had met him. She hoped that he had followed Rayne's advice about being ready to leave at a moment's notice.

As her mind wandered, Tug's voice brought her thoughts abruptly back to the present. "Company," he called out from his position at the front of their group. "A lot of company by the look of it."

The tone of his voice bore the clear message that his two companions should be ready for any eventuality. Sara didn't really see what they had to worry about. At most, they would face more awkward questions. Though she was no longer gagged, her fear of Tug ensured that she dare not say a word against them.

Before long, a troop of mounted men appeared from out of a cloud of dust on the road ahead. At first, Sara thought that they must be Rangers. That thought was quickly dispelled, however. Though they were armed, some of them bore lances, others had bows strung across their backs, and all seemed to have swords strapped to their waists, they clearly lacked the more rigid discipline of regular soldiers. Nor could she see any sign of the distinctive brown and green garb she had come to associate with the Algarian Rangers.

As they drew level with Sara and her captors, the leading men of the group drew rein on their horses and within a few moments, the whole troop had drawn to a halt and all eyes were turned to Sara and her three fellow travellers. Now that they were so close, Sara could see that there were a dozen or so of them, most of them barely more than lads, though there were two or three that looked to be older than all of the rest.

"Ho there," cried Tug, obviously wanting to seize the initiative. "Where are you bound for lads?"

Just as with the Rangers at Novistor, he seemed to be able to turn on the charm, or at least put on its mask, whenever it was required. It was so at odds with his true persona that Sara couldn't understand how people were so easily taken in by it. They were though, that was clear, and she saw no reason why this conversation would prove any different from all of the others.

"We're on our way to Keerêt," responded a tall bearded man from the second rank, one of the few older men in the group. Sara guessed he would be about forty or so, perhaps a touch younger. She also noted the way the other men turned to him as soon as Tug had spoken. It seemed he was their leader, or at least their spokesperson.

"We've come up from the Marches to help in the war," the man continued. "Where are you off to? From what I hear, the Algarians need every man they can get at the front. You seem to be headed in the wrong direction. And might I ask, why have you bound that girl? Surely three burly men like you don't need measures like that for a slip of a thing like her. What's she done and where are you taking her?"

"I wish I had a crown for the number of times I've had to explain that today," answered Tug in an exasperated tone. "This so-called slip of a girl is a runaway, if you must know, and she's led us a pretty chase. Her father is man-servant to the Guardian, Golkar."

At the mention of the wizard's name, Sara could see that her assessment of the situation had been an accurate one. These men would be no different to the rest of the people they had met since they had left Novistor. Many of them raised their eyebrows at the mention of Golkar's name and she saw a number of them exchanging glances. His name was like a talisman just by itself.

"About two weeks or so back," continued Tug, "she ran off with a young Marcher lad who turned her head with his slick words. Her father's been worried sick ever since. We caught up with them in Novistor where the Rangers handed 'em over to us. As you can see, the young lass is of a mind not to go back home. She still thinks she's in love." At this, he gave a little chuckle, as if to say, 'you know what young girls are like'.

"The young lad quite turned her head," Tug continued when the man said nothing in response, "and I daresay they've been up to a bit of mischief together, if you know what I mean."

Sara saw Tug wink at the man as he finished speaking and she felt a blush come over her face. Her predicament was so demeaning. To have Tug mock her like this in front of strangers when she knew she could do nothing to defend herself just added to her misery. It was enough to be in the mess she was without everyone being led to think she was some back-woods slut who couldn't manage to keep her pants up.

When Tug got nothing but a blank response to his comments from the Marcher leader, he continued. "If we didn't bind her, she'd run away again at the first opportunity."

The man Tug had been speaking to idled his horse closer to Sara and gave her a searching look. Sara kept her eyes down. She dare not look at him. She knew that Tug was watching her closely. In any event, it wouldn't matter what she said, or did. In the end, Tug would produce the Ranger's token, or if needs be, the ring that marked him as an aide of Golkar's, and these men would acquiesce just like everyone else had. It would do no one any good, least of all her, for her to say anything to contradict the draghar's story.

"Are you all right Miss?" asked the man in a voice that was soft and full of concern.

Sara nodded ever so slightly in reply, fighting to keep her feelings in check as she did so. She knew that she was trembling but she didn't know how to calm her nerves. She dare not open her mouth. She was sure she couldn't do so without betraying her seething emotions.

"Is what he says true, Miss?" the man pressed when she continued to remain silent.

Sara fought to control the feelings that were boiling within her. This was her chance. There were more of them than her captors. If she poured her story out to them, they might help her. It was clear their leader was concerned about her. What was she waiting for?

After the briefest of pauses, Sara knew that the decision she had made earlier must stand. Her courage was gone. It would do her no good to cause trouble anyway, she would never convince them she was telling the truth. More importantly, she couldn't bear to face what Tug would do to her afterwards. Her only response to the man's question was to lower her head even further and remain silent. She felt so deeply ashamed. Rayne would have had more courage than this. She was a coward. She sniffled, turning her head to one side in an attempt to wipe her nose against her shoulder as she did so.

"She'll be all right once she gets back home to her father," said Tug when Sara remained silent. "Right now, I think she's thinking of what he'll say to her when she gets back home. Deep down, I'm sure she knows she's betrayed his trust. I thank you for your concern though. May Mishra ride at your shoulder, Sir. We must be on our way. We've a long way to travel. Good day to you."

With that Tug kicked his horse into a trot and Nell dutifully followed his lead. As they moved forward, Sara turned and cast a final glance behind her. She feared that the group of men they were leaving in their wake had been her last hope.

As the distance between the two groups grew, Sara could see that the man who had spoken to them was still watching her. She managed to smile wanly back at him, then forced herself to turn away. *There are still some kind people in this world*, she thought. *I mustn't forget that.*

CHAPTER 8

It was some time later that they pulled away from the road and set up a camp amongst a copse of trees, far enough from the road to avoid attention from anyone who happened still to be on the road at such a late hour. Once they had eaten a small meal, and her captors had sat around talking quietly amongst themselves for some time, Ter had been assigned the first watch and the rest of them had settled down in their bedding. Sara, of course, was still bound, but somehow managed to get into a position where she thought that sleep might be possible. If she could stop her mind from running, that is.

A million thoughts crowded her mind, each demanding its place. She thought back to the days of her captivity, when Ruz and Tug had been her jailors. She remembered how she had given up hope when they had thrown her into that cell, and how she had eventually rekindled that hope, how she had fought back and broken free. It had all been futile though. She saw that now. It had achieved nothing.

Nothing, that is, unless you counted the death of Josef, possibly of Ruz, of those two men from the settlement, and of Ter's brother. What was that? Five people, five deaths that wouldn't have occurred if she had just accepted her fate. And then, of course, there was Rayne. Where had all this got him? He had wanted to join the Rangers, not get arrested by them. What would that do to him? What kind of future could there be for him now?

Those were certainly achievements, she thought bitterly; achievements only she could accept responsibility for. And, for all her efforts, she would soon be right back where she started from anyway. So much for fighting the good fight. She had fought, but at what cost? Fighting back had only dragged others into her nightmare. It was useless to try and fight them. Besides, even if she could find the will to fight any more, she couldn't do it alone, not against all three of them. Just one of these cutthroats would be more than she could handle by herself.

And where could she hope to turn for help here in the wilderness? As Rayne had once said to her, the people she was likely to run into here were likely to be just as bad as Tug and his friends, if not in league with them. And what could escape mean here, in any event? Where could she go? How could she find her way out of the wilderness? And what of the sligs? Were they out there still, searching for her? Escape from Tug, even if it were possible, might only leave her at the mercy of hunters far worse than him. Surely the concept of escape was dependent on there being somewhere or someone to escape to. No. She had made that mistake once already. It would be pointless to try and repeat it.

It was hard to regret the time she'd had with Rayne though, for all that. She wondered where he was right now. Would he be fast asleep or would he be awake too, thinking of her as she was thinking of him? It would be nice to think so. She knew him well enough to know that if he were awake he would be missing her, just as she was missing him, and that he would be worried about her, just as she was worried about him. They had become too close for it to be any other way for either of them.

Hopefully, he would be fast asleep. It was, after all, the middle of the night and she couldn't imagine that he would have been mistreated since his capture in anything like the way she had. He would be under guard too, of course, but his guards would be Rangers. He would probably have sat around a campfire with them earlier in the night chatting amiably about the war, or about what they had done before it had started, or what they would do once it was over. For him, despite his predicament, life should soon return to normal. They would take him to Keerêt, and then they would probably release him.

Wherever he was, though he would undoubtedly be worried about her, he would be unlikely to guess at the treatment she had been receiving since her recapture. Rayne had virtually no real direct experience of Tug. Yes, he knew that Tug would stop at nothing, even murder, to recapture her, and he had to know that they would be taking her back to Golkar, but he wouldn't have any idea of the torment she was enduring at the hands of these monsters along the way.

Though she drew comfort from the thought that he wouldn't have to endure that knowledge, it also heightened her feeling of loneliness. In many ways that was the hardest thing to bear about her plight. Not only was there no one out there to help her now, there wasn't even anyone that would ever really know what she went through before they finished with her.

What was it her grandmother used to say? *A heart makes no sound when it breaks.* She was right. Hers was broken now and no one even knew, or cared. Love was such a personal experience; neither the happiness nor the grief it could bring were things you could share with others. The people you met, that you really cared about, they left footprints on your heart that only you could see or feel.

She told herself that Rayne would eventually convince himself her death had been a swift and a painless one. Any other course would be too painful for him. Self-preservation alone would probably prevent him from considering the blacker of the paths she may be destined for. She couldn't blame him for that. Even now, she dare not consider some aspects of her future herself.

Sara remembered another time when she had lain bound beside a fire and Josef had stepped out of the blackness to rescue her. Unfortunately, that wasn't going to happen this time. Josef was long gone, and a good thing too. Though he had known what she was facing, he had seen enough horrors in his life without adding this one to his burden. *Who was he, anyway?* she wondered. There were so many unanswered questions there, like how he had known so much about her and Rayne, and how he had come by his magical powers. Sara realised she would never find out the answers to those questions now.

If only she had been able to achieve what Josef had eventually suggested would be her best hope, to contact one of the other Guardians. She had failed, of course. What chance had she had after all? In some ways, it had been cruel of Josef to have built up her hopes. Even trained warriors would have found what they had set out to do a daunting task, with Golkar bringing all of his forces to bear to thwart them. Sara guessed that Josef's desire to avert the evil future he believed Ilythia was destined for had blinded him to that small fact. She couldn't blame him for that, either. She was too tired to apportion blame. It would serve no purpose.

And where were Golkar's adversaries, anyway, those former colleagues of his, those great 'protectors' of Ilythia? Wasn't that why they called them the Guardians? If they were supposed to guard Ilythia, then where were they? Had he defeated them already? She was sure he would. Even Josef had been sure of that. Nothing could escape from Golkar. Ilythia and all of its inhabitants were doomed to their fate just as surely as she was.

If only she had never been brought here, never been chosen by Golkar in the first place. And why had he chosen her? How had he picked her out? What had drawn him to her? Had it been simply chance that had led Ruz and Tug to her particular bedroom on that fateful night?

Thoughts of home inevitably drew an image of her parents to Sara's mind. She hadn't given much thought to them for a long time now. *Why was that?* she wondered. Was she shielding herself from that grief?

They would be distraught by now, of course. She wondered if they would have given up hope now, too. It had been weeks since she had been taken from them and there would be nothing to indicate where she had gone. The police would have been brought in. They would have scoured her room, the house and the surrounding area, all to no avail. How mystified they must have been at finding no signs of forced entry to the house, no signs of foul play or any other indication of where she had gone or who with. Perhaps they would assume that she had run away from home. How ironic that would be. They probably thought that she had run off with some unknown lover, just like the story Tug had put about to secure her recapture. How else could they possibly explain the circumstances of her disappearance?

That would be hard for her parents to bear, to have to think their daughter had run away leaving them to despair with no word of where she had gone or who she had gone with. What must they think of her now if they had come to believe that was the case?

Sara was glad when she felt the need for sleep starting to take a hold of her. Where in all of the morass she had sunk into would she find a pleasant thought to hold onto? How would she find the will to bear what was yet to come? She had no answer to that. She knew that there was none.

It seemed to Sara that the trip back to Golkar's home, to Tu-atha as Tug called it, took a lifetime. She lost count of the number of days that had passed, or whether the trip should really be counted in weeks, or months. She could no longer reckon in such terms. Time had long since ceased to have meaning for her.

Day after interminable day they trudged along through the dreary landscape of the Western Wilderness. Westward ever was their course and each day brought them closer and closer to what Sara knew would be her final resting place. Tu-atha would be the end of the road for her.

At times she wondered if it was only her state of mind that made their surroundings seem so drear and sinister. Had her circumstances been different, and her company more abiding, might she not then have found the forest a beautiful, peaceful place, full of life and wonder? She didn't dwell on the thought. Her circumstances were what they were, and her company, well, let's just say that she thought she would be unlikely to find a worse set of companions though she journeyed through hell itself, if that wasn't where she was already. That's what her trip was in her eyes, after all, a senseless sojourn through a living hell, having to suffer again and again the daily torments and indignities her captors seemed to delight in dishing out to her. As if her fate alone wasn't enough of a torment.

Sara remembered stories from her history books at home, of how she had read that in the Middle Ages they would sometimes draw and quarter their victims before they hanged them. Wasn't hanging enough, she had always wondered, not understanding the need for any more cruelty beyond that. Now she was the victim being tormented unnecessarily when she was already destined for a horrible death at her journey's end. The little mind games they played with her seemed endless. And they clearly derived so much fun from them. It still didn't make any sense to her. Not that anyone would ponder over her circumstances. No history book would ever be written to tell of her fate.

Given the horrors of her current circumstances, it was no small wonder to Sara that she hadn't already succumbed to the pressure of it all and altogether lost her sanity. She suspected the reality was she was only keeping her head together by the barest of margins. She also wondered whether she was still capable of judging her own state of mind anymore. What was her benchmark, after all? Certainly not Tug, or Ter, or even Rewin. Whatever the state of her mind, even if by some miracle this nightmare did come to an end, Sara knew that she would never again be that girl she had been back at home with her parents. That time of innocence was gone now, forever.

Finally, one day, about mid-morning, they came to a split in the road and Ter and Rewin drew their horses to a halt. The trail before them branched in two directions. Neither was sign-posted, and Sara hadn't the faintest clue which led to Tu-atha or where else the road might take them. She had long since lost any sense of direction. The sun at her back told her their trail still led in a westerly direction and that was all she knew.

"Good speed, Tug," said Rewin to the draghar, who had also halted and had turned in his saddle to face his two companions. Nell stood dutifully to the rear of Tug's mount, nodding her head contentedly. She was still tied by a short length of rope to the back of the draghar's saddle. "This is our road," the thin man continued. "I expect you'll be there before nightfall, same as us. Can't say as I won't relish a soft bed for a change."

Tug grinned broadly at the last comment. "It ain't the bed you're looking for, you rogue, it's the company. Margret will give you a good welcome home, I'm sure. Just remember to pace yourself. You ain't as young as you used to be."

While Rewin could manage only a wry grin at the comment, Ter threw back his head and roared with laughter.

"You too, you big oaf," laughed Tug. "My guess is you'll be straight over to the Swamp to see Ida. Just remember to stop long enough to have a bath, you stink worse than a bandy-legged skunk. And make sure she doesn't winkle all that gold out of your pocket on your very first night."

"Don't worry about that," chortled Ter. "I got plans for my share. Didn't go traipsing halfway across the land just to spend all me pay on one fat wench . . . gunna spend it on a dozen fat wenches . . . har har."

Ter's good humour was infectious and soon all three of them were laughing uproariously together. The whole scene had an air of unreality to Sara. Anyone would think they had just come back from a trip to the county fair. It was hard to believe, seeing them right now, that these were the same murderous villains that had hunted her down and dragged her back here beaten, bound, and subdued.

"Drop over and see us as soon as you can," called Rewin from over his shoulder, as the two men turned their horses towards the left of the two trails that lay before them. "And some more work'd be handy too. Can't say as I wouldn't mind taking some more of Golkar's gold off his hands. Right neighbourly of him to stimulate the local economy." By the time he'd finished speaking he was yelling and had nearly disappeared from sight behind some intervening bushes.

"I will," called Tug in reply as he turned his own horse to the right, forcing Sara and Nell to follow.

The rest of that day passed in total silence. Not that there was usually much chatter among the group. Sara never spoke at all any more, unless she was spoken to, or a reply was expected. The others had occasionally chatted about this or that but she had long since given up paying any attention to them, preferring to retreat to the safety of her own inner world as much as she could.

Still, the deathly quiet of the day had an unnerving effect on Sara. Perhaps it was because they were so close to Tu-atha now. It was hard to force away thoughts of what her return there would mean anymore; not when they were but hours away from it. It was more than that, though, she realised. The silence had an unnatural air to it. It was as if the forest itself was holding its breath. Hadn't Rayne said something similar when he had found her here? She seemed to remember him commenting on the eerie feeling he had felt in the valley that housed Tu-atha. That was how it was now. Even the birds had stopped chirping.

And so it was that they had good warning of the rider that approached them as their horses stepped slowly along a winding forest trail late in the afternoon. The sun was before them now and dipping down towards the horizon, casting long shadows and causing its light to flicker in and out through the boughs of the trees before them as they moved forward. Though their sight was constrained, however, their hearing was not.

Tug was the first to hear it, and when he stopped and turned to the right, peering off into the undergrowth, Sara could hear it as well. It sounded like a big animal was coming towards them from just beyond a thicket of bushes, not far to the right of where they had stopped. Sara watched as Tug took his bow, quickly stringing it and expertly fitting an arrow with a deftness that had to be admired. Sara felt her heart begin to race.

At that moment, a horse and its rider emerged from between two of the bushes they had both been looking at. Sara felt her stomach do a quick flip as she recognised the rider instantly.

"About time," said the rider as he drew on his rein.

CHAPTER 9

Ormuz. Its very name had once been enough to inspire awe, though none now lived who could tell that tale. Today it was nothing more than a desolate ruin. The hands that had raised its walls had long since crumbled to dust. The feet that had trodden its streets, the bejewelled slippers that had paced its corridors of power, they were nothing now, not even an echo in some long, lost, corridor of history. In fact, their passing had been so complete that none but the gods knew whence they had gone, what they had achieved, or why they had failed. Time, that most relentless of hunters, had long since thrown its cloak of obscurity over their deeds.

Nor did the isolation of the citadel do anything to enhance its memory. With its crumbling walls perched on the crest of a lonely hillock, deep inside the Northern Wastes, far from civilisation, far from any of the trade routes that crossed the waste and even farther still from the nearest oasis, its very location had long been forgotten. The remains of the paved road that led to its gates could still be found if, one looked hard enough, but none ever did.

For the Northern Wastes were aptly named. Most of its travellers stuck to the caravan routes. They were well marked, and for good reason. Those that strayed from these paths were rarely seen again. In fact, it was said that only the Gu-anth, the wandering tribes-people of the dunes, could survive away from the string of oases that traversed the desert's heart. Not that many could tell of them either, for they were a miserable race, pitifully few in number and rarely seen by others. They cared little for strangers for they were wanderers, nomads, a forlorn people living lives of constant struggle. The desert was a harsh environment and the Gu-anth weren't inclined to share its few resources.

For the moment, then, Kell sensed they would be safe; though for how long was uncertain. The wizard lifted his weary eyes and gazed around the structure in which they had finally taken refuge. Thyfur was still asleep, he noted, as his eyes passed over the sleek form of the beast that lay curled up like some gigantic misbegotten feline against the far wall of the ruined temple they had chosen for sanctuary.

What better spot could they have picked, he mused, then a Temple of Mishra; for despite its ruined state, that was unmistakeably what their current abode had once been. The broken statuary, the distinctive frescoes, faded though they were, the low altar stone with its shallow depression, the two niches in the back wall with plinths that had once held life-sized statues, all of these marked the ruin for what it had once been, a place of worship to the most revered of all the Ilaroi, to Mishra, and her consort, Tarquin.

Perhaps, thought Kell, this choice would bring them the turn of chance they so desperately needed, for it would take nothing less than the intervention of a god to get them out of the situation they now found themselves in. The battle was over, but not the war. Golkar wouldn't rest now until he had finished it. He would know that Thyfur was far too powerful an enemy to be left unchecked.

Turning his attention to the sleeping beast, Kell couldn't help but wonder at the remarkable change that had come over the creature since they had reached Ormuz. When they'd arrived at the place a few short hours earlier, the gryphon had been exhausted. Both the wounds he'd received in the battle and the gruelling flight away from the scene of combat to this remote fastness had taken its toll. It had taken all of the creature's remaining energy just to heave his vast bulk inside the crumbling walls of the temple precinct. Thyfur had all but collapsed in the corner once he'd completed that task.

And yet now, to look at the beast, even though he was sleeping, he showed all the signs of being well on the way to recovery. The sheen had returned to his metal plumage. Inexplicably, the raw wound across his hindquarters had closed. And the beast's breathing, where formerly it had been laboured and shallow, now seemed to have returned to an even and healthy state. All this in a few short hours.

Kell knew that this wasn't normal. From his earlier experience, he'd expected Thyfur to need days to recover, at the very least. And yet, here in this place, the creature was undergoing a remarkable transformation.

For not the first time, the Guardian wondered if there was a connection between the gryphon, or indeed the gryphons, and the long forgotten race that had raised the once mighty towers of Ormuz. This wasn't the only time he and Thyfur had been here together. Indeed, it was Thyfur who had first shown it to him many years ago. Perhaps the beast's interest in the place went beyond what Kell had formerly assumed. Perhaps there was some link here that he hadn't previously discerned.

Though the phenomenon intrigued him, Kell put the mystery aside. If he hadn't been able to divine the way of it before this, he sensed he was unlikely to do so in his current state. Thyfur might seemingly be on the mend, but the wizard was far from being in any condition to continue the fight with Golkar.

Kell raised his hand to the bandage across his cheek, flinching as his fingers gently brushed the thin gauze. The left side of his face had been badly burned by the same bolt that had wounded Thyfur. Unlike the gryphon, however, his wound was still badly in need of attention. Though he had made a perfunctory attempt to dress and clean it while Thyfur slept, he couldn't see that it had been to much avail. His face still felt as if it was on fire, and it was taking a fair measure of his mental control just to handle the intense pain he was still experiencing. He guessed that the injury required more attention than he had been able to give it. Tarak, or even Nim, would have known how to treat such a wound, but he didn't, least of all with the limited supplies he had available to him here in their hideaway. What he needed most, though, was time to rest, and time wasn't a luxury he had at his disposal right now.

That Golkar would be looking for him, he was certain of. How long he would take to find him, though, he had no idea. His knowledge of his fellow Guardian's powers could no longer be relied upon. Who knows what new sources of power may now be available to Golkar. Nor did he know whether the wizard had acquired additional skills, or spells, or if his mysterious ally had become the more immediate threat.

Tactically, Kell knew that he had only a few options available to him, and all of those seemed marred. He could either keep moving in a bid to ensure that Golkar would find it difficult to locate him, or he could stay put and try to regain his strength. The latter option seemed to have more merit. He had drained a considerable portion of his power in the recent battle and it was clear he would be in no shape to attempt anything dramatic again until he got some much-needed rest. Whether Golkar was in similar shape remained unknown.

The other option, that of keeping on the move, was, he knew, dependent on his ability to secure effective transport. Thyfur was his best option, though it would grieve him if he had to further endanger his friend. Without the gryphon's aid, however, and with his own magical powers at such a low ebb, he wouldn't be able to move far or with much speed, and that was a serious limitation. To be caught by Golkar or his ally in the open could prove fatal.

To stay put and rest then was the more attractive option, though its risks were also higher. That Golkar would find him eventually if he stayed put was certain. Were their positions reversed, Kell knew that he could find Golkar anywhere in Ilythia given sufficient time. His timing would need to be finely judged then. He would need to stay where he was long enough to recoup his powers, but not long enough for his adversary to discover his location.

There was a third option, mused Kell, though it wasn't one he relished. That would be to take the battle to Golkar again, as soon as Thyfur was rested. Golkar had been wounded in the recent battle too, and though he had won the day, who knows what the cost had been to his powers. There had been no sign of his ally in the recently completed battle and there was a chance that Golkar may not currently be in a position to enlist the mysterious stranger's aid, for whatever reason. There might, in fact, never be a better time to try and bring an end to both his colleague and his ruinous plans. The support of Thyfur again, especially if he had recovered as much as he seemed to have, and assuming he was still willing to take the risk, might just swing the day in Kell's favour.

Kell knew that this was a choice he wouldn't normally have considered. He wasn't usually one for gambling all on one throw of the dice. It was that very fact that could make it the best of all his options, however. Golkar knew him well. A bold move like that wasn't what he would expect from Kell, and the chances were he hadn't planned for such an eventuality. Maybe, for once in his life, Kell should act out of character. It could be just what was needed to bring an end to this whole conflagration.

Kell wondered if it was the surroundings he now found himself in that had inspired such a stratagem. Was Mishra guiding his thoughts?

That was an interesting thought. Perhaps this was her way of intervening. If a choice had to be made, then why not this one? At least it would end this madness, if not for Golkar, then for him.

But not right now, thought Kell. *Right now I must rest. Such a choice will wait till Thyfur awakes. Until then, I need sleep too.*

~~~

Mardur groaned as she collapsed onto the scaly chest of her lover. "That was good Norag," she gasped between breaths, "very good. How can I ever give you up?"

"Don't."

"If only it were that easy," she sighed, smiling contentedly as she stretched out her legs on either side of Norag's, luxuriating in the feel of his thick leg muscles rubbing against the smooth skin of her inner thighs.

It had to end, though, and she knew it. And she knew that Norag knew it as well. They were both simply delaying the inevitable, playing that dangerous game lovers sometimes do, ignoring the consequences while they wallowed in their lust.

They had both agreed that tonight would be their last tryst, one last night together before they took a more sensible path and brought their affair to the end they should already have given it. Mardur was determined to stick to the plan. They had already pushed their luck to the limits. Any more of this foolishness, delicious though it was, and they would both end up spitted on the end of Grartok's spear.

Mardur didn't kid herself that the lad was in love with her. She knew the attraction for him was purely a physical one. She had known it would be thus right from the start and she had made sure she had shown him things few if any of the inexperienced young women of the tribe could emulate. She knew she would need to do so to maintain his interest, this was a serious business for her, after all. She had needed more than a one night stand.

The level of her success had surprised even her, however. The lad had just kept coming back for more and more and it had taken some effort on her part to keep up with the pace he had set, though she had to admit to enjoying the challenge. Too much so, it seemed, for now, she was ensnared herself, hooked on the power she had come to hold over the young warrior.

And why not? thought Mardur. Norag was a young warrior of barely sixteen summers. He was a fine specimen of slig manhood. He could have any of the pretty young things around the camp; and yet he spurned them all, night after night, in favour of her. She knew that it was foolish but she couldn't help feeling proud of the attention he paid her. She hadn't lost her power over men yet, not by a long shot.

Mardur knew just how jealous the other women must be. First Hrothgar, Second Warrior of the Sagath, had chosen her as tent-mate. That alone was an achievement of some significance. Then she had borne him an heir, and a male heir at that. Sons were of the utmost importance to slig warriors. Many sligs, both warriors and their tent-mates, reckoned their worth by the number of their sons. That Grartok had risen to be leader of the tribe without a son and heir was testament to his unmatched skill in battle. He'd had to fight long and hard before the rest of the warriors realised it was foolish to challenge him in open combat. His childlessness still gnawed at him though, as Mardur well knew.

Hrothgar had been proud of her. She knew it even though he would never admit it to her openly. Maybe a large part of his pride was due to the advantage she had given him over his childless brother, but that didn't matter to Mardur. She had held her head high nonetheless. With Grartok unable to find a suitable mate, there had been no other woman of higher standing in the whole of the tribe.

Then Grartok had cast his eye on her. Though her path since then had been a perilous one, now she was tent-mate to the First Warrior of the Sagath, a position that couldn't be surpassed within the tribe. And soon the Sagath would take their position as foremost tribe in the slig nation. Where would that leave her? Tent-mate to the leader of the slig nation, that's where.

Mardur felt the beat of her heart quicken within her breast. It was hard not to wonder at the speed of her rise. Maybe she had underestimated herself for too long. Men were easy to manipulate, after all, she thought, smiling to herself as Norag began to snore beneath her. They were all captives to their lust. As long as you gave them what they wanted, as often as they wanted it, and with as much variety as possible, and as long as they thought that they were the ones in charge, you had them in the palm of your hand. It was as easy as that. They simply had to believe that you wanted them even more than they wanted you. It didn't matter whether it was true or not; all that mattered was that they believed it. If only the young ones knew, thought Mardur, chuckling to herself.

Norag stirred beneath her. *That's right, little one*, she thought, *get your rest. Soon I will wake you and we shall do it one last time.*

Mardur knew she would have to return to her own tent soon, certainly before the change of the watch. Grartok had kindly arranged for a guard on her tent, to protect her in the event that Hrothgar returned unannounced and tried something foolish. He would think twice about attacking one of the First Warrior's guards. It wasn't that he couldn't best them. To kill one was to sign one's own death warrant; only the First Warrior himself could challenge their authority. Such was the custom of the sligs.

Mardur had made a point of befriending the guards that Grartok had chosen. Glok was the one that usually took the early watch and tonight she had put enough sleeping draught into his ale to ensure he wouldn't awaken before she returned. It wasn't the first time she had done it, either. She would need to wake him before the guard was changed though. Glok didn't like sentry duty, for all its authority. He thought it was soft, especially when others were off at the front, taking Algarian heads as trophies of war. That was fine by Mardur. It made him all the easier to handle. It wouldn't do, though, for him to be replaced by a less tractable sentry. And being caught sleeping on duty in front of the First Warrior's tent wasn't something she would wish on her worst enemy. Then again, she thought, smiling to herself and thinking of Hrothgar, maybe it was.

She was in a good mood tonight, and it wasn't what they had just done that was the only source of her happiness. That very afternoon she had visited Urtok, the tribe's midwife. The old woman had given her the very news she had been so desperate to hear. She was pregnant. Her courses were well overdue and Urtok's examination had confirmed her hopes. Whether the child was Norag's or Grartok's meant nothing to her. She was with child!

If that wasn't enough, Urtok had then proceeded with a reading of the bones. Mardur had never been sure what to think about that little ritual. She had become an instant believer after today's reading though. From the moment the seer had lifted the small cloth bag into her hands and pulled its drawstring apart, an eerie atmosphere had descended on the confines of the tent. Even the smells had changed. She hadn't been able to put her finger on the feeling at the time, but now, with some time to have absorbed the whole experience, Mardur knew what it had felt like. It had been as if, suddenly, there had been others with them there in the tent. It had made her skin crawl, she remembered that quite clearly.

Urtok had shown no sign of any reaction to the change, however. The old crone had scattered her assortment of teeth, knuckles and shards of bone across the floor of her tent. Then she had thrown some nameless but pungent herbs onto the fire of her small brazier and begun to chant, closing her eyes and rocking back and forth on her spindly legs as she did so. Mardur had looked on nervously, uncertain as to what to expect.

Urtok had to have seen close on to a hundred summers and Mardur had wondered if she were about to finally depart this world. She remembered having the strange feeling that the old woman was going to keel over right in the middle of the ritual. It was silly really, but the thought had just popped into her head, along with a very vivid image of that actually occurring. Mardur had gasped involuntarily when, just as that thought was passing through her head, Urtok's eyes had suddenly snapped open and she had begun to speak in a thin reedy voice that didn't really seem to belong to her.

"I see a warrior," she had said. Mardur felt a shudder go through her just at the memory of it. She had never liked the seer. It wasn't right for someone to be able to see things that hadn't happened yet. It was unnatural in her view. "And a male child," Urtok had continued, causing Mardur to gasp yet again. "I see the child on a horse. I see you beside him. The child is yours, the one growing inside you. I see a mass of warriors spread out on the plains before him, more than I have ever seen gathered in one place. The sky behind them is aglow with flames." With that the old woman had abruptly slumped forward, almost knocking over the brazier as she did so.

Well, that had been the end of the reading, and not soon enough, Mardur had thought. She had heard enough for her liking and she didn't want to tempt fate by hearing any more. As soon as Urtok had recovered, Mardur had returned to her own tent, exultant at the news. What she had prayed and hoped for had finally happened. Now she would be safe.

She had been on a high ever since. Now the lie that she'd told Grartok was no longer a lie. All of her troubles were over. Well, almost all of her troubles. Mardur was far too happy to let her few remaining difficulties intrude on her good mood.

Hrothgar remained to be dealt with, of course; though, as far as she was concerned, that was Grartok's problem now. She had little doubt he would deal with it in his normal efficient manner. She doubted if Hrothgar would ever get the chance to call for the *Shüglac* he longed for. Grartok was too wily for that. He would probably have his brother despatched long before he even returned to the tribe.

Then there was the matter of Hrothgar's son. Mardur didn't allow her mind to dwell on that little problem either. She had already begun to prepare herself for the inevitable. The child was being looked after by one of the younger women at this very moment, and had been for days. Mardur had feigned illness and her position as Grartok's tent-mate wasn't without its perks. She was distancing herself from the babe, knowing deep within her that there was nothing she could do to save it in her current situation. She had already begun to tell herself that the child was bound to be trouble anyway. It was Hrothgar's spawn after all.

No, she wouldn't allow anything to put a blot on her mood now. This was a good day and she meant to keep it that way.

"Wake up you," she cried, sitting up and shaking Norag as she spoke. "I'm ready for more boy. What's the matter? Can't you keep up?"

~~~

"Where's that son of a putok Larnük? What kind of a mess can the cur have possibly gotten himself into?"

It wasn't the first time Hrothgar had asked the questions and, just like on all of the other occasions, he could feel his anger rising steadily as he spat out his words. "I can't wait in this stinking wilderness forever. If we don't get away from here soon, there'll be nothing left of those Algarian dogs for us to feast on but ash and bones."

Though there were more than a dozen warriors within earshot of Hrothgar when he spoke, not one of them dared to answer his question. Not that Hrothgar minded. He hadn't expected an answer, he was just venting his frustration and they knew it as well as he did. He and what was left of his small group of warriors had pitched their camp in a small clearing beside the ford that had been their pre-arranged meeting point. Of the twenty men he had set out with, thirteen of them were here with him, waiting. Seven were missing.

Like everyone else, Larnük and the three warriors he had taken with him had been due at the camp three days earlier. Only, they hadn't turned up when they'd been due. When they still hadn't shown up by the next morning, Hrothgar had sent out another four warriors to find them. Now it wasn't only Larnük and his men that were missing. Three of the second group hadn't returned either. They had been due back at high-sun the previous day.

Hrothgar was beginning to wonder if his mission was cursed. There was simply no explanation for what had happened to any of the missing men. The only firm conclusion he had been able to reach was that to send any more of his warriors out on search parties would be foolhardy in the extreme. If the missing members of his hunt didn't turn up soon, he would just have to leave without them.

Rhontar, the one warrior who had returned, had seen no sign of any of their comrades. The last he had seen of the three that had gone with him to look for Larnük had been when they had split up to widen their search area. Of Larnük and his group, there had been no sign at all. Rhontar said that he had found a campfire of theirs that seemed to have been disturbed in some way, but he could find no clear indication of either what might have happened to them or where they had gone. And Rhontar was one of his best trackers!

The whole thing was a complete and utter mystery and Hrothgar could feel his frustration growing. He also knew that his mood was rapidly turning to anger. If only one of his men would give him the excuse he was looking for. He watched with contempt as they averted their look from his as he cast his eyes over the group assembled about him. Not one of them dared to meet his gaze. A few of them were taking the time to clean and sharpen their weapons; others were attending to long overdue repairs to their gear. Most of them simply stood around, leaning casually on the shafts of their spears or their long-handled axes, idly chatting with their companions. They knew their place, he thought to himself. They were capable warriors, but there wasn't one of them that would dare to challenge their hunt leader.

Hrothgar liked to run his hunt with an iron fist. 'Keep 'em scared and keep 'em on the edge', was what his father had always said to him and his brother, and experience had taught him his father was right. It made for better warriors and it kept them in line. He'd seen how some of the other hunts operated, like a pack of dogs, each one waiting for the next one up the line to make a mistake so they could feast on his carcass. Not an ounce of loyalty in the whole of the hunt. Hrothgar had nothing but contempt for those hunt leaders.

His failure to find Larnük and his men bothered him though, and the seeming loss of three more warriors searching for them was nothing short of a disaster. It wasn't just that Hrothgar was itching to get away to join the battle against the Algarians; it rankled to lose good men with nothing to show for their loss. He prided himself on his prowess as a leader. Good leaders didn't waste their resources needlessly.

Warriors would often be lost achieving an objective; that was to be expected. But Hrothgar knew that he hadn't achieved his. That cursed human female was nowhere to be found. He couldn't even say that his men had died valiantly in battle. Perhaps they had, but unless they turned up, no one would ever know. They had just disappeared without a trace.

Hrothgar could hear that swine of a brother of his now. He would relish this little bit of news, that was for sure. And he wouldn't forget it in a hurry either. Seven warriors lost in a search for one defenceless human female, and after all that, they hadn't even found their quarry.

Hrothgar kicked at the embers of the fire in frustration. The dog had set him up for failure and he had been fool enough to let him. How could anyone hope to find one female in all this wilderness? And what was the point of this ridiculous mission anyway? She was probably dead by now, fallen down some ravine, or drowned in a river. Let the Guardians play their games with each other, the sligs had no need of them. Where was the honour in hiding behind the robes of a wizard? Cold steel, thought Hrothgar, that was what the sligs had built their reputation on.

Hrothgar's eyes, which had been wandering over the warriors spread around the campsite, came to rest finally on a solitary slig. He was smaller than the rest of the warriors and was seated alone, away from the bulk of the group. It was Norvig. He was always alone. Hrothgar knew that none of the rest of the hunt cared for his cousin. And Norvig had never been one to cultivate friendships.

He had turned up at the ford two days earlier, as agreed, having successfully delivered the information which Hrothgar had wanted sold to Kell. Though he welcomed the bags of gold Norvig had returned with, he found little else to celebrate about his cousin's arrival. First, there was the simple fact that he just couldn't stand the sight of the snivelling little runt. But secondly, and more importantly on this occasion, his report of his meeting with Kell and the message that the Guardian had sent back with him had served to turn Hrothgar's foul mood even fouler, as if he didn't have enough on his mind as it was.

The Second Warrior had never had any liking for any of the Guardians, least of all Kell. He wondered how he would have reacted to the insults Norvig claimed he'd had to endure at the wizard's hands. He was certain he wouldn't have been able to show the restraint his cousin had exercised. Perhaps he would have finally found out just how good the wizards really were. From what Norvig had told him, it sounded as if Kell had pulled off one almighty bluff, and Norvig, of course, hadn't had the guts to call it. Hrothgar wondered if the Guardian would have dared such a sham if it had been him instead of his cousin he'd been dealing with.

The Guardian's offer of further money for more information was equally galling. Five hundred gold crowns was a lot of gold, by anyone's standard. What was annoying, however, was that Hrothgar didn't have the information Kell sought. He knew that the girl was important, but he didn't know why. Then again, maybe it was a good thing he hadn't been able to locate her. If Kell placed that much value on finding out more about her, then perhaps it would be better if she was still out there somewhere. Perhaps she would keep Kell and the other Guardians busy tracking her down while the Sagath got on with dismembering the Algarian empire.

For the moment, then, it seemed that Norvig had outlived his usefulness. In fact, if anything, he was now a distinct liability. Hrothgar could see that it would be difficult to extract any more gold from Kell for the moment. By the time he found out what the wizard wanted to know, he'd be unlikely to be in any position to negotiate its sale. In fact, if he had his way he'd soon be back with the bulk of the army. There'd be little opportunity for that kind of maneuvering then.

Besides, the whole arrangement was becoming just a little bit too risky to Hrothgar's way of thinking. His brother had played his hand and Hrothgar had done what he could to ensure that all would not go exactly as planned. As far as he could see, it was in the hands of Zar now. There was nothing more that he could do other than ensure that he was ready to seize whatever fresh opportunity the God of Battles should decide to throw his way.

Norvig, however, was another matter. Hrothgar didn't like loose ends. Better to take your blade and chop them off before they have a chance to unravel, that was his motto. Something would have to be done about his little cousin and Hrothgar realised this could be just the opportunity he'd been looking for. Why take his anger out on some unfortunate member of his hunt when little Norvig was so close to hand? Besides, if he played his cards right, he might be able to make himself look good at the same time.

Hrothgar felt better now that he'd decided what to do. If Larnük and the rest of the missing warriors didn't turn up by high-sun, he would send the remainder of his hunt off to join the battle against the Algarians. He was the hunt leader, though. He wouldn't abandon his missing men without first ensuring he had done everything he could to find them. He would stay behind for one last, albeit brief, search; and Norvig would help him.

There would be no one else around to interfere with Hrothgar's plans then. And if Norvig got a bit careless and met with a little accident, then who would know that he didn't go missing, just like all of the others. Hrothgar could feel his mood brightening already. He couldn't help the smile that spread across his face as his mind filled with a vision of cousin Norvig kneeling before him, snivelling like a baby and begging for his life.

CHAPTER 10

The surface of the mirror shimmered and rippled as Golkar passed through it, settling once more as the last portion of his body cleared its frame. The wizard stood still for a moment, taking a deep breath and steadying himself as he surveyed his surroundings and allowed the thrill that accompanied the passage to course through his body. His eyes came to rest on the sole occupant of the room he had entered.

"I'm not sure how you do that," exclaimed the woman who stood facing him, "but it's very distracting. Can't you use the door like everyone else? I might have been in the middle of dressing, or just about to hop into my bath. Can't you knock . . . or something."

Golkar laughed. He wasn't taken in by her charade of modesty for an instant. "Then the pleasure would have been mine, I'm sure. Perhaps if you hung the mirror on your parlour wall instead of in your bedchamber you wouldn't have to worry about such things."

"Hmmm. Perhaps." The woman's smile betrayed her good humour. "To what do I owe the pleasure of your company this time, my lord Golkar?" she continued, seemingly ignoring his jibe. "Is this business, or . . . something else? My room is a mess today." As she spoke, she turned her head coquettishly in Golkar's direction, batting her eyelids gently and peering at him from beneath her long lashes with twinkling eyes.

Golkar couldn't help but smile in return. The room didn't look at all messy to him. It looked just like it had the last time he'd visited Tay-rala, cozy and inviting, even if it was just a touch too feminine for his taste. His eyes wandered to the large four-poster bed he knew from experience had the softest mattress he had ever laid down on. It all looked very inviting indeed. But that was how a woman's bedroom should look as far as he was concerned. Golkar knew from experience that the other chambers of her small cottage were much more pragmatically furnished.

In his view, it was Tay-rala herself who added the touch that gave the room its real warmth though. Without her, the room was just a room; but she was something special, a striking specimen, tall and slender with thick, long, brown hair that seemed to cascade down her back like a shimmering waterfall, catching the soft candle-light in the room as she moved to and fro, pretending to busy herself at her dresser. Her features were fine and her slender face matched her physique. She was an attractive woman, even more so when she used just a hint of Glamour to enhance her looks, as Golkar could see she had done today.

She had probably cast the spell as soon as she'd seen him coming through the mirror. She had no real need of it, nor had she the skill to make anything more than subtle enhancements to her appearance, but Golkar guessed that vanity compelled her to try and look her best for him. Having won his friendship, she seemed to work hard at maintaining his interest in her. Though she was clearly attracted to him physically, it wasn't hard to see that she was equally drawn to his power and standing and he, in his turn, found that particularly gratifying. There was nothing more pleasing than bedding a woman who knew the full value of his place in the world, *and* who adored him for it.

Perhaps it was the after-effects of the transport spell, but for a moment he was tempted to put his business to one side for a while. Tay-rala was, after all, his closest female companion, with the twin virtues of being both an occasional lover of some skill and a charming companion. And it was not as if she didn't know her place. He knew that her pretence at ease in his presence was just that, a sham. Though she had some small capacity for magic herself, she obviously knew she was hopelessly outmatched by his power. That scared her a little; he could sense that, and he liked it. But he also knew that, like him, she was incredibly ambitious. She had skills of her own after all.

She was a seer. She had the gift of foresight and what's more, when the circumstances were right, she could focus her skill quite tightly. Without that, her visions would have been nothing more than an interesting jumble of snippets of what was to come. Many could claim that ability. It was only when those visions could be harnessed that they became an asset rather than a liability. Very few could achieve that, and Tay-rala was one of those few, the best in fact that Golkar had ever known.

And that was what drew him to her even more. She knew where his plans were taking him. He had confided in her just enough to see what would happen, knowing she wouldn't be able to resist exploring where his schemes would take him. And yet she had stood by him. If anything, her devotion to him had increased. Clearly, whatever she had seen of his future, she'd decided that she wanted to be a part of it as well, or perhaps she had simply seen the alternative and didn't want to be a part of that.

Golkar didn't mind. Her motivation was her affair. One needed company at times after all. What were friends after all but people you used when your own company was no longer enough? Even a Guardian had to unwind occasionally. After the day he'd had thus far, he could do with some time to relax. Unfortunately, now was not the time. It was her talents, both as a healer and a seer, that had brought him to Tay-rala's abode.

"Business this time," he replied. "You don't know how much I would love to spend the afternoon in your arms, my dear, but right now I need your assistance." Easing his coat down his back, Golkar turned to display the bloodied bandage he'd managed to wrap around his shoulder. Though the wound the gryphon had given him was still throbbing, he kept a tight rein on his feelings. His pride wouldn't allow him to let Tay-rala see the extent of the pain he was in.

Pride or not, however, he knew that the wound was in bad need of attention. He had lost a considerable amount of blood already and even he could tell that if something wasn't done to properly seal the wound soon he would find himself in dire straits. He needed to recuperate his strength after his battle with Kell and he wouldn't be able to do so properly until his shoulder was seen to.

"Ahhhh. I see, my lord. And I thought this was just a social call. Let me take a look at that. Come into the parlour and let's get that dressing off. And then you can tell me how it is possible that a Guardian can be given a wound like that!"

Golkar's assessment of Tay-rala's skills wasn't unwarranted. Within a short time, he was seated before her fire sipping a herbal brew which she assured him would do him the world of good in his current depleted condition. His wound had been cleaned, stitched, poulticed and freshly dressed, and he felt immeasurably better than he had done when he'd arrived at her house. Already the pain in his shoulder was receding.

"It was a clean tear and nothing major was damaged," announced Tay-rala, who was seated beside him. Her words had startled him for an instant. Apart from the occasional question, and a brief nod when he had responded, she had barely said a word while working on his injury. Golkar had been happy to remain silent; he'd sensed her need to focus her powers on the task at hand. Her words now were the first the two had spoken to each other for some time.

"The healing spell I used will speed up the regeneration process. The stitches are only a precaution really, in case you don't keep it immobilised like I've told you to. My guess is that you won't rest until you've settled this affair. Now that your plans are exposed, no doubt you'll want to see them through to their conclusion. I don't think your injury will hinder you for long now that I've seen to it. A wound from a gryphon is just like any other, it would seem. I detected nothing of concern in the wound. There was no magic at work there that I can discern."

"It feels better already," replied Golkar, nodding thoughtfully. "I've always said that your talents are many and varied."

"Hmmm. Don't try your sweet talk on me. You need a good night's rest and then you should be fine. That draught you're drinking will pick you up in no time at all."

"Good. Now to my other business. As you said, now that my plans are in the open I must allow my opponents no time to plan an adequate response." Golkar saw no need to let Tay-rala know that he had been forced to declare his hand somewhat prematurely. The girl was a detail he'd not shared with her either; though, for all he knew, her powers had already allowed her to see how he meant to achieve his aims.

"I have a need to draw on your other talents as well. I need to find out where Kell and the gryphon have gone. I'm sure they were in no better state than I was when they withdrew from our encounter. I mean to follow them up and finish them off as soon as I can. The old fool has no idea how long I've prepared for this or he wouldn't have challenged me so openly. Now that I've rebuffed him once, I need to finish off before he can make better preparations for his own defences, or before he can do anything to put my other plans in jeopardy. But before I can do that, I need to know where he is."

"I see." Tay-rala sat quietly for a few moments before she continued. "Very well. I've not spoken to you of this before, but I've already had a vision of a confrontation between you and Kell. I sought and was given a glimpse shortly after you first confided in me. I couldn't resist exploring that line, as I guessed you knew I would. You must have known my curiosity would be piqued, and I think you wouldn't have confided in me in the first place if you'd not wanted me to seek such a glimpse." The seer paused for a moment then, watching Golkar with an anxious look on her face. "I hope I did no wrong."

"No, no. Of course not. Go on."

Visibly relaxing, Tay-rala continued. "The glimpse I was given was quite a vivid one. Though I couldn't see the actual outcome of the confrontation, I distinctly remember the feeling that Kell had fallen and that you were left as the sole Guardian of Ilythia. That last feeling, in particular, came through to me remarkably strongly. I couldn't tell what had become of Tarak, but I had the sense that he was no longer a force to be reckoned with. I remember one portion of the glimpse quite clearly. I saw you standing alone at the top of a flight of broad stairs. As I said, you were alone, and you had your hands raised above you, as if in victory. The sense of exultance that radiated from you was unbelievably powerful. That was how the vision ended."

Having related her tale, Tay-rala paused for a moment, watching Golkar's face. She could see that she'd surprised him. "It was a very powerful glimpse, Golkar. Even now some of the images are still clear in my mind."

"Really? Why didn't you tell me about this before now?"

"I . . . I was worried you'd be angry with me for prying into your business. And I saw no need to tell you. In my experience, it's a dangerous business revealing the future. My visions are only one view of what may happen. They're glimpses, nothing more and nothing less. At times, the very knowledge of how something may unfold can lead to a different outcome. Complacency, for example, when the utmost preparation may be called for. I've learnt it is often better not to share such visions.

"But as for what you seek. I may already be able to help you there as well. While I was tending to your wound just now, I had another . . . 'vision'. Not a glimpse this time. It was something different to that, but nonetheless, I believe that what I saw was real. It came to me as I was cleaning the wound, as my hand touched the torn skin. It was a vision of a beast that could only have been a gryphon. I've never seen one, of course, but that is what this must have been. It was large, very large, and it looked like a lion, except that its head was like that of a hawk, or an eagle, or some such similar bird, and it had two great wings folded against its sides. Its sides shone in the sunlight. They are very magical beasts, as you well know. Its recent touch to your wound must have left a residue that I could sense.

"I saw it lying, as if asleep. It was lying amidst the ruins of a temple. The whole structure was old . . . very old. Then that passed and I saw what I took to be the same scene, but from afar. I could see the ruins of some ancient place atop a small hillock. The whole thing was surrounded by desert. The sun was beating down on it and the hill stood out as if it was an island surrounded by sand. I'm not sure, but think it might have been somewhere in the Northern Wastes, unless it was somewhere on Liricor.

"Interesting," replied Golkar, rubbing his chin thoughtfully. "That is very interesting indeed. It does sound like the Northern Wastes, doesn't it; and I know of a place there that fits your description quite well. I must say, my dear, you are full of surprises. Did you see Kell in this vision."

Tay-rala smiled at Golkar's compliment. "My skills are nothing compared to yours, but I'll be happy if I can play some small part in helping you achieve your goal. What are friends for after all? No. I didn't see Kell. But that isn't surprising. The connection was with the gryphon, with the wound he gave you and the magic that resides in the beast. It isn't unusual for such a vision to be localised just to that aspect of the connection, to the beast in this case."

"That makes sense. I expect that he won't have strayed far from the creature in any event. If I find the gryphon, my guess is I'll find Kell somewhere very close by. You have done me a service Tay-rala, a very great service. If your vision was a true one, and if I'm right about the place you saw, then you'll have given me just what I need to finish that meddling, old fool off once and for all. I won't forget this."

Golkar eased back in his chair and took another sip from the draught Tay-rala had brewed for him. For the first time since the human girl had gone missing, he felt that his plans were back on track again. Though he'd had no word from Tug, regardless of what Tarak may have known, it was clear that Kell, at least, was unaware of her presence here in Ilythia. He would never have acted so precipitously if he had been. He would have bided his time, or worked out some way to use the girl's power to thwart him. Instead, all the old fool had done was expose his own weakness. Clearly, Kell hadn't the faintest idea how to stop him from achieving his aims. Now that he'd played his one and only card, and failed, it would be a simple matter for Golkar to finish him off.

He was glad he hadn't let Josef die just yet. He would come in handy now. Not as good as the girl would have been, and certainly not enough if his colleagues had been more challenging adversaries, but, given the circumstances, adequate for the task at hand. The girl was simply a bonus now. He would be able to use her power to better effect without having to waste it in dealing with his two colleagues as he'd originally planned.

He would rest now. When he was rested, he would strike, and strike quickly. Kell would have no chance at all this time. Then Golkar would be *the* Guardian of Ilythia, sole Guardian that is, not just one of three. Then all of Ilythia would see how powerful he had become. He would need to make a demonstration or two of his powers, of course, finish off the girl and ensure that all would bow to his will in one and the same breath.

"No indeed," he said softly, turning to look once more at Tay-rala and reaching out to take her hand in his. "I won't forget this, my dear."

~~~

Count Regulus leaned forward with his elbows resting on top of the rough stone wall of the parapet as he gazed out at the scene before him. The view from the walls of the city was little different from what it had been the day before, or the day before that, or the one before that. The smell of smoke and ash was stronger than it had been yesterday. That was one difference he noted. Today, he could see four separate plumes of smoke rising from beyond the distant hills, whereas yesterday there had been only two. The overall colour of the sky was different too. Looking out as far as the horizon, he could see that a smudgy brown haze now separated the green of the hills from the clear blue of the eastern sky. If only it would rain again, he thought. That might douse the flames. It might even slow down the sligs' seemingly inexorable advance.

They were out there, and he knew it, as did everyone else in Keerêt. Somewhere beyond those distant hills, beyond the horizon, they would be fighting skirmishes with Algarian regulars even now. Hopefully, the army had their measure by now. Hopefully, the tide had finally turned.

That didn't stop the frantic preparations that were going on closer to home, however. The Marshal was too seasoned a fighter to be caught with his guard down. Regulus knew that he was working just as hard at preparing the defences for the city as he was at directing the tactics for the front line troops. One had only to glance at the wide expanse of plain between the walls of Keerêt and the distant row of hills to see that.

From where Regulus stood, he could make out small figures scurrying across the plain. The smaller groups, he knew, would be citizens in the main, maybe a farmer, with a bundle of his belongings across his shoulders, hastening to move into the safety of the city, or some merchant rushing to see to his goods before he too sought shelter. The larger groups, he knew, would be Algarian regulars. A whole regiment had marched out only an hour beforehand and he could still make them out by the plume of dust he could see rising skywards way in the distance. It wasn't hard to guess their destination, even if you weren't privy to the details of imperial strategy as Regulus was.

The road they were following would take them straight to the Mendobar Hills. That was where the last stand would be made if the sligs weren't held at the river. Not that that was likely now. After a fortnight of bad news, the situation was slowly but surely changing. The weather hadn't turned, even though Count Brassilius, the Marshal of the Realm, had been quietly praying for more rain for a week, but the slig advance was being slowed nonetheless. Indeed, from the more recent reports, it seemed it might even have ground to a halt. The Algarians had finally stopped retreating.

Brassilius had formed his defensive line along the eastern shore of the Sarrowmar River, knowing that if the regulars couldn't hold them there then they could rapidly pull back across the river, bring down the bridges behind them, and defy any attempt to cross the river in force. Though the deep and swift-flowing river would provide an almost impenetrable line of defence, however, it would also prove difficult for the Algarians to re-cross. Once yielded, the eastern shore would prove difficult to regain should the sligs decide to stay there. And that meant virtually giving up some three-quarters of Algaria to the enemy. They would be able to plunder and ravage the eastern parts of Algaria with impunity. And so Brassilius had formed his line on the eastern shore, and his strategy seemed to be working.

He and his commanders had considered a wide range of scenarios. Regulus and the rest of the Council had been briefed on their deliberations only the night before. In the unlikely event that the army couldn't deny the sligs passage of the river, Brassilius' plan was for them to fall back to the line of the Mendobar Hills. There they would re-group before completing a more orderly retreat to the walls of Keerêt.

Of course, Regulus knew only too well that if that happened they were all doomed. The Mendobar Hills couldn't be held for more than a day or so. A stand there would merely delay the sligs while the bulk of the Algarian army retreated with some dignity. What was left of it, that is. A retreat from the river would only occur if the army's losses were too great for it to remain there any longer. There would be nowhere else to go then. They would be bottled up in Keerêt and the doom of the Algarians would be upon them.

None of that was likely though, realised Regulus, shrugging off his gloomy thoughts. Brassilius was simply covering all eventualities. That was why he was Marshal of the Realm. The eastern shore of the Sarrowmar was well fortified. The Algarians could hold that line for years if need be. And, in any event, they would surely find a way to re-cross it even if they were forced back. The Algarians weren't done for yet. If anything this war was just starting. Now that the army had stopped retreating, the sligs would see what they were really up against. They'd had it all their way till now, but no more.

Regulus felt his spirits lifting. The Algarians were a great people, with a great leader. Elissa would lead them out of this situation. She would never allow them to go under without a fight that would ring down the ages. He could hear her words now, echoing in his mind. The speech she had given the Council last night had been one of the most stirring he had ever heard. Even her father would have been proud to see her. One part kept repeating over and over in his head.

"We have only just begun to fight," she had said. "The sligs will curse the day they started this war. It will go down as their great day of mourning, if any of them live to tell the tale. They will rue the day they took on the might of the Algarian empire. They will find that instead of a sleeping dog they have roused a mighty lion, one that will chase them back across the land, nipping at their heels, devouring their fallen, tearing at their stragglers. There will be no place in all of Ilythia for them to hide from our wrath."

It had roused the Council members just at the time they needed it most, and their fervour would soon spread through the Algarians like a fire. They had been the right words at the right time. Regulus couldn't help the feeling of pride that coursed through him as he remembered the emotions that had swept through the chamber when Elissa had delivered her speech. They were a mighty people and they wouldn't go down into the dustbin of history without a fight.

"The sligs have broken through at Jeeluk, Sir. Our outliers are falling back to the river."

Count Regulus turned to face the military attaché standing before him, drawing his eyes away from the eastern horizon. He had been so engrossed in his thoughts that he hadn't heard the man right.

"Sorry, What did you say? The sligs have broken through where?"

"At Jeeluk, Sir," the attaché responded, with just the hint of a tremor to his voice. "The Queen has called an emergency meeting of the Council. You're required urgently."

"But that can't be right," responded Regulus, ignoring his demand for the moment. What the man was saying didn't make sense. "Brassilius had the defences on the Northern Frontier bolstered. The last report said that all of the bridges were down except the one at Landorion, and Landorion is well garrisoned. Where did you get this information, soldier? It can't be right."

Regulus' eyes widened in horror as the attaché answered his questions. He could see that the man was rattled, and the more he heard, the more he understood why.

"From Count Brassilius, Sir. I've come directly from him. They've got across the river on the northern front. Landorion's been cut off and they're sweeping south towards Keerêt. Jeeluk has already fallen, Sir. There's nothing between them and the capital this side of the river. The order's gone out to pull back across the Sarrowmar immediately, before the army's caught in a pincer. They've got to abandon their positions there before they get trapped between two slig armies."

CHAPTER 11

If ever Sara had been in any doubt, the horrible images Ruz had conjured up of what they would do to Rayne confirmed her worst fears. She was in the hands of cruel and sick monsters. Not content with simply killing her, as she knew they would do in the end, for the moment they seemed to be enjoying the mental abuse they were inflicting upon her too much to bring her ordeal to that chilling conclusion.

They would hunt Rayne down, Ruz had told her. It might take some time, but in the end, they would find him. And once they did, they would use their authority to insist the Algarians hand him over. And she should be in no doubt. The Algarians would not dare to refuse such a demand from Golkar.

Then they would torture him. And she would be made to watch. It would be slow, and it would be painful; that much was certain. Regardless of what else they did, that would be their payment for her refusal to tell them what they wanted.

But it wouldn't end there. Not if she kept on denying them. Tell them everything now, Ruz had demanded, and Rayne's end would be painful, but at least then they would put him out of his misery. They would kill him and that would be the end of it. Continue to deny them, he had assured her perversely, and they would let him live; if you could call living what it would be like for him after they had removed certain parts of his body. His right arm, certainly, and both of his ears, perhaps, and his nose, maybe even his legs.

Sara took a deep breath as Ruz stepped back for a moment to give her a chance to consider his repulsive threats. She was grateful for at least that moment of respite, but knew that he wasn't done with her yet. Not by a long shot.

"Answer me, hu-maan," the draghar screamed at her. Though the volume of his voice was unnecessary, both that and his shrill tone had the effect he no doubt wanted. Sara cringed in response.

She knew that she couldn't keep this up for much longer. *Why am I holding back*, she thought, watching for a sign that he was about to move in closer and continue his vicious verbal assault. *I'll tell them in the end. I know I will. They won't stop until they've broken me, so what am I proving by denying them. If I tell them now, maybe they'll stop and put an end to all of this torment.*

Before Sara could complete her line of thought, she whimpered involuntarily as she saw the draghar take the step forward she had known he would, closing the distance between them before she could even begin to think of how to answer his question.

"I'll ask you one more time you little bitch," Ruz snarled, leaning in so that his face was almost touching her own. "How do you know the old man? Who is this Josef and where did you meet him? Where did he come from?"

Sara could smell his fetid breath as he spoke. She wished that her hands were free so that she could reach up and wipe from her face the spittle he was spraying as he scowled at her. She knew deep down though, even if her wrists hadn't been bound tightly to the arms of the chair they had chained her to, she wouldn't be game to do that.

She was confused. Although she wanted her torment to stop, fear was muddling her thoughts. Right at this moment, she didn't dare do or say anything that might further fuel his barely-contained rage.

But she had to say something. She had to stop them from continuing their interrogation. She couldn't take it any more. To think that they might do these things, that she might have to watch while they did them, that Rayne might have to endure such things. It was just too horrible to contemplate. Her whole body was trembling now.

Her mind was equally agitated, with contradictory thoughts swirling around, jostling for attention, first suggesting one way of responding, then, only moments later, another.

She was afraid to speak, lest it not be what they wanted to hear. At the same time, she wanted to tell them. She wanted it to end. But she couldn't betray Josef, not after everything he had done for her and Rayne. But then, maybe he would understand. Maybe he already knew that she was no hero. She was a coward really. She knew that now, and surely he must too. If only she could ask someone. She didn't know what to do.

"I . . . I don't know. Ho . . . hon . . . honest I don't. I . . ." she finally managed to stammer.

As Sara spoke, she turned her head towards Golkar, pleading with him with her eyes in her desperation. Surely he would see that this couldn't go on for much longer. Surely there must be some vestige of decency left in the man. Surely he would step in soon and bring an end to Ruz' horrific inquisition.

The tears in her eyes as she stumbled over the words, combined with the direction of her gaze, prevented her from anticipating Ruz' reaction to her silent plea to his master. The scream he shrieked from his position just a few inches from her face shook her to the core.

She almost blacked out in response, the fright he gave her was so extreme, so unexpected. For a few moments, she seemed to lose track of what was happening, of where she was and what was being asked of her. It lasted for only a few moments, and then, in a sudden rush, it all came back to her, the memories washing through her like a flood from a collapsing dam.

She was in Golkar's lair. That was it. After the wizard had met them on the path to Tu-atha they had brought her back here and they had been tormenting her ever since. She wondered if what she had been through in that time had served any purpose other than to satisfy their sick needs and to drive her to the brink of insanity. All those questions and all those disgusting threats. Why? What was the point? What could they possibly gain from finding out what she knew?

They had asked her about Josef a number of times. At first, she had been surprised to hear they were even aware of his existence. Then she had been about to reveal what little she did know when it suddenly dawned on her that they had been using the present tense when they spoke of him. That meant he was still alive! She had been certain he was long dead. Before long, she had ascertained that he was not only alive, he was here, here with her in Tu-atha. They were holding him captive too.

The glimmer of hope that had formed then had been just as quickly dashed. Ruz had told her that he *was* all but dead, that Golkar was using him, like he had used that young girl he had killed the night she had arrived in Ilythia, like he intended to use her once he was finished with Josef. Unfortunately, Josef's particular nightmare hadn't ended yet either; he was in the same predicament she was.

Now she remembered why she had refused to tell them what she knew. Josef was alive. She couldn't betray his friendship while ever he was still alive. Who knows whether it mattered or not; she just couldn't do that. They were going to kill her anyway, the least she could do was to honour his friendship. It was all she had left now.

"That'll do, Ruz," she heard Golkar exclaim wearily from where he sat on the other side of the room. "It doesn't really matter, anyway. He's been useful, whoever he is."

Turning her head to one side again, Sara watched apprehensively as the wizard slowly rose from his chair. "You're an enigma, Sara," he exclaimed as he approached her, "that's for certain. As is this Josef. But who'd have thought I'd get two for the price of one?"

Sara closed her eyes so that she didn't have to look at the smile on the wizard's face. It was so horrible, so false. Turning her face away from him, she tried to swallow. She had been so terrified of Ruz and his threats she hadn't thought to do that while his intense questioning had been going on. Doing so now only served to remind her how parched her throat felt. Though she knew that her face must be covered in sweat, her mouth felt incredibly dry.

"Please," she begged, taking advantage of the wizard's seeming decision to end her torment, at least for the moment, and hanging her head, not daring to look at either of her tormentors as she spoke. "Can I have some water?" Her voice sounded croaky.

"Yes, of course you can, my dear." It was Golkar's deep voice that responded. She opened her eyes and turned to face him once more. "Must keep your strength up," he continued. Though his tone was pleasant enough, it gave her little comfort. She knew that the end must be close for her now.

As if to confirm the thought, the wizard turned towards Ruz and spoke again, reaching out across the table that stood against one wall of the room and filling a small goblet with water as he did so. "Fetch Josef back up here again," he said in an off-hand manner to the draghar, "and get him ready. Tug can help you."

With a final snarl in Sara's direction, Ruz moved to obey his master. She knew what his look meant. *You think what I gave you was bad. You're really in for it now*, he had said to her, as plainly as if he had spoken the words. She felt her lower lip tremble ever so slightly. She knew he was right. She watched as the draghar left the room, then shivered as she realised he had left her alone with Golkar.

In all of her time in Tu-atha, both since Tug had brought her back, and when she had first been brought there, she had never been totally alone with the fiend. Either Tug or Ruz had always been present when he had been with her. Now, for the first time, she was alone with the maniac. She felt the goosebumps rise on her skin as the wizard approached her with the goblet of water in his hand. She knew he could see the way she was squirming futilely against her bonds, but there was nothing she could do to control her actions. For some strange reason, his very presence unnerved her. Hard though it was to believe, she would rather be left alone with Tug or Ruz than with him. He made her skin crawl, and it only got worse the closer he came to her.

Having reached her side, Golkar stood there for a moment, obviously relishing her discomfort, then lifted the goblet to her lips, tilting it ever so slightly so that some of the water within could flow into her waiting mouth. She saw him smile as she flinched when his arm brushed against her tunic as he held the drinking vessel up to her lips. For a moment, she hesitated, wondering if the water was drugged, then relaxed as she realised that would actually be a godsend. As she opened her mouth, she closed her eyes, not wanting the wizard to see the fear she knew they would betray. Greedily, she gulped down the cool fluid, swallowing repeatedly until the goblet had been drained. Her automatic 'thank you' as the wizard placed the goblet back on the table drew another unwanted smile from Golkar. Sara wondered if any of his other victims had been so polite on the eve of their death.

"So now we come to it, my dear," he said, approaching her once more. Halting directly in front of her, the wizard reached out and pushed a strand of hair that hung down over her eyes back into place, carefully avoiding touching her skin as he did so. "It will be better for us both if you try to stay calm," he continued. "I'll finish with Josef first, and then it will be your turn. I promise not to keep you waiting long."

Somehow, she managed to hold back the tears that sprung to her eyes until he turned away and began to busy himself at his table once more. As she felt the salty fluid beginning to run down her cheeks and onto her lips, she tried to focus her attention on the wizard, knowing that if she allowed her mind to wander she would quickly lose all control of her emotions. Images of her parents, of Rayne, of her house and her friends all sprang to the forefront of her mind, jostling with each other for attention. Taking a deep breath, she pushed them all away, trying to calm herself by focusing on what the wizard was doing.

She watched as he lifted a small pot that had been simmering for some time on a brazier beside the table. As he poured some of its contents into a slightly larger bowl which he had placed on the table, Sara caught a glimpse of the fluid within. From what she saw, it appeared to be nothing but water. She had automatically assumed it would be something more sinister than that, and perhaps it was. Looks, as she knew, could be deceiving.

Once that was done, he reached up and took down three porcelain jars from a shelf that ran along the wall behind the table. As he opened each container, he held it to his nose for an instant, then reached in and took a pinch of its contents and added it to the bowl of heated liquid. When he had done that with all three, he took down a bunch of what looked to be dried herbs and began to add some of their leaves to the mixture as well, crushing them with his hand as he did so and gently stirring the resulting concoction. This continued for a short time until he seemed satisfied with the result and put the mixture aside.

Into a smaller bowl, he then placed three or four seeds which he extracted from yet another jar on the shelf above the table. He then took a small, black pestle and began to crush the seeds against the side of what she now realised was a mortar. Once he had reduced the seeds to a powder, he added that too to the larger bowl and began to stir the mixture once again. Within moments, the room began to fill with a heady aroma that belied the small quantities he seemed to be using.

For some reason, despite her circumstances, Sara felt her spirits beginning to lift as the aroma permeated the room. Her pulse, which had been steadily rising as she had watched Golkar preparing his strange brew, began to slow. Her breathing, which had been shallow and laboured, began to return to a steadier rhythm as well. Even her eyes, which had felt heavy and downcast, began to lift and clear.

She watched in fascination as Golkar then seated himself at the table once more and leaned down, right over the bowl, breathing its fumes in deeply in steady, measured breaths. Even from where she was, bound to her chair, she could see the way the colour of his skin slowly, but noticeably, began to change. Whatever the concoction was, it was clearly very powerful stuff.

Sara wondered what the seemingly innocent ingredients must really have been. Certainly, they cannot have been simple garden herbs. His normally pale skin was slowly but surely acquiring a pinkish hue that hadn't been there before he had begun to inhale the brew over which he was now slumped.

Sara's focus on Golkar was suddenly interrupted as two sounds in quick succession interrupted her thoughts. The first came from Golkar himself. Quite unexpectedly, he began to chant. What began as a murmur, quickly rose in volume. Before long Sara could distinguish words, clearly recognisable as such, though they were from no language she had ever heard before. Despite what she'd been told about the translation spell which had been embedded in the portal that had brought her to this world, she couldn't understand what it was he was saying.

The second sound was that of the door opening. It was the two draghar. They had Josef with them. He was slumped between them, apparently unconscious. If anything, he looked even worse than when Sara had last seen him . . . skinnier, if that were at all possible, and more emaciated; older too, and sicker. His right wrist was wrapped in a rough bandage that was stained with blood and she could see a large bruise on the right side of his forehead.

She watched, silently, as Golkar's two henchmen dragged him across the room and lowered him onto one of the other chairs in the room, pulling it out from the table so they could maneuver his body into it. Once they had done that, they bound him in place as well, using manacles as they had done with her, and chaining each of his ankles and both of his wrists to the legs and the arms of the chair in succession. Another chain was wrapped around his waist, binding him to the back of the chair in what seemed to Sara a completely unnecessary final flourish

The result was that, just like her, Josef was almost totally immobilised and certainly completely at the mercy of his captors. Not that it seemed to matter to Josef, who remained unconscious throughout the operation.

Sara looked on with mounting apprehension as they carried out their task. It was so hard to accept that what she was witnessing, what she was taking part in, was really happening. It all seemed so surreal, especially with Golkar's chanting adding such an eerie touch to what was already such a macabre scene.

Having bound Josef to the chair, Ruz then untied a bandage that had been wrapped around the old man's wrist. Sara's eyes widened at the sight of the wound it had covered. Craning her neck to see what was happening, she looked on, enthralled in a ghoulish way she found she couldn't resist, as Tug took a knife from his belt and ran its sharp edge across Josef's wrist, making an incision parallel to two that were already there. She drew in her breath sharply as the blade sliced open his sallow and wrinkled skin.

With a mixture of horror and fascination, she continued to watch as Tug took a bowl that Ruz offered him and held it just below the arm of the chair Josef was bound to, collecting the dark blood that began to flow freely from where he had made his fresh cut and ran down over his wrist and onto and over the arm of the chair. All the while, Golkar sat at the table, chanting and inhaling the fumes from his mixture, ignoring the sinister task being carried out by his two minions.

Sara watched the colour draining from Josef's face as the bowl slowly filled. So much blood. Too much for an old man just barely alive, she thought. They're killing him, it suddenly dawned on her, just as Golkar had said he would. She heard the low groan that he gave then, like a death rattle must sound, she thought absently. His left eye-lid fluttered for an instant, revealing a glimpse of some small spark of life that remained in his ruined and battered body. Then, it seemed to Sara, the spark, all of a sudden, was extinguished. He slumped forward, lifeless again. Dead this time, surely. Finally, and thankfully, dead.

Tug turned around and carefully handed the bowl of blood to Ruz. It was as if what it contained was extremely precious. The wizard was still chanting. He hadn't stopped for an instant while all this was going on. The sound he was making reminded Sara of a Buddhist monk kneeling at a prayer wheel. *So this is how Golkar kills them*, she thought to herself, marvelling at her detachment. She watched as Ruz carefully placed the bowl on the table, well away from where Golkar still sat.

That action was the signal for a change in the whole proceedings. At the very moment the bowl touched the table, Golkar stopped his chanting. The sudden and unexpected silence was almost as eerie as the chanting itself had been and Sara found her attention riveted to the change in the wizard's behaviour.

Pushing back his chair, he slowly rose from his seated position, then stood uncertainly for a moment, swaying slightly, gripping its back tightly for support. Gradually, he steadied himself. Once he had done that, he turned to look, first at Josef, and then at Sara.

Sara gasped as his gaze locked on to hers, shocked at the transformation that had come over him. He seemed taller now, for some reason, but that wasn't all. It was his eyes that really held her. His gaze, which had always been intense, now held her transfixed. Though she was still firmly bound to her chair, she suddenly felt as if she was falling, towards Golkar . . . no, not just towards him . . . into him, into the deep well of his eyes!

She wanted to blink, but couldn't. His gaze held her more surely than the bonds about her wrists and ankles. It was like a rope had been stretched taut between them and it was now being reeled in, slowly pulling them closer and closer to each other, though she knew that neither of them was actually moving. She stared back at the wizard, her own eyes gritty, unable to blink or turn away, though she desperately wanted to.

A sense of power seemed to emanate from him now, unlike anything she had ever experienced. The room and all of its contents receded into the background of her vision. There was just Golkar now. Golkar and her. She felt the dryness of the air around her, vaguely remembering she had experienced a similar sensation twice before. Her hair seemed to be standing on end. Every nerve in her body seemed to have come alive and was tingling . . . waiting . . . waiting expectantly for something to happen.

Then, suddenly, the spell seemed to break. Golkar abruptly turned his gaze from her and began to move, very slowly now, as if in a trance. Turning back to the table, he reached out and took a hold of his wand which lay there beside him, on top of the pages of an open book. With that in his hand, he turned towards her again. She was relieved when his gaze passed her by this time. His attention was now directed to Josef. She flinched as the uneasy silence of the room was suddenly broken once more. Golkar began to chant again.

As he chanted he moved towards Josef, crossing in front of Sara as he did so. She noticed that Ruz and Tug were as equally transfixed by what was happening as she was. As Golkar reached Josef, he took a hold of the old man's bleeding wrist with his left hand. She could see the skin of the wizard's hand whitening as he tightened his grip on Josef's arm. Slowly, he raised his other hand, chanting all the while. He placed his palm flat against Josef's forehead, and then slowly allowed it to form an arch, with just the tips of his fingers touching the old man's skin. The chanting continued unabated. It was as if he was trying to draw something from the old man's head.

Sara shrieked in alarm as Josef's eyes suddenly flew open. She had thought him dead. Now his eyeballs were bulging from their sockets and his lips had drawn back, exposing his teeth and gums. Somehow, Sara managed to tear her eyes away from the ghastly scene, vaguely aware that she was sobbing.

Unable to resist the lure of the ghastly scene being played out before her for long, however, she raised her eyes again a moment later. Golkar's chanting had risen to a crescendo. As she looked up, he was lowering both of his hands. Josef's head had slumped forward on to his chest once more. If he hadn't been dead before, he certainly looked it now. His face was as white as a sheet.

Golkar looked down at his own bloodied hand, turning it over and idly examining it as if it was something he had never seen before. She noticed a slight smile form about his lips. He looked up then, directly at her. For the briefest of moments, his eyes flashed as he held her gaze, then he turned and strode purposefully across the room. She cried out in surprise as she watched him walk right into the mirror that hung on the wall opposite. In the blink of an eye, Golkar was gone. He had disappeared right before her eyes.

It was some time later when the commotion started, at least it seemed that it was to Sara. She had fallen asleep for a while and had no idea how much time had actually passed, whether it had been only a few minutes or some hours since she had drifted off. She hadn't believed sleep would be possible, still chained to the chair as she was, but she had obviously under-estimated the depth of her exhaustion.

She awoke to find herself still in much the same situation she had been in when Golkar had made his incredible exit. Josef was still there, bound to the chair next to her and Ruz was still sitting in the chair she had last seen him in; only, now he was leaning back with his feet resting on the edge of the table. Tug was nowhere to be seen. Presumably, he hadn't returned from wherever it was he had gone to when he'd left the room shortly after Golkar's alarming departure.

Sara clenched her hands together two or three times and tried to wriggle her toes. Her limbs were beginning to cramp and she thought that some movement might help the circulation. What she really wanted to do was to walk around a bit and to bend and twist her back and stretch her limbs like she sometimes did when she woke at home.

Home, what a meaningless word that was now. Sara forced the thought from her head, fighting down the despair that threatened to engulf her. It had risen so suddenly it had shocked her. She sensed that her nerves were hanging by a thread and she tried to think of something else. She didn't dare turn her eyes to the mirror. That was where Golkar would come from when he returned from wherever it was that he'd gone.

Turning to her left, she cast her eyes over her fellow sufferer. Josef looked in no better condition than he had earlier. It was hard to believe he was still alive but she could see no reason for Ruz to lie about the matter. The draghar had checked the old man's pulse as he and Tug were preparing to take his body away, only to find that he still lived, despite everything he had been through. His pulse was barely a flicker, Ruz had said, but it was there nonetheless.

At first, Sara had thought they'd been teasing her. She had seen what they had done to him earlier, the amount of blood they had taken from his body, and what Golkar had done to him before he had left. It was hard to credit the old man surviving that experience.

For some reason, they seemed to regard his blood as a particularly precious commodity. Ruz had taken the bowl from the table after Golkar had gone and had placed two small stones that looked to Sara just like polished amber within the fluid. He had then covered the bowl with what seemed to be a silk cloth and placed it on a small table on the other side of the room. It still sat there now, right where he had left it. Sara couldn't even begin to fathom what they hoped to do with it.

She guessed, however, that while ever Josef was still alive he could still provide them with more of his precious blood. Perhaps that was why they had decided to leave him where he was. As if to confirm her suspicion, Ruz had told Tug it would be better to let Golkar decide what to do with him. He had said that the wizard might still find some more use for him yet.

"Don't worry, little one," he had sneered at Sara at the time. "Your time will come too. Be patient." They had both had a good laugh over that.

Sara had tried to ignore them. She didn't want them to see how afraid she really was. She hadn't succeeded though. Once Ruz had realised how much he had upset her, he had only teased her even more. He hadn't stopped until she was crying again. Even now, the thought of some of the things he had said to her brought the tears welling up in her eyes again. Thankfully, he had eventually tired of that game and had sat back to wait for the return of Golkar. Tug had gone off on some unnamed errand and she had been left alone with her thoughts until, mercifully, sleep had claimed her. And now she was awake again. Awake, but still in her own private nightmare.

Sara's thoughts were interrupted by a sudden commotion from somewhere beyond the door. She heard someone cry out and then a crash, as if some item of furniture had fallen over, spilling its contents on to the floor. Ruz was up and out of his chair in a flash. Drawing his sword, he rushed out of the room and disappeared from sight down the corridor. Once again, Sara was left to wonder at the sudden departure of one of her captors.

CHAPTER 12

As Rayne had expected, the door to the wizard's home was shut. Unfortunately, it was also locked. He had crept up to the entrance as stealthily as he could, and had slowly turned the handle, only to find it wouldn't budge. For some reason, he hadn't anticipated that.

When he had peered in through the glass panels of the window moments earlier he had seen that the front room of the house was empty. From where he had stood, he'd been able to discern another doorway and a staircase that led to an upper floor. He had quickly decided that, once inside, his first move would be to see where the doorway led to. The stairway looked too grand to lead to the cells where Sara should be, assuming she was still alive. Taking a deep breath to calm his racing pulse, and gripping the hilt of his sword as tightly as he could, he had slid across to the wooden door and moved his free hand to its handle.

And now his whole plan was stymied by such a simple thing as a locked door. He had known it had been a foolhardy venture right from the start, but he had thought he would get further than this. What was he to do? *Think, Rayne, think*, he told himself. He knew that to tarry on the wizard's doorstep would only invite disaster.

The window. That was it. Sheathing his sword and moving back to where he had been standing only moments earlier, Rayne took his knife from his belt and cautiously slid it into the crack between the two window frames. Twisting the blade slightly, he pulled back with a flick of his wrist.

To his surprise, the window opened slightly, emitting a small creaking sound as it did so.

He quickly flattened himself against the wall of the house again. After a few moments, when he had heard no indication of any response to the noise he had made, he tentatively peered around the edge of the window again. There was still no sign of life from within the house. Keeping his knife in his hand, he used his fingers to prise the window open further. Once he could get a proper grip, he pulled the two frames completely out and open.

Leaning in over the windowsill, Rayne looked up and down the length of the room. It looked safe enough. If there was anyone at home, then they were in some other part of the house. Perhaps the house was empty, he thought hopefully. As much as a part of him wanted that to be true, he knew that if Sara wasn't there he would have no idea where to look for her. She would be lost to him for good then, that was for sure.

Pressing on, Rayne clambered in over the sill, dropping to the floor as quietly as he could once he had cleared its edge. Once more, he waited, as still as could be, knife at the ready. All he could hear was the pounding of his own blood against his eardrum. Yet again, he exchanged weapons, sheathing his knife and drawing his sword. The swishing noise the latter made as it left its scabbard seemed impossibly loud within the confines of the room. He pushed the thought from his head. He was being ridiculous. He had been as quiet as a dormouse.

Rising from his position below the open window, he moved forward, towards the closed doorway he had seen through the window, staying crouched over as he moved and continually scanning the room, particularly the staircase that led up into the house, ready for any eventuality. Looking down at his hand, he realised that his weapon was shaking. He tried to steady it, but it only seemed to get worse. He knew that his heart was beating faster then he had ever thought possible. It was too late now; there was no turning back from here. He had made his decision back when the Rangers had let him go. All he could do now was to see it through to its conclusion.

Perhaps he would have been better off if the Rangers who had been assigned to take him Keerêt had done their job. They hadn't, though. They had taken pity on him; said that they couldn't see the point in wasting time over such a simple matter when the whole country was at war, said they would say that he had escaped and that they had searched high and low for him to no avail. They had told him to go back to the Marches and change his name and start a new life. They had made him promise, too; made him promise to forget about Sara and get on with his life without her, told him there were plenty of other pretty girls in Ilythia.

Of course, he had agreed to everything they'd suggested. He had assured them he wanted nothing more to do with Sara, that the last thing he wanted was to end up in an Algarian gaol over a girl. He had lied through his teeth, knowing that as soon as they were gone he would head right back where they had come from, that he would search for her until he found her.

He hadn't been afraid then. He had known he was heading for certain death; that the task was an impossible one. But he hadn't hesitated for a moment. He loved the girl. He couldn't abandon her.

So why was he scared now? Was it because he had gotten so much further than he had thought he would? Or was it because now his whole plan had become a reality, not just some vague idea he had in his head? Perhaps because he might die right here in this house. He shook his head at the dark thought. What did it matter, anyway? He was here now. What had to be done, had to be done.

Rayne reached out and turned the handle on the door in front of him. This time it turned easily. He pushed the door open and stepped through, into a corridor. Still he could hear nothing. Silently, he crept down the corridor. There was another door at the end of it. He reached for its handle, turned it ever so slowly and began to push it open. A voice from the room beyond startled him as the door swung open, gradually revealing the contents of the space in front of him.

"Just in time. I've brew ….."

It was Tug. The draghar looked up from his position beside the pot-bellied stove at the same time that Rayne saw him. Their eyes met for a brief instant and Rayne felt his legs turn to jelly. Luckily, he still had his hand on the door handle or he might have stumbled in his shock.

They both recovered at the same time, though Tug was the merest fraction of a second quicker than Rayne. As the draghar lunged for the table beside him, grabbing his sword and drawing it from its scabbard in one fluid motion, Rayne stepped into the room with his own weapon up and ready.

The draghar was waiting for him now. His own weapon was up and, like Rayne, he was crouched and ready to spring. The two combatants began to circle each other, the small table in the centre of the room all that separated them. They were eyeing each other, each appraising his opponent, planning his next move. They had almost completed half of the circuit of the room when Rayne suddenly realised what the draghar was up to. A small flicker of his eyes had given the villain away. He was angling for a position closer to the door that Rayne had entered by. Like a fool, Rayne had left it wide open.

At that very moment, Tug sprang for the doorway, bringing his blade up to parry the slashing blow Rayne aimed at his side as he did so. The ring of clashing steel reverberated in the confines of the small room. Rayne's blow had little other effect though, for the draghar was out and into the passageway.

Having completed the maneuver Tug slowly began to back down the corridor towards the other door. Rayne could do nothing but follow, with his own blade held out in front of him, its tip a hand's breadth from that of the draghar's. He knew what the draghar was doing. He was retracing Rayne's own path into the house. He was doing what Rayne's father had always told Rayne he should never let an opponent do; he was choosing his own ground to fight on. Tug wanted to get out into that front room. Perhaps from there he could call for help to whomever else might be in the house. Whatever the reason, that was clearly his intent. Rayne knew that he couldn't let that happen. When the draghar slowly began to move his left hand behind his back, searching for the door handle that was now only a short space behind him, Rayne lunged at him with a furious assault.

Though his attack took Tug by surprise, the draghar fought back with some skill. Their swords clashed together a number of times in quick succession, then Tug grunted as a lunge from Rayne caught the edge of his left forearm, slicing through the exposed skin. Rayne tried not to look at the blood that began to flow freely down the draghar's left arm. He knew that he had to keep his eyes on Tug's own weapon, for the blow only seemed to spur the draghar on to a fresh effort.

Rayne felt himself being pressed backwards as he tried to parry a furious counter-attack. As Rayne edged backwards, the draghar stopped and quickly reached behind him, finally turning the handle of the door he had been so desperately trying to reach. In a moment, Tug had stepped back into the open doorway, with Rayne following closely on his heels.

The fight now moved into the wider room. The clashing sounds of their swords as thrusts and lunges were met with parries and counter-strokes rang through the room. Both were fighting desperately, Rayne with the constant fear that the draghar would call for help at any instant. He could feel the sweat on his body beneath his jerkin. It was on his brow too, but he dare not pause to wipe it away. The furious pace of the deadly duel he was engaged in would clearly not allow such a respite.

His arm was beginning to tire, but surely so was the draghar's. A thought flashed into Rayne's head and he acted on it in an instant. Swinging his blade at the draghar with all of his might, he felt his arm jolt to a halt as Tug's blade came up to parry his stroke. As their blades locked together, Rayne pushed with all of his might, denying Tug the chance to free his own blade from the tangle. At the same time, he quickly reached for his belt with his left hand. Drawing his knife, he swung it up and into the draghar's rib-cage with all of his force, twisting it viciously as he felt it crunch against bone somewhere deep within his opponent's chest. As the draghar opened his mouth and screwed up his face with a mixture of both pain and surprise, Rayne pulled the thin blade out and swung it once more into the draghar's vitals. This time, Tug screamed out in agony. As Rayne pulled his blade from the wound, he pushed the draghar from him and watched as Tug slumped against a small table, spilling its contents to the ground with a loud crash as his lifeless body slid to the floor.

Rayne's chest heaved as he looked down at the body of his opponent on the floor beside him. Tug's vacant eyes still stared up at him defiantly as his blood began to pool around him on the wooden floorboards. There was no doubting that the draghar was dead.

Bending down, Rayne wiped the bloodied blade of his knife on the draghar's shirt. A mixture of emotions and thoughts swept through him. He was exhausted. Their brief but furious fight had sapped his strength, more from the mental and emotional exertion than the actual physicality of it he guessed. The whole thing had been one big blur, his actions governed more by instinct than any capacity for strategy or forethought.

And now a man lay dead at his feet, or a draghar did, at least. He had only ever killed someone like that once before, that night in the forest when he and Sara had been jumped by those two men from the settlement. The earlier one, the man he had killed at the falls, had been different. That had been from a distance, and it had been no more than a split-second reaction.

But this was face to face, this was to the death. If he hadn't won, it would be him lying there dead, not Tug.

A blood-curdling scream scattered Rayne's thoughts. Swinging his head around, he was horrified to see yet another draghar rushing at him from the direction of the staircase with a sword brandished above his head.

His new assailant was on him before he could rise. Frantically bringing his blade up to parry the draghar's blow, Rayne could do little but deflect the angle of the blade as it slashed down towards him. As he felt the steel slice through the sleeve of his jerkin and into the skin of his upper arm, he tried to roll with the force of the stroke. Surprisingly, he managed to do so, stunning even himself when he ended up back on one knee and with his blade ready to parry the next blow. Neither instinct, nor his father's training, it would seem, had deserted him yet.

The wound to his arm was serious, however, and the jolt of the next blow sent an arc of pain across the breadth of his shoulder. He almost lost the grip on his blade as he struggled to ignore the injury and to move quickly enough to counter yet another blow. Somehow, he managed to get to his feet, though the rain of blows from his foe continued unabated. Ruz, for Rayne realised that was who his new opponent must be, seemed determined to keep the initiative, not letting up for one moment on the furious assault he had launched as soon as he had caught sight of him.

Gradually, Rayne gave ground under the weight of the draghar's blows. Though he was smaller than Rayne, Ruz seemed as strong as an ox, and he was using his strength to good advantage. When a second stroke pierced the skin of his thigh, Rayne knew that the end was near. He was no match for his opponent, especially drained as he was from his earlier encounter. Still he held on though, digging deep into reserves of strength that only a fight to the death could inspire.

A third time the draghar drew blood, this time splitting the skin on his left hand when it flailed carelessly to one side as Rayne parried yet another stroke. He was almost done. In desperation, he reached for an ornament with his bloodied hand and flung it in the draghar's direction. Ruz bared his teeth as it sailed harmlessly over his shoulder. He was moving in for the kill. Rayne flicked his eyes momentarily to the left of the draghar, towards the staircase.

"No, Sara, don't," he cried out suddenly.

To his eternal surprise, Ruz took the bait. As the draghar instinctively turned his eyes for just the barest fraction of a second, Rayne lunged with his sword, driving it deep into his opponent's chest with the whole of his weight behind it. He heard a gurgle struggle up out of the villain's throat as he staggered backwards on faltering legs, then collapsed to the floor heavily. Rayne's sword still lay embedded in the draghar's chest. For the second time, Rayne bent over and sucked deep breaths into his lungs. It was all he could do to stop himself from falling to the floor beside the second of his victims.

He stayed like that for a few moments, unable to think of anything but the need to pull himself together in case there were still more of them to deal with. He hoped that would not be the case. One look at the wound to his shoulder told him he would have to find a way to bandage it soon or he would be in serious trouble. Blood was running freely down the back of his arm from the deep and jagged cut the draghar's blade had left there. His left hand was also sticky with blood. The cut he had sustained just below the knuckle of his index finger had gone almost through to the bone and to say that it stung like hell was an understatement of no mean proportions. The red patch that had formed around the tear in his leather trouser leg indicated that the cut to his thigh was taking yet a further toll.

Limping across to the window, Rayne pulled strongly on the curtains that framed it, bringing the whole thing crashing down to the floor. The noise no longer concerned him. If there was anyone else in the house then they must have known he was there by now. It took him but a few moments to shred the material into something that could pass muster for bandages, then he set about doing what he could to bind up his wounds.

Within a short while, he was done. The crude bandages he had tied over the wounds to his thigh and his left hand would last for a while, if necessary, but his attempt at binding the wound to his shoulder was, he knew, little short of laughable. All he really seemed to have achieved was to stop the flow of blood down his arm. For the moment, the wad of material he had bound to his shoulder was soaking up the fluid that continued to flow freely from the gash he had sustained. It was too awkward to get at for him to hope to achieve much more than that by himself.

It didn't look pretty but it would have to do for the moment. As he hobbled towards the staircase, with his sword in his hand once more, he wondered what he must look like. Not the warrior he would need to be if he found Golkar up there waiting for him, of that he was sure.

~~~

As Golkar's body emerged from the shard of looking glass that lay half buried by sand on the floor of the ruined chamber, his senses were on full alert. Those first few seconds, when he had just completed the passage, that was when he was always at his most vulnerable. He was getting better at it though. The speed at which he could gather himself and assimilate with the new environment had improved immeasurably since when he had first learnt to use the spell.

In fact, this time, with the extra power he had gleaned from Josef, he didn't think he had taken more than a heartbeat or two to adjust. It had certainly been a lucky day when Josef had fallen into his clutches, he thought, despite his niggling concern over where the old man had acquired his power. He had thought that only the Guardians held anything like it, them and the girl Sara. Still, Josef's existence, anomalous though it was, was a windfall, and he had made the most of his unexpected catch.

That was such a feeling, he thought to himself, having all that additional power flow into your being. It was as if he had just finished consuming the most exquisite meal he had ever laid eyes on, only this had been a pungent meal of fabulously raw energy. Golkar, for the first time in his life, felt satiated with power. Any more would have probably been beyond him in his current form.

He made a mental note to remember that when he used the girl. He would have to be careful. Too much of a good thing could, in this case, be disastrous. He would need to make sure he remained able to stay in control of the overwhelming power available to him.

It was worth it, though. He knew, both from his earlier use of the old man and from the breathtaking feelings he was now experiencing, that his power had been augmented far beyond anything he or any of his colleagues could ever have achieved on their own. Kell would not even know he was here. The masking spell he was using was at a level he would never have thought possible before he had tried tapping into the old man's essence. If the girl were anything like this, there would be nothing he couldn't achieve.

Golkar forced himself to rein in his thoughts. There was still a task to be done. Though he harboured no doubts as to what the outcome of this battle would be, it would still be his greatest challenge yet. Or perhaps his greatest triumph would be a better way of putting it. Once Kell was out of the way, he could relax and take his time with the rest of his plans.

Glancing around the chamber, Golkar quickly confirmed there was no sign of either Kell or the gryphon in the area he had chosen for his arrival. He would have been surprised if there had been. The scan he had performed as he had opened the gate, while verifying Kell's presence in Ormuz, had indicated that his fellow Guardian was not in the immediate vicinity of his chosen point of arrival.

Golkar slowly ran an appraising eye over his surroundings. Though the ruins looked much as he had expected them to, a strange feeling was tugging ever so gently at the corners of his awareness. There was something . . . something different here. The old city had an odd feel to it. It had been a long time since he had been here; at least a century if not much more. It had been a ruin then, of course, but that was all it had been, ruined, deserted, empty, nothing more. Now it felt, well, almost as if there was something more here than just the ruined buildings.

Golkar dismissed the thought. It must be his new powers. His awareness was heightened to such a state now that his mind was brimming with new sensations and unfamiliar feelings. It would take a bit of getting used to. Or perhaps it was just the presence of his colleague, and the gryphon, if it was still with him. After all, the latter was something he had virtually no experience of.

Golkar knew that he had injured the beast; but how badly remained to be seen. For a moment there, Kell and the beast had given him a run for his money. Though he had ended up sending them both packing with their tails between their legs, he had to admit that his colleague's use of the beast had been quite a coup in its own way. Not that it had saved him in the end. Still, Golkar didn't like surprises, least of all ones of that magnitude.

Reaching out with his senses in a broad sweep of the surrounding area, Golkar quickly pinpointed the location of both his opponent and his magical companion. The fact that Kell's life-sign was weaker than he would have normally expected confirmed that he hadn't yet recovered from the injuries he had received in their earlier encounter. Though the gryphon was close by, it was harder to read. Golkar had no benchmark against which to read what he sensed from the beast. The fact that they were both together would make things easier for him though. Without any further hesitation, he put his plan of attack into action.

Leaving the building he had arrived in, Golkar strode down a few steps then purposefully across the courtyard beyond, weaving a path through the columns and broken statuary that littered his path. His eyes were fixed on the open doorway of the temple at the top of the stairway that led up of from the broad avenue that ran through the centre of Ormuz. It was an unnecessary and instinctive precaution, for he knew that his opponents were still blissfully unaware of his presence. In a few strides, he was up the broad marble steps that led to the temple.

Golkar halted there for the briefest of moments, readying himself, then strode boldly into the inner sanctum of the temple, lowering his masking spell as he did so in an ostentatious display of his power. Though a tremor of excitement ran through his body, he knew no fear. When his sudden and unannounced arrival drew an immediate reaction from both of his opponents, he was more than ready for them. Raising the wand he held in his right hand, he instantly flung a holding spell in the direction of the crumpled form of his colleague.

The result was both immediate and effective. Kell, who had been in the process of attempting to rise from where he had been resting, sitting with his back against the temple wall, had already raised his own wand and was rapidly hurrying to complete a spell of his own when the holding spell struck him. Golkar smiled to himself at the ease with which it held him. For the moment he was content with a stalemate, neither allowing his foe to complete his own spell or attempting to take any further action against him.

As Kell strained with all of his will to overcome the holding spell and draw his own power forth, Golkar turned to deal with the second of his two protagonists. The first few moments of the battle had confirmed what he had known before it had started, that Kell alone would not have the power to vanquish him. The combination of his recent injuries and Golkar's own greatly enhanced power made it certain that without some external assistance the wizard was doomed. Golkar, however, hadn't forgotten that he had more than one score to settle here in Ormuz.

And Thyfur, it seemed, might prove to be a more worthy opponent for him than his colleague had been thus far. Unlike Kell, the beast had responded quickly to his sudden appearance at the door of the temple. The gryphon had risen up to its full length and was towering menacingly over the diminutive form of Golkar when the wizard turned to face him. For a brief moment, Golkar was stunned. Thyfur presented an awesome sight as he slowly drew back, unsheathing his razor sharp claws and preparing to leap at his prey. The sun glinted off of his plumage as his head twisted threateningly towards his foe and his terrifying beak opened to reveal the huge cavity of his mouth. Then, just as he was about to pounce, Golkar raised his left hand.

The air shimmied in front of the beast as a huge net suddenly winked into existence and hung there, as if suspended from some unseen structure way up in the sky above the open roof of the ruined temple. With a flick of his wrist that belied the drain on his power necessary to complete such a maneuver, Golkar flung the magical mesh at the gryphon, instantly covering him from head to toe and effectively binding the beast as surely as if he had been caged. Though Thyfur struggled mightily against the strange bonds, the net stuck to him like a spider's web. Its gelatinous looking strands glimmered with a pale translucence that belied its actual strength. It was as if Thyfur had been bound within a web of steel cables, sticky and flexible, though stronger than any constraint he had ever encountered.

Feeling that he had the beast's measure, Golkar turned his attention back to Kell once more. His former colleague hadn't rested for a moment and was still struggling against the holding spell, unable to complete his own attack despite his best attempts to break free. Though Golkar felt his confidence strengthened, if anything, by the opening salvos in this grim duel, he knew that this would be a fight to the death now. There could be no retreat from this encounter. Each of the combatants would fight till his last breath before he'd surrender to the will of his opponent.

And so Golkar steeled himself to put forth all of his might. He could already feel the awesome drain on his power from the exertion of dealing with both of his opponents at the same time. Despite the apparent ease with which he had contained the gryphon, the spell with which he held the beast had taken some effort to raise. That had been nothing, however, compared to what it was taking to maintain it in the face of the gryphon's determination to break free of his bonds. To add to that, his duel with Kell was also taking its toll on his resources. He was pushing his new power to its very limits. Yet still he felt supremely confident. He had their measure; he was sure of it.

It was time to up the ante. Ignoring the wrenching pull of the gryphon's will on his own, he began to apply a crushing force around the upper body of his fellow wizard, slowly but surely constricting his chest, crushing it as if in a vice. He watched detachedly as Kell's face began to contort with the effort of trying to resist this dual attack from his rival. And as he did so, he wondered at his own power, revelling in the strength that allowed him to deal with multiple opponents and multiple attacks at the same time. They had been fools to even attempt to resist him.

It was then, just when his power seemed to approach its zenith, that the first doubt entered his mind. At that very moment, when he felt that the final victory was within his grasp, that all he had to do was reach out and take it, and crush them both once and for all, Kell first, then the gryphon, began to make a supreme effort, acting as if in concert in a simultaneous effort to throw off the control with which he held them. Incredibly, the intensity of the battle began to rise to an even higher level still.

Somehow, Golkar managed to stay with them, drawing even deeper on his own power in answer to this new challenge. For the first time, however, he began to feel his strength ebbing. He was being pushed to a level beyond anything he had ever anticipated he could achieve. His concentration began, for the first time in the whole of this deadly battle, to waver. There were limits after all, he began to realise, to his new power.

Golkar felt his limbs beginning to tremble as the fight approached a critical point. Someone or something would have to give way soon, he could feel it. Both of his opponents were drawing on every resource they could muster, each knowing that they had to exert the maximum effort possible, or end their existence right here in the ruined Temple of Mishra. It was all that Golkar could do to quell their combined resistance. Kell's he had anticipated, but not the gryphon's, or at least not to the level it was now clear it was capable of. Perhaps he had miscalculated. The beast seemed so much stronger than he had believed possible.

Desperately, Golkar strove to maintain his three-way focus, the dual attack on Kell and the constraint with which he held the gryphon. As he dug deep into the well of his own power, striving with all of his might to complete his ascendancy over his rivals, he felt himself teetering, as if on the brink of a precipice. How to control so much force? How to sustain multiple attacks in the face of such a call on his will? An abyss seemed suddenly to open beneath him, beckoning and repelling him at the same time with its paradoxically simultaneous promise of peace and utter oblivion.

With a shudder, he remembered that he had seen its like before, when he had opened the portal to Sara's world. He had nearly succumbed to it then, and that had been without another Guardian and a gryphon throwing all that they could at him in a desperate bid to overthrow him. Though his instinct told him to resist, he felt himself being drawn towards it, against his will, against all of his attempts to defy it. His assessment of it began to change. It began to seem desirable, appealing, something he had to have, even though at the core of his being he knew that he had to deny it. It offered a quick and seemingly logical way out of his current dilemma. He could barely resist its deadly appeal, was no longer sure he even wanted to. As he lifted his feet to take a first step towards it, he felt the floor of the temple shake beneath his feet and a low rumble begin to sound in his ears.

Despair washed over him, threatening to sweep him into the darkness in its wake. Knowing that he was about to lose, he determined to take his colleague with him. With a sudden and final effort, he strengthened the grip he had on Kell's chest, squeezing with all his remaining strength in one last almighty effort. As he fought to maintain his holding spell and the constraint he had placed on the gryphon at the same time, he felt his own strength slipping away, rapidly now, like a stream racing towards the edge of a waterfall.

Golkar felt a shiver run down the length of his spine, chilling his heart to its very core as a series of tremors rippled throughout his body. Suddenly, a flash of blinding light burnt painfully into his retina and a piercing cry rent the still air of the precinct. He felt a hot wind sear his heart as the soul of a Guardian shot past him into the abyss, thrusting him out of its way in its haste to be gone from this world. Golkar felt a chill race across his soul. For a moment, he stood there, confused, blinking uncontrollably as he struggled to regain his vision. Then he realised what had happened. He had won. He had defeated the last of his colleagues. He was the sole surviving Guardian of Ilythia.

As Golkar began to exult in his victory, he quickly pulled up short. The battle had still not ended. Kell was no longer, and yet the force that opposed him had diminished only a little. Incredibly, though he had just vanquished his fellow Guardian in a head to head duel, victory still eluded him. Something . . . something strong and very ancient still opposed him.

The gryphon, in fact, seemed to be gaining in strength with every passing minute. Golkar could feel his spell of constraint beginning to weaken in the face of the beast's growing determination, a determination which seemed to have leapt a notch or two with the passing of Kell, as if that great cataclysm had awakened some new source of strength within the beast. If things kept going the way they were, his spell would not only give way, but in the aftermath of its collapse he could be in very great danger of being swept into the same abyss that had taken his colleague. It would be like trying to stand in front of a tidal wave.

Golkar felt the despair rise within him as his energy steadily ebbed from him. Though his destruction of his colleague had been both spectacular and utter, the drain on his own power had also been colossal. He wouldn't be able to hold out for much longer. Yet the gryphon, if anything, was continuing to grow in strength. It was feeding, he realised with horror, feeding on this place, drawing energy from it in some way that Golkar could not understand. He *had* miscalculated. He had chosen the wrong place to confront his enemies.

A gleam of light reflecting on the face of a gemstone took his attention as he looked frantically about the shattered room, desperately seeking for a way to avoid his impending doom. A small piece of black crystal stood embedded in the face of one of the walls, above a vacant plinth. Even at this distance, Golkar knew that it was the same as the ones Tanis had given to each of the Guardians. Here in the temple, it had been a symbol of some kind, no doubt, an adornment for a statue that had long ago fallen and shattered on the temple's floor perhaps. Someone had taken the shard of crystal and set it into the wall of the now ruined and abandoned temple.

The jet black crystal was rare, extremely rare, and precious, priceless even, of the type jealously sought after by all with even the slightest of magical abilities. Once acquired, such items were hoarded and venerated for their unique qualities, for their capacity to augment and store mana.

Golkar had thought only four had ever existed here in Ilythia, shards of a singular larger crystal the Ilaroi had brought with them when they came to Ilythia. There was the one Tanis had owned, and had taken with him when he had left, and there were the three shards he had bestowed upon his pupils, on the three Guardians. At least one of those had been destroyed when Golkar had killed Tarak and, no doubt, another had been removed from this plane of existence with the demise of Kell, only seconds earlier. Golkar still carried his. So that accounted for all four.

And yet, here was a piece, sitting among the ruins of an old building, apparently unnoticed and unwanted. It had probably been there for centuries, if not aeons. Surely fate must have placed it here for him to find it in such a time of need as this.

Golkar had to do something, and fast. In an instant, he took his opportunity. Leaping back out of the doorway through which he had entered and relinquishing the spell of binding that held the gryphon at the same time, he quickly focused all of his remaining power on one single purpose. In the blink of an eye, the crystal turned from rock to liquid and expanded to fill the space that the walls of the room had once bordered. In a fraction of a second, it had gone from a small crystal to a mass the size of a large room. And for a few moments the previously black substance became translucent.

So quick was the transition and so unanticipated that Thyfur could now be seen within, caught in full flight in the now rapidly hardening substance as he reached towards his foe, like a monstrous fly caught in rapidly cooling amber. His mouth was open, his teeth bared. A look of anger, of a beast about to devour its prey, could still be seen, reflected in his wild eyes. The moment was frozen, caught as surely as sculptor catches an instant and renders it in stone for all of posterity to admire.

As the substance snapped back to its crystalline form, though to all appearances immensely larger in volume now than the small and innocuous crystal shard that been it genesis, Golkar knew that its magical properties would prevent any attempt by the gryphon to free itself. It wouldn't even try to escape. To all intents and purposes, the huge square of crystal now held the beast in stasis. It could no more move or act than it could think or age. It was held, frozen in time, and would remain so for eternity. Nor could the gryphon be seen within now. As the crystal hardened, it assumed its normal colour, completely obscuring its contents. No-one, other than Golkar, would even know of the beast trapped forever within.

Golkar allowed himself the ignominy of sagging to the floor as his exhaustion washed over him. He had never felt so depleted in all of his life. Nor had he ever been so close to failing. And yet, he had triumphed in the end. Even the powers of the ancients had been insufficient to vanquish him. *I have become a god*, he thought, as sleep began to take him. Even as the thought took hold, he chose not to acknowledge that he was weak now, weaker than he had ever felt. He had exhausted all of the power he had acquired from Josef, and much of his own to boot. He knew that he needed rest. With rest would come recovery. Once he had recovered, he would return to Tu-atha and complete what he had begun.

CHAPTER 13

The soft rosy light of the dawn that had barely begun to stain the edges of the eastern sky was a welcome sight for Thom as he opened his eyes and slowly surveyed their surroundings. It was a breathtaking sight, and one that always evoked the happiest of memories. For a while he lay still, peering up at the limitless depths of the cloudless sky above him and setting his mind free to roam back, searching for happier times.

It didn't work, though. Try though he might, the solace his spirit sought eluded him. Those memories were from another time. Thoughts of the terrible things he had been forced to witness in the past few days could not be that easily banished, he realised, sighing at the despondent thought. For the moment, the life he had led before the sligs had come was little more than a dream, too dear and too cherished to be anything more than a liability in his current situation.

Reluctantly, Thom brought his gaze down from the ever-brightening cloudless sky to examine his more immediate environment. Shrugging off his gloom, just as the new day was now shrugging off the black mantle of night, he strove to focus on what was before them. Better that than looking back at this point. Perhaps today would be a better day he thought without any real conviction as he surveyed their surroundings.

The stained and crumbled edges of the wall that formed the horizon from his vantage point on the floor of the ruined shell of what had once been The Four Bells offered a stark contrast to the clear morning sky above him. In better times, the hostelry had been one of the finer establishments Kurandir had to offer travellers. All that it offered now to the two refugees who had passed a cold and uncomfortable night within its confines was a welcome respite from a bitter and piercing wind.

As Thom struggled to sit up and throw off the remnants of the drowsiness that still shrouded his thoughts, he felt Jinny stirring slightly beside him. By chance, he happened to look down at her face just at the very moment when her fluttering eyelids finally popped open. The broad smile he received in return for his effort lifted his spirits in a way that the dawn had somehow been unable to.

"Good morning sleepyhead," he whispered softly, not wanting to disturb the tranquillity of Jinny's own gradual wakening.

"Good morning," Jinny yawned in response. Rolling over and stretching her slim body along the length of his torso, she snuggled in closer to the warmth of his side. "I'm hungry. Don't guess there's any chance of sending for breakfast in bed."

Thom smiled wanly at the thought of such decadence. Breakfast in bed. What an idea. Did people really do things like that? Was there really a time when that was possible? And where did Jinny get such a notion?

"I'm sorry," she murmured despondently, after a few moments of silence had passed. "I guess that's not very funny. It's hard not to think about food though. Especially when your tummy keeps rumbling."

"That's okay. Don't worry. We'll find something today. There must be plenty of food here somewhere. I don't think we were in a very good frame of mind to think clearly yesterday. I hadn't expected it to be like this. We both needed that sleep pretty badly too. We'll get up soon and then we'll turn this place upside down until we do find something to eat. And if we don't, I'll send our complaints to the owner."

"Deal," smiled Jinny as she pulled herself up beside him and began to look around at what had passed for their lodging for the night. "Looks like the wind's died down a little. The sky looks a lot better too."

They sat there among the ruins for a while then, chatting softly to each other and trying to forestall what they knew was before them, another search through the ruined buildings and bloated bodies of what was left of the provincial capital. Finally, the hunger that gnawed at their stomachs induced them to be up and about their task. Once they had risen and stowed their meagre possessions into the makeshift bundle Thom carried slung over his shoulder, they began once more to scour the remnants of the building they had chosen to spend the night in.

It had been no accident that had led them to that particular establishment. From the moment Thom had seen the painted sign flapping about in the breeze he had been determined The Four Bells would be their resting spot for the night. He had told Jinny that, although it offered nothing any one of a dozen or more similar buildings could provide, he had always wanted to spend a night in a fine hotel in one of the big towns. This might be his only chance to realise that dream. The fact that the hostelry had been severely damaged by the fire that must have ravaged the town when the sligs had sacked it hadn't deterred him in the slightest. The lack of a roof wouldn't matter a jot he had told her. They'd been sleeping under open skies for days, what difference would another night make?

He had decided not to share with her the thought that he didn't want to get caught unawares in a place without the means for a quick exit. In the broken ruins of The Four Bells, he knew they would not only easily hear if anyone came their way but they would also have little difficulty in making a rapid escape in the unlikely event that trouble did put in an appearance.

He had also known that he was probably taking an unnecessary precaution. They had spent some time picking over the ruins without the faintest sight of either man or slig, live ones that is; there were plenty of dead ones. Though they had taken their time approaching the town, wary of the prospect of encountering any more stray sligs, they'd still had sufficient hours of daylight left to at least satisfy themselves that they were alone in the smoking ruins. Anyone with any sense, and that included the slig army, had obviously long since left.

Unfortunately, they had also done a pretty good job of taking whatever there was worth having with them. Thom and Jinny hadn't been able to find more than a few mouldy scraps which in better times they wouldn't have dreamed of putting into their mouths. Those times were gone, however, and they had quickly and greedily consumed the few morsels which they had found.

Thom knew they had to do better today. Though they had found plenty of drinkable water, they were both beginning to weaken from the lack of anything substantial to eat. By his reckoning, it could still be some time before they found a way back to wherever the Algarian lines now were. If anything, food would probably only become harder and harder to come by.

The slig army was somewhere out there between them and the Algarian lines. From what he had seen so far, the creatures were living off the land as they went, stripping it bare of whatever supplies they could lay their hands on. That wouldn't leave much for him and Jinny, assuming they made it that far. It also meant that, for the moment at least, finding somewhere safe to sit out events wasn't really an option either.

Food was quite critical to their survival and would only become more so as time went on. The promise he had made Jinny, that they should be able to find provisions somewhere here in Kurandir, may very well prove to be a hollow one, and he knew it. That was why they couldn't afford to leave the place until they were sure they had given it a good going over. If there was food here, then they were going to find it.

And so, with the new day, the search began again. When their exploration of the building they had slept in revealed no trace of anything worth having, they widened their search, rummaging through building after building in an increasingly desperate hunt for something edible. The place seemed to have been swept bare of any such thing. It looked to Thom as if someone had already done what they were trying to do, whether slig or human he couldn't tell. Perhaps there had been some survivors who had stayed on just long enough to strip the place bare. If so, then they had left by now. Kurandir was nothing more than a ruined shell. Even the dogs seemed to have deserted the place.

They weren't totally alone, however. Thom did see a stray cat or two in the course of the morning and for a while, he considered whether he should try and catch one of their feline observers. At least he and Jinny would have some meat for their dinner. He knew that Jinny wasn't ready for that though, and if he were honest with himself then he would have to admit that he wasn't either. The time might come when desperation would force such squeamishness aside, but they weren't at that point yet.

A low whistle from Jinny, one of their pre-arranged signals, drew Thom's attention back to the task at hand. Turning in her direction, he saw that she had crouched down behind an upturned table and was frantically waving at him to take some type of cover himself. They were in the basement of what had at one time been a house. The floorboards from the ground floor were half gone; their burnt remains butted up against the stairway that still led down to what had once been the lower level. He and

Jinny had ventured down into the cellar hoping to find some old store of provisions that might have been overlooked in the previous occupant's haste to leave.

As Thom quickly crouched down next to a twisted jumble of wooden furniture that must have at one stage stood on the floor above, he saw that Jinny was peering over the top of the table at a large wooden cupboard which stood against the rear wall of the room, leaning back precariously against the stonework but otherwise relatively undamaged. As he watched she risked a furtive glance at the floor space between her and the bottom of the staircase that had led them down into the basement, then quickly turned and faced the cupboard again, as if to make sure it hadn't changed in any way in the few moments she had taken her eyes away from it. He knew what she was doing, she was assessing the time required to cover that ground in the event she had to flee.

When she looked his way again and saw him looking at her, she began to point frantically at the cupboard. From her gestures, it seemed that she thought there might be something, or someone, in it. Thom had no idea what had led her to that conclusion but he didn't intend to take any chances; the look of anxiety on her face told him that something had definitely frightened her. In their situation, they couldn't afford to ignore even the slightest hint of danger.

Thom took a good hard look at the battered old cupboard Jinny seemed so intently focused upon. It was big, certainly big enough to hold a man, or a slig, though the latter would be a tight fit. One door was slightly ajar, as if it had been twisted on its hinge and would no longer close properly. In all other ways it looked fairly innocuous; though of course, he thought, if someone had chosen it for a hiding place, then that was exactly how they would want it to look.

Drawing his knife in a display of bravery which he knew was more for Jinny's benefit than anything else, Thom waved to her to move back towards the staircase, as quickly and quietly as she possibly could. He waited while she scampered across the floor and stopped at the bottom of the staircase, one foot poised on the first step, ready to flee at the first sign of trouble. Her doe-like eyes flitted back and forth in a way that went straight to his heart. He knew that she was counting on him to keep her safe.

With one eye still on the cupboard, Thom stooped down and picked up a piece of broken rubble from the floor, trying to quell his own racing heart as he did so. Swinging his hand forward in a gentle underarm loop, he flung the makeshift missile across the room, aiming for the wooden door of the cupboard. His heart seemed to miss a beat as the rock hit its mark and bounced harmlessly back on to the stone floor of the basement. He felt the air rush out of him as he suddenly began to breathe again; he had been holding his breath as he watched intently, waiting for any reaction to what he had done. If there had been some small animal in or behind the cupboard he would have expected to hear or see something, some movement or sound in response to the clatter of the rock against the wooden door.

Still not daring to move, he waited a few moments more, keeping his eyes glued to the tiny gap left by the twisted door. Jinny, he knew, was still crouched on the bottom step, waiting and watching just as intently as he was. There was no other way, he decided. He would have to go and have a proper look. Forcing his legs to move, he began to cross the space that separated him and the cupboard.

Though one part of him kept telling him that what he was doing was foolish, that they'd be better off just leaving the place and searching somewhere else, the other was saying that if he did that he would spend the rest of the day constantly looking over his shoulder, wondering if something had been there and whether it had simply waited until he had left to follow him, looking for the right opportunity to take him by surprise and kill him. He knew that he was being overly melodramatic, that there probably wasn't anything in there at all. In some ways, he felt a bit foolish. Whatever Jinny had seen or heard, it could have just been a mouse, or another cat, or nothing at all.

Better to be cautious all the same. As he approached the cupboard, he picked up a long piece of burnt timber. Holding it with his left hand, he reached out and slowly began to prise the door open. The other still held his knife, though he knew that if there was a slig hiding inside the cupboard he would just turn and bolt for the stairs, and hope that Jinny was long gone before he even got that far.

All of a sudden, the door burst open and before he could even think about turning and running a hairy shape jumped out from within and sprang at him, snarling like some wild monster as it did so. As Thom crashed to the floor, struggling desperately to fend off the beast that had landed on top of him, he felt a strong hand take a murderous grip on his throat. His opponent had taken a hold of his wrist with its other hand and was twisting it painfully in a clear attempt to get him to drop his knife.

He thought that he must be dreaming when he heard a familiar voice snarl from right next to his ear. "Drop it or I'll squeeze the life out of ya right here and now." It couldn't be.

"Pa?" he sobbed, unable to believe his ears. "It's me, Thom. Thank God. Is it you?"

When his opponent made no attempt to release him, Thom realised that he must have been mistaken. He felt the grip on his throat tighten as he struggled to get out from under the weight of his adversary. The message was clear, stop struggling or run the risk of having his windpipe crushed. Thom chose the former course. As he did so, his opponent slowly drew back, maintaining his vice-like grip but enabling the two combatants to get their first good look at each other.

It *was* his father. He looked haggard and thin, wild and dishevelled, but somehow, incredibly, it was him. The strange look he was giving Thom was hard to understand, though. Though his father was looking straight at him, he gave no sign that he recognised who Thom was.

"I been 'round too long for that one, boy," his father scowled slowly. "My Thom's dead. Don't even look like you much, anyway. Drop your knife ya thieving cur or I'll throttle ya just for the fun of seein ya die."

From the crazed look on his father's face, Thom could see that he meant what he said. As he opened the fingers of his right hand, he felt his father shake it violently, forcing the knife to rattle across the stone flags of the floor. A thin plaintive voice drifted down from somewhere above them as the weapon slid to a halt against the far wall.

"T-Thom," he heard Jinny call out hesitantly. "Are . . . are you okay?"

~ ~ ~

Hrothgar was in a good mood. He was finally back where he belonged, back among his fellow Sagath as they prepared to storm the defensive line the Algarians had hastily thrown up along the line of the Mendobar Hills after their retreat from the Sarrowmar. This was where a warrior belonged he thought idly, surveying the landscape with a practised eye as he listened to the voice of the slig beside him. This is what they were born to do from time immemorial.

Kurg, the hunt leader in charge of this section of the line, was bringing him up to date on the progress of the war. It was going well for the sligs, very well indeed if Kurg's news was accurate. And if Hrothgar was in any doubt of that, all he had to do was to look about him. After all, they were already over the great river. Apparently, the Algarians had retreated from the eastern shore the previous day in such a panic that they'd been unable to prevent the Sagath from crossing over behind them. The bulk of the main slig force was now assembled here on the western bank and, from the look of them, they were more than ready for battle. They had got a taste for it now and they wanted more, anyone could see that.

Hrothgar knew that he was lucky he had come back when he had. If he had waited much longer it might have all been over. He'd ridden hard to get there and by the will of Zar, it seems he'd arrived just in time for the final throw of the dice. From everything he had seen and heard so far, it should only be days before the Sagath were at the gates of Keerêt itself.

That was something he wanted to be part of, the sack of Keerêt. There was nowhere else for the Algarians to run to now. Once they were bottled up in the city, their fate would be sealed. The sligs would pull down its walls then and the Algarians would run from their blades like women. Its streets would run red with blood. That had been a slig dream for untold generations, and now they were actually about to live it. It made Hrothgar proud to be a slig warrior. Oh yes, he was in a good mood. Then Kurg told him the news about Grartok.

"So, he finally found someone who could spawn a brat for him, did he?" he laughed, slapping his side with his free hand as he rolled back in his saddle. Far from being annoyed, as he'd always thought he might if his brother ever produced an heir, now it had happened he found the whole thing quite amusing. The very fact that it was such a big deal to Grartok said it all really. From the way he'd apparently been carrying on anyone would think he'd started shitting gold nuggets. "The bitch must have spent the night buried up to the waist in horse shit to grow something from his seed," he roared between bouts of laughter. "Which of the whores split her fat legs for the great Grartok this time?"

As he spoke, Hrothgar looked up at the Algarian defences, perched on the crest of the hilltop that stood just under a league or so from where he and Kurg sat astride their mounts. Though Kurg's mount stood placidly,

idly cropping the row of churned up vegetables that ran beneath its feet, his own was constantly moving, still panting and fretting, slowly cooling down from the hard ride he had given it over the last few days. He was only half listening to Kurg's voice now. Grartok's need to prove himself was all very well, but he for one was itching to get some blood on his axe.

"Mmmm. I'm . . . I'm not . . . I'm, I'm not sure," Kurg finally responded, licking his lips nervously as he spoke. "They look dug in, don't they," he grunted after a moment, when he realised that Hrothgar's attention was wandering, nodding his head towards the enemy lines as he spoke and glad to have changed the subject. "Nice of them to save us the job of digging a hole for their stinking bodies."

They both laughed at that, though Hrothgar thought he detected a slight touch of nervousness in his fellow hunt leader's mirth. He must be worried about the coming assault, he decided. Nothing wrong with that; better to be anxious now than later, when it mattered. "Well, may Zar be with you," Hrothgar mumbled without much conviction, raising his clenched fist to Kurg in salute as he turned his horse away and proceeded on down the line of waiting men, nodding to this one or that as his horse slowly picked its way through the rich loam of the floodplain on which their force had been drawn up in readiness.

Though the sligs were clearly itching for the word to be given for the long-awaited assault to commence, they seemed in a strange mood to Hrothgar. All he seemed to get from many of the warriors as he rode past them was strange looks. Many more wouldn't even meet his eye. They seemed nervous, unsure of themselves in some indiscernible way. Though only a few were veterans, he had known most of the others since they were young bucks. They didn't know the meaning of fear. Perhaps they'd had a harder time getting there than Kurg had let on. Something was spooking them, that much at least was clear to Hrothgar. Eventually, he pulled up alongside an old friend who greeted him with a nod as he pulled on his rein and eased his horse into the line alongside his.

"When did you get back?" drawled Tarnk in his usual sardonic fashion, turning his gaze back to the Algarian lines way off in the distance as he spoke. "Thought you might have had something better to do."

"This morning," scowled Hrothgar, glancing at the angry scar that ran diagonally across his companion's face. "Thought you might need some help. Looks like you could need it. Where'd you get that?"

"Forgot to duck."

The rustling of leather against leather and the stamping of horses hooves rose up over the uneasy silence that followed Tarnk's laconic reply. Eventually, realising that his companion wasn't going to volunteer anything further, Hrothgar's curiosity got the better of him.

"Where?"

"Kurandir."

"Some fight, huh?"

"It was that. They'll sing about that one for a long time to come. You should'a been there."

"Hmmm." Hrothgar knew that he'd missed too many good fights because of his worthless errand into the wilderness. "Lose many?"

"Yuh."

"Bet that pissed Golkar off."

"Could say that."

After another uneasy silence, Tarnk suddenly spoke again. "When you gunna sort him out?" he asked, keeping his voice steady and his eyes fixed on the ridgeline in front of them.

"What do you mean?"

This time Tarnk turned slowly and looked at Hrothgar for a long moment before he replied. "You spoken to anyone else since you got back?"

"Yeh, Kurg. Why?"

"He bring you up to date?"

"Pretty much. Said it was a bit of a stroll in the woods so far."

"Told you about the child?" asked Tarnk, turning his face away again to look down the line.

"Yeh." Hrothgar's face split with a wide grin. "Never thought Grartok had it in him. Who's the bitch that made him a man? Kurg didn't know."

"He knew."

"What do you mean?"

"It's Mardur."

A sudden silence fell like a dead weight over the two warriors. Even those near them seemed to have stopped chatting. Hrothgar strained to keep a hold on his rein as his horse suddenly tossed its head back and forth. An image of his brother's face reared up in the forefront of his mind. Grartok was looking down at him, sneering.

"So. When you gunna sort him out?" asked Tarnk when Hrothgar seemed to have his mount back under control.

"Where is he?" Hrothgar knew that his voice was hoarse, his words tight and clipped. It was all he could do to retain his composure as his anger flared like a bonfire within him. His eyes were glaring at Tarnk now, almost daring him to say the wrong thing.

"Back at the bridge," Tarnk replied in a flat voice. "Seen a rider come in from the north not long back. Looked like one of Nargal's boys. Must be a big . . ."

Hrothgar didn't bother to wait for him to finish. He wouldn't have heard him anyway as the rush of blood through his ears rose to a sudden crescendo. With a rough twist of his wrist, he swung his mount around and dug in his spurs. As his horse surged forward, he reached down with one hand to loosen his axe from its sheath.

~~~

The scene before the city was not an edifying one for the ruler of a once great nation to have to see. Panic had broken out among the Algarians and their forces were in almost total disarray. Standing on the balcony of her apartments high up on the gleaming walls of the palace which commanded the highest point within the city, Elissa watched as her nation slowly began to come apart at the seams.

On the plains below, the stream of refugees had swelled to a throng. Dragging their meagre belongings along on their backs or, if they were luckier, on rickety carts, they were streaming across the broad plain and into the city from almost every direction. A smaller number, she could see, were doing exactly the opposite, making their way out, scrambling to flee a city they had become convinced could no longer protect them.

Elissa knew that the streets below her were choking in a pandemonium the likes of which had never been seen in Keerêt. There was no longer anywhere for these new refugees to be housed, and many had simply dumped their belongings and set up camp in the narrow laneways and passageways of the inner city, adding further to both the confusion and the congestion. In all of this, the army, or what was left of it, was struggling to stay intact and to maintain the discipline that would be needed if the whole debacle were not to turn into a rout. If that happened, then all hope would be lost, if it wasn't already.

Elissa turned away from the view and strode back into her apartment with her head held high, sweeping past her maids and attendants in a thin attempt at bravado. She, at least, must maintain her decorum in this their most trying of times. "Send for the Marshal," she cried out as she bent over the maps strewn across the broad mahogany table that formed the centrepiece of her anteroom. *There has to be a way*, she thought as she began to pour over the charts for the umpteenth time that morning. *There must be somewhere they can be held.*

"And get me some fresh koohlar," she shouted to no one in particular, not bothering to look up as quick hands grabbed the silver jug that stood beside her. The quick patter of feet across the panelled floor told her that her command had been instantly obeyed. Ignoring the knock at the door that followed a short while later, Elissa finally sat down and took up her eyepiece, keeping her eyes glued to the charts in front of her all the while. She couldn't for the life of her imagine why they had to make the print on the maps so damned small. How could anyone be expected to read them?

Her concentration was interrupted when a familiar voice broke into her thoughts from just beyond her left shoulder. "Count Regulus begs admittance, Madam," announced her maid. "Shall I tell him to wait?"

"What? No. No. Show him in. Thank you, Brina."

Reluctantly turning away from the maps, Elissa watched the girl cross the small room and open the door to admit the count. Her handmaiden had been a faithful companion for many years. Was she right to allow her to stay on when her family had already left, even if the girl had insisted they would have to take her away in chains before she would leave her Queen? Elissa knew that she could have ordered the girl to go, and yet she had not done so. Was selfishness to be her only reward for years of faithful service? Thankfully, the formal bow from the count as he entered the room commanded her attention and denied her the opportunity to further pursue her line of thinking.

"Please don't do that," she exclaimed in an exasperated tone, beckoning Regulus to rise and approach her. "It seems an outrageous extravagance to allow such formalities when my realm is collapsing around my ears." She cursed herself for her lack of composure, knowing that the slight catch in her voice wouldn't go unnoticed by her closest friend. "Damn you, Regulus," she hissed, suddenly angry. "Why is it always you that makes me feel like I'm not strong enough for all of this?"

"Come," soothed the count, placing his hand gently on her shoulder as she turned her back from him and took a deep breath. "Don't be angry with me. Not now. You know why. You know it's because I'm your friend. You're human Elissa, not some edifice of stone and precious metals like the statues of your predecessors. You have a heart, just like I do, and just like the rest of your subjects. Unfortunately, there are precious few you can open yours to. I'm glad you can at least let your guard down with me. And don't think that I haven't shed a tear or two for our fate too. It would take a heart of stone to look at what is happening here and not feel something strong stirring within us."

"I'm sorry." Elissa had managed to regain her composure once more, the soft shine to her eyes the only reminder now of her momentary loss of control. "Thank you, Regulus. I truly am sorry. I feel the weight of the whole realm upon me today."

"You're not alone in that, my Queen. We all feel it. The court will stand with you, though. A few have left, but not many. It's the common people that are most at sea now. They're scared Elissa, frightened out of their wits. I've just come up through the city now. It's not a pretty sight. If we don't get them doing something, there'll be an even worse panic than there is now and that will be the end of us. We'll never be able to defend the city then. I've taken the liberty of doing a few things. I'm sorry, but there wasn't time to consult anyone."

"I think the time for consultation and meetings is over. What have you done?"

"Don't wait for Brassilius to respond to your summons. I ran into Halin on the way up here. I told him not to bother looking for him. Brassilius is busy. When I came across him he was having a bit of a crisis, blaming himself for the current situation and on the verge of losing it. I told him to get a grip on himself and to open the armoury and get every able-bodied man up on the walls with some kind of weapon in his hand. He'll be all right now. I know I had no business giving him orders but, frankly, he needed it. I think he just had a bad moment there for a while. Mishra knows we've all had some of those since yesterday. He's going to commandeer a couple of warehouses and get a few more kitchens going. That'll get some of the women and children off the street and get their minds off their troubles for a while."

"Well. You have been busy. You're sure he's all right now? He's going to have a lot more on his shoulders before long."

"He's fine now. I didn't suggest anything he wouldn't have thought of himself anyway."

"Mmmm. Have you heard any news from the East? I haven't heard anything up here for some time now."

"Yes. The sligs have begun their assault. It's not the East that's our main problem, though. It's the northern front. A message has just come in from Jakic. That's what I was coming here for before I ran into Brassilius."

Regulus held out his left hand, offering the rolled up scroll he held there to Elissa. The Queen looked down at the scroll blankly for a moment, then lifted her eyes to meet his once more, ignoring the offer, wanting him to go on, though dreading what she was going to hear.

"I'm sorry," he continued, blinking nervously as he lowered his hand, "but I'm afraid it's even worse than we thought. Our whole northern front is in full flight. Jakic says there's nothing left to rally. Apparently, Jeeluk was considerably worse than we'd thought. The survivors say it was a bloodbath. It appears that any hope that Jakic might still buy us a few days can be forgotten. If Marlor stays where he is now, by the morning our one remaining force of any size will be surrounded and cut off. The Mendobar Hills can't be held any longer, Elissa. We've got to pull them right back to the city, now. That's too big a decision for me to make. It will need your seal on it. We can't afford to waste time while they send someone back to verify my authority to give an order like that."

Elissa felt like Regulus had just told her that her closest relative had passed away. Her jaw dropped and she felt her cheek tremor as her mind struggled to accept what she had just heard. Surely he wasn't serious. "But the plain's full of refugees. We need more time to get them all into the city."

"It's too late for that. You must send the order now, Elissa. If Marlor is cut off away from the city walls, his fate will be sealed. And so will that of the rest of us. The refugees will be cut to pieces before even a quarter of them get into the city. And what chance will the rest of us have once Marlor's gone? We can't defend the city without his men. Even with them, our chances look grim. Send the word out onto the plain at the same time. Give the word for everyone who can to fly for the gates now, while they still can."

"Oh Mishra," sobbed Elissa as she sank back into her chair. "Why have you forsaken us?" She knew that Regulus was right. Even when they'd heard that the northern front was being overrun they had still pinned their hope on buying more time, thinking that something could be salvaged from the wreckage. There *was* no more time now. She felt hollow, like someone had just snatched away all of her will to go on.

Elissa looked up at Regulus. Despite the composure his tone suggested, he looked agitated. She hadn't noticed before, but his face was pale and gaunt. It was his eyes, however, that were the most telling. They kept shifting focus, looking this way and that but never directly at her. Regulus was scared. If it was reassurance she needed, it was not to be found in the look on her friend's face.

"We knew it would come to this," she heard him continue in a voice that sounded stronger than he looked. "It's just come sooner than we had hoped. We're not done for yet, my Queen. The walls of Keerêt are strong and Brassilius has done all that he can to prepare us for a long siege. There'll be many in the council who'll remember in the days to come that they opposed him on that."

His words were sound enough but they carried little conviction. For Elissa, his transparent attempt at optimism only made things worse. If even he had lost hope, then what was there left to cling to?

"I know that," she responded wearily, unable to hide the despondency she was feeling. "I will send the order. We have no choice, do we? But to whom will we turn for hope once we're penned up in the city? It's just us now. The gods have forsaken us, and the Guardians too, it would seem."

"Don't give up on the Guardians yet," urged Regulus after the Queen had sent for a scribe. "Remember what Nim said, that Tarak and Kell intend to join forces and that they've both promised to come to our aid as soon as they can. While ever those two Guardians live there is still hope, Elissa. Tarak wouldn't have sent Jekira here if he intended to abandon her to her fate. They *will* come to our aid . . . I'm sure of it."

CHAPTER 14

The sudden departure of her chief tormentor had done nothing to calm Sara's nerves. If anything its effect had been more akin to pouring gasoline on an already blazing fire.

Even though she too had heard the noise that had prompted Ruz' abrupt exit, she had been so frightened when the draghar had sprung up and grabbed his sword that she had been certain he had finally determined to do away with her, regardless of his master's plans. To her relief, he had headed straight for the door. She had heard a few more noises after that, but then everything had gone quiet again. What it all meant was anyone's guess.

Probably just Tug dropping something or knocking something over somewhere, she thought, unwilling to have to deal with anything more than she already had on her plate. Ruz must be just as much on edge as she was. She took a few deep breaths, trying desperately to keep the panic she knew was simmering just below the surface of her seething emotions under some sort of control, lest she lose all grip on her sanity altogether.

Though Ruz seemed to be gone for an eternity, she knew that she had no ability to maintain any sense of time, least of all in her current state. It may have been just a few minutes even though it seemed to her to have been much longer. Not that she was in any hurry to see the evil creature again. If anything, she realised, she should be grateful for the respite from his attention, no matter how brief it might be.

Then, just as she had begun to feel her pulse rate coming back under control and her frayed nerves had started to subside, even if only fractionally, the impossible happened. She couldn't believe her eyes when she suddenly saw Rayne's head cautiously peering around the edge of the door out of which Ruz had run seemingly only minutes earlier.

"Oh my God. It's not possible," she cried out in amazement. "What are you doing here? Rayne, tell me I'm not dreaming."

"What have the bastards done to you?" gasped Rayne as he limped across the floor of the room and threw his arms around her. "Are you okay?" he asked as they attempted an awkward embrace. Though Rayne had put his arms around her shoulders as he stood beside her, all Sara could do was try in some way to press her own upper body back against his, her manacles and her seated position prevented her from achieving anything more than that. When he bent down and she felt the soft skin of his cheek touching her own face as he hugged her to him, she drew in her breath sharply. She hadn't expected to ever experience such feelings again.

"Yes, yes. Of course I am," she sobbed, unable to restrain her emotions any longer. "Oh, Rayne. I can't believe this is happening."

Before Rayne had a chance to respond, Sara groaned as if she was suddenly in great pain. For a moment she had forgotten the terrible danger he had put himself in by coming there.

"Ruz," she gasped, as he stood back to look at her. "He went out there looking for you only a few minutes ago. And Golkar, he'll be back at any moment, he will, I'm sure he will." She was tripping over the words in her rush to get them out. She had to make him realise the danger he was in. "You've got to get out of here. Leave me. You can't save me now, Rayne. Save yourself. They'll only kill you too."

She was close to hysterical now. Rayne couldn't possibly hope to fight them all off. How he had got there was irrelevant. If he stayed, it would just mean another senseless death. She couldn't let him do that. "Quickly," she urged him, looking wildly from the door to the mirror and back again as she spoke. "Go. Now. While you can."

"Calm down," Rayne responded in a frustratingly calm voice. "Ruz and Tug are dead. I killed them both, Sara. They're dead. They can't hurt you anymore."

"But . . . but Golkar, he . . . "

"Let's get one thing straight," interrupted Rayne, turning around and looking about the room as if he were searching for something. "I know we have to hurry, but I'm not leaving here without you. Where are the keys to those manacles? I've got to get you out of that chair."

"By all the demons in Kornok," he suddenly exclaimed as he caught a better look at the man shackled to the chair beside her. "What's *he* doing here? Th . . . that's Josef."

"I don't know. He's still alive, I think, but he can't last much longer. Oh, Rayne," she cried, losing control once more. "They did terrible things to him." She was sobbing again. She could feel her eyes filling with tears, the fluid quickly blurring her vision.

"It's okay," she heard Rayne say as she felt him take her hand in his.

"I wish I could hold you," she cried plaintively as she pulled at her manacles in a futile attempt to free herself. "I'm so scared, Rayne."

Rayne gave her one last squeeze with his hand and then began to move around the room, turning over everything he could see as he searched for the keys to her bonds. There was nothing Sara could do but look on helplessly. *It's useless,* she thought as he roamed about the room, methodically examining every possible place the keys could be. *It just isn't meant to be. I'm not going to get away from here. I know it.*

"Think Sara, think," cried Rayne, as his search became more frantic. "They're not here. Who locked you into them? What did they do with the key?"

"I don't know. I can't remember, Rayne. You don't know what it was like. I just can't remember everything. I don't want to remember everything. Oh please, please go. Please, Rayne. I beg you. I don't want to see you die too." She knew she was in no state to think clearly about anything. What was Rayne doing here, anyway? Then, all of a sudden, she remembered.

"It was Tug," she shouted excitedly. "Tug had them. He put them in his pocket." She could picture him doing it quite clearly now. They must be still in his pocket.

"Excellent," replied Rayne, with a broad grin on his face. With that, he rushed over to Sara and kissed her passionately on the lips. "I'll be right back," he said as he rushed from the room. "Don't go away." With a final wave of his hand, he disappeared around the corner of the door.

Sara laughed madly at his playfulness, realising as she did so how long it had been since she had last felt able to feel anything even approaching joy. It had been in Novistor, at The Spreading Fig, she remembered. The happy mood quickly dissipated, however. They weren't in The Spreading Fig now. They were dicing with death here. How long did they have? How long would it be before Golkar returned? And even if they did get away, how far could they hope to get?

Try though she might to not get excited, however, she couldn't suppress the sense of hope that began to grow in her heart. She had got away from this place once before, she reminded herself. Maybe she . . . correction, maybe *they* could do it again. She wasn't alone this time.

As the feeling of hopefulness began to take hold of her, Sara lifted her head and began to look round the room. *Josef*, she thought suddenly, feeling her heart sink back into a pit of despair. What would they do with him? How could they possibly get away with him in tow? That would be almost a certain guarantee that they wouldn't get far. And yet, they couldn't just leave him there.

Just at that moment, just as her newfound hope reached its zenith, and peaked, she heard a sound from the other side of the room. Sara turned her head, seeking its source, and as she did so, she opened her mouth in horror. A leg was emerging from the surface of the mirror that hung on the far wall. She recognised the golden slipper and rich maroon of Golkar's pantaloons instantly.

There was nothing she could do but stare, horrified, as the wizard stepped into the room and stood for a moment, eyes downcast, breathing deeply, obviously allowing himself to become accustomed once more to his own chamber. He looked tired compared to when she had last seen him, drained in some way, exhausted.

Appearing to compose himself now that he'd had time to adjust to his new surroundings, he took a few deep breaths, then slowly raised his head and looked about the room. He stopped when his gaze met Sara's. Though obviously tired, he returned her stare with a look of bemusement, and eyes that blazed like crackling fire.

As their eyes locked, Sara finally found her voice, screaming out her fear in one long, loud, piercing shriek. It was the sound of terror, sheer, unadulterated, terror. She knew that their doom was upon them.

Golkar stood silently, staring at her malevolently but otherwise patiently, as Sara screamed her lungs out. When she finally had to stop and draw breath, he spoke.

"Calm yourself, my dear," he drawled, in his usual patronising manner, giving her one of his phony smiles as he did so. "You have a little while yet. Right now, I'm tired, and I'm ravenously hungry. Taking command of this plane of existence," he continued as his facial expression slipped greasily from a smile into a smirk and the fire in his eyes began to slowly diminish, "is very demanding work, don't you know?"

Recovering from her initial surprise, Sara strained to rein in her own emotions and keep her own face expressionless as he spoke. She knew that Rayne had to have heard her scream. What he would do as a consequence was yet to be seen. She hoped to God he wouldn't come rushing blindly up the stairs to save her. Not that she had any idea what she *did* want him to do. She was too busy trying to cope mentally with the wizard's sudden reappearance to think that far ahead.

"I . . . I'm sorry," she responded, deciding that her best move would be to try to delay the wizard by engaging him in conversation. "You startled me. Where did you go? I mean, just now, when you left us. Wh . . . Where did you go? What have you done? Why can't you just leave everybody alone? You have all that power. Isn't it enough to know that everyone is so scared of you? Why do you have to hurt anyone?"

As she finished, she saw the wizard turn suddenly towards the open doorway. "Nooooooo," she wailed as she turned her own head and saw Rayne standing there, with what appeared to be a long spear in his hand. Before she could warn him to run, Rayne drew back his arm and threw the weapon with all of his strength, straight at the wizard's chest.

Sara wasn't surprised when Golkar batted it aside with a simple twist of his arm. She watched despondently as the deflected spear flew past him harmlessly and thudded into the wooden beams of the wall behind him. Rayne showed no sign of any similar disappointment, however. Apparently undeterred by the ease with which the wizard had repelled his initial attack, he drew his sword and stepped cautiously into the room.

"No," she shouted, sensing her plea would go unheeded but determined to try to stop him just the same. "Run, Rayne. It's too late now, just run."

Rayne showed no sign of heeding her advice. With his sword arm up, he began to advance cautiously towards the wizard, crouching in a fighting pose as he did so. Sara couldn't bear to watch. As she swung her head away from the scene being played out before her, she heard the wizard's voice once more. He was laughing now as he spoke.

"Well, now I've seen everything," he chuckled disdainfully. "This little sprite comes with a most impressive entourage, I must say. What shall I do with this one?"

When she heard Rayne gasp, she knew that she had to look back. She had to know what was happening. Turning to face the two combatants again, she watched in amazement as Rayne's body lifted up from the floor and then was flung with some invisible but incredible force against the wall beside the door. Sara sobbed as she heard him cry out in pain as his body hit the wall and then dropped limply to the floor. It was there for only a second or two when it lifted again and was then flung across the room and against the opposite wall, just missing by inches being impaled on the hilt of the spear which still protruded from the timber beams. As he crashed to the floor for a second time, Rayne looked more like a rag doll than a human being. His crumpled and twisted form looked broken and lifeless as it lay slumped where it now lay, against the wall of the chamber.

"No" Sara screamed when she saw his body begin to rise into the air for a third time. She felt the fury rising within her and this time when she screamed at the wizard she did so with all the intensity of her being, hurling her rage at him in frustration as she desperately tried to pull herself free from her bonds.

"Leave him alone you monster," she shouted in her rage.

Sara watched in surprise as, inexplicably, Rayne's body suddenly came to an abrupt halt only a metre or so above the floorboards. Golkar, who had been directing the motion of his victim's body with his own right arm stretched out in front of him, stopped and slowly turned his head in her direction. Though the suddenness of his change of behaviour surprised her, the look of consternation on the wizard's face was even more perplexing.

Sara's surprise soon turned to apprehension, however. As rapidly as it had appeared, Golkar's look of consternation was quickly displaced by one of wrath. In the blink of an eyelid, the wizard swung his right arm around and flung it towards her, throwing it out in front of him with his flattened palm facing directly towards her, as if he was trying to push her away, though there were easily some four or five paces of floor space between them.

Sara gasped in alarm as she suddenly felt both her body and the chair it was manacled to forced joltingly back across the chamber, the wooden legs scraping noisily on the floorboards as it did so. She gave a little shriek when the chair's backwards motion was brought to a shuddering halt as it slammed against the wall behind her.

Though her backwards motion was thereby halted, however, Golkar made no attempt to release her from the extraordinary power he had somehow managed to bring to bear against her so quickly and so unexpectedly. Sara winced as she felt her body being pressed back uncomfortably against the frame of the chair by the unnatural force the wizard was now bringing to bear against her. It was as if a fierce and almighty gale had suddenly sprung up and swept through the chamber, pinning her to the wall, though the air in the room was both dry and still.

"Don't dare to interrupt me . . . ever," the wizard roared, after a moment of silence had passed. The quivering of his outstretched palm was a clear indication of the barely contained rage that had fuelled his change of attack from Rayne towards her. Sara felt herself quailing under the combined impact of his scrutiny and the bizarre force which pinned her to the frame of her chair more securely than any bonds ever could.

Golkar's face had taken on a contorted look, his chest was heaving and his eyes were flickering, dancing with an infernal fire that seemed to her to be not of this world, as if it was sourced from the bottomless pit of some nameless and unspeakable hell. Though he had, for the moment, stopped what he had been doing to Rayne, clearly, she had now become the sole focus of his malice. Having seen what he had done to Rayne, Sara dreaded to think what he might now do to her.

Just as she began to brace herself for the onslaught she felt sure he was about to unleash, Golkar lowered his hand once more and the pressure he had been applying to her was suddenly released. When the chair she was bound to suddenly rocked forwards alarmingly before settling in its upright position, Sara felt a surge of relief rush through her body. She allowed herself to breathe in deeply. Without realising it, she had been holding her breath the whole of the time the wizard had had her under his terrible scrutiny.

Unfortunately, her relief proved to be short-lived. When Golkar turned away from her again, satisfied that he had cowed her into silence once more, and obviously intending to finish what he had started with Rayne, she felt her own anger rapidly returning, despite her foreboding.

In the brief interval her confrontation with the wizard had allowed Rayne, he had somehow managed to roll over onto his back. To Sara's surprise, though he was clearly injured quite badly, he was still conscious. He was in the process of struggling to raise himself up on one elbow when the wizard renewed his attack. Sara sobbed as she watched Golkar send him sprawling to the floor again with a simple wave of his arm.

"No," she cried out defiantly, silently cursing her impotence in the face of Golkar's awesome power. "Leave him alone." She knew that her demands were pointless, but they had sprung from her quite involuntarily. The sight of Rayne being toyed with so cruelly was pressing buttons she seemed to have little or no control over.

For the second time, the wizard abruptly stopped what he was doing and spun round to face her. Sara recoiled as she waited for the force of some spell to hit her, mentally steeling herself to absorb whatever punishment he chose to dish out, thinking that this time she was prepared to endure whatever she had to if it would buy even the briefest respite for Rayne. Closing her eyes as tight as she could, she pushed back at the wizard with all of her might in an instinctive attempt to fend off his anticipated blow. The result surprised her even more than it did Golkar.

Something very strange began to happen. Sara sensed that a wall had suddenly arisen between the two of them. Not a wall that could be seen; this was an invisible wall. But she knew for a certainty that it was now there. How, she couldn't explain.

It was as if two storm fronts had met and collided and were vying for ascendancy, each determined to supplant the other. Sara could feel it swaying back and forth between them, moving slowly towards her at first, then back towards Golkar again as she pushed back at it, trying to repel the wizard's attempt to hurt her. She didn't really understand what was happening, but she realised that it must be something she had done. In some strange way, her anger at what Golkar was doing . . . no, more than that, her determination to stop him from what he was doing . . . that was it, that was what was fuelling this wall. And it was if they were both buffeting it with their will now, probing it, looking for a way to break down the other's defences.

The realisation that she might be able to resist the wizard's efforts as long as she focused her mind and all of her will to that purpose suddenly flowed into Sara's consciousness like a stream of light flooding into a dark room through a suddenly opened door. Though she had no idea how this could be, the evidence before her seemed clear and undeniable. Where Golkar had easily thrown her back against the wall in his earlier assault, this time he seemed unable to achieve his purpose. She had somehow stumbled on a way to resist him.

Unfortunately, the very act of considering this discovery only served to weaken her capacity to maintain it. As soon as she began to think about it, about what it was and how she could use it, she felt the wall giving way before the wizard's mental onslaught. Hastily, she resumed her focus, pushing any extraneous thoughts from her mind and striving to rebuild the barrier that had almost crumbled as swiftly as it had first arisen. Once again, the forward progress of Golkar's assault came to a grinding halt.

What now? she thought, tentatively trying to maintain her resistance while simultaneously exploring the prospects before her. To her surprise, this time she managed to achieve her purpose. It was actually possible to partition a small part of her mind away from the grim mental duel she was otherwise engaged in. It wasn't easy though, and she quickly realised that anything but the simplest of thinking would probably be totally beyond her if she hoped to maintain a reasonable defence against the wizard's attack. She didn't even really know exactly what it was she was doing. She was just doing it, that was all, and she dare not allow herself the luxury of questioning how it was so.

A groan from the direction that Rayne lay in distracted her attention and suddenly the wall between her and Golkar was down. In an instant the full might of Golkar's will swept over her, both mentally and physically, slamming the chair she was bound to back against the wall behind her again with a loud crack. Her whole body shook with the jar of the impact and she felt the wizard's mind sweep into hers before she could even begin to think how to resurrect her mental defences.

All of a sudden, her head was filled with ghastly images, mental pictures of the destruction Golkar promised he would inflict on the people of Ilythia once he took full possession of the power she held within her. Sara gaped at the horror unfolding within her thoughts, wanting desperately to close her mind to the atrocities being laid out before her but knowing she was utterly unable to do so. She watched with mounting dismay, wondering at the sickness of the person who could have conjured up such evil thoughts.

While her mind was powerless to resist the onslaught, forced to look on like a helpless observer, her body was under no such constraint. Sara felt her stomach begin to churn as the images being forced upon her moved from one hideous scene to the next. She felt the gorge quickly rising within her throat. With a slight jerk of her torso, she suddenly retched, then gasped and retched again, absently aware of the dampness across her blouse as the contents of her stomach spilled out of her mouth and ran down her chin and onto her heaving breasts.

Golkar's wicked laugh only added further insult to her injury as Sara's chin sagged against her chest. She felt drained, both physically and mentally, broken and beaten in a way she had never before experienced. Resistance was pointless, there was no longer anything left to cling to. Nothing, that is, except her despair. Bound as she was, she couldn't even wipe the remnants of her vomit from her chin. Her soft little whimpers only seemed to goad Golkar into further laughter. Then, just as suddenly as they had begun, the nauseating display of mental images ceased.

"Had enough, my pretty?" she heard Golkar sneer from across the room as she hung her head in shame, despising herself for how quickly her resistance had crumbled. Her most fervent wish now was that he get it over and done with, that he finish her once and for all, and quickly.

A moment passed and not a sound could be heard in the room. Sara felt herself jump as the roar of Golkar's voice shattered the silence like a hammer smashing a pane of glass into thousands of pieces. "I SAID, HAD ENOUGH, MY PRETTY?"

"Y . . . Yes," she stammered, suddenly realising that the wizard's rage was due to her own silence. It seems he wasn't done with tormenting her yet. Her heart was hammering against the wall of her chest. She felt even more vulnerable now than before she had tried to resist him.

"I thought so," he snickered, obviously amused at her sudden submissiveness. "Or perhaps you'd like to see what I'll do if you dare to defy me again."

The image that suddenly flashed into Sara's mind was so revolting she could do nothing to stop herself from retching again. For a few moments, her chest and stomach heaved as she emptied what little remained inside her onto the floor of the chamber. Her wretchedness was now all but complete, the taste of bile in her mouth a bitter reminder of what she would have to endure if she tried to resist the wizard further.

"Now watch," he said, spitting his words out at her with venom as she struggled to regain her composure. "Watch while I take your would-be rescuer here and turn him into meat for the dogs." Once again, she looked on helplessly as Golkar turned his back to her and began to lift Rayne up from the floor, levitating his body up into the air with the same astonishing ease he had done before.

No, Sara thought to herself. *I won't be able to live with myself if I don't try to stop him.*

She knew that she couldn't defeat Golkar. Regardless of that, she also knew that she had to try, even though her heart quailed at the thought of the torment he would inflict on her when she failed. Hadn't Rayne somehow found his way to this place in what he must have known would be a doomed attempt to rescue her? She owed him the same, at the very least.

Girding herself once more for the onslaught she knew she could expect by way of reply, Sara hurled all of the mental energy she could muster straight at the wizard. As she did so, she tried to form a picture in her mind of him being thrown to the floor by the force of her will. The immediate result she obtained was encouraging, though not as effective as she had hoped. Not surprisingly, this time he was ready for her. This time his defences were up and waiting.

Her immediate goal was met nonetheless, though Sara cringed at the way he allowed Rayne's body to drop unceremoniously to the floor again with a sickening thud. At least the muffled cry Rayne gave as he hit the floor told her that he was still alive.

That positive thought was quickly dispelled as Sara found herself reeling under the impact of yet another assault from Golkar. Though she fought to maintain the defensive barrier she quickly put in place, she knew that this time he wouldn't be taken by surprise, this time there would be no easy impasse. And she was right. Slowly but surely, Golkar began pushing the barrier between them back towards her.

Yet it wasn't Sara's strength that was failing her. It was more than that. She simply didn't know how to conduct such a fight. Push back, that was all she knew. Yet she knew that she would need to do more than that. This was more than a contest; it was a deadly battle. Her life, and Rayne's, were at stake, if not those of all Ilythians. Just pushing wasn't going to be enough to stop Golkar. That knowledge, that she couldn't actually hope to win this deadly battle, only seemed to further undermine her attempts to fend him off.

After all, he was a wizard. He was a Guardian with centuries of experience. Maybe Josef was right and she did have as much or even more power than Golkar did. Perhaps she had even caught him at a bad time. Twice now she had been stunned at the impact of her attempts to stop him from harming Rayne. But even so, *he* knew how to win a battle like this. This was what he did. It was one thing to have such power, but another to know how to use it.

Deep down, Sara knew that, whatever minor victories she might have had thus far, in the end, she was going to lose. How could it possibly be any other way? And failure would bring heavy consequences. All she was achieving was making him even angrier than he had been when she had first tried to intervene. With mounting horror, Sara began to see that her attempts to confront the wizard might only end up bringing even more pain and suffering to Rayne than he would have otherwise had to endure.

Sara felt her will to resist Golkar steadily diminishing as the realisation of what she had done slowly crystallised in her mind. Fight on she still did though, even though it was futile. She just couldn't sit there and watch him hurt Rayne anymore without at least attempting to stop him, to fight back. Wasn't that what she had originally set out to do, she reminded herself as the barrier separating their two wills was inexorably being driven back towards her. Wasn't that what she had said she would do when they had brought her here and locked her in a cell? Wasn't that what she had told her father she would do so many years ago?

Despite her resistance, Sara felt the last vestiges of the mental barrier she had erected beginning to collapse. Then, as the prospect of defeat seemed to loom ever larger in her consciousness, she suddenly became aware of a voice. It came from way down in the deep recesses of her mind, weak and barely discernible. She tried to ignore it at first, for she knew that it must be Golkar. He had finally broken through her defences and was trying to undermine her resistance from within. There was no way left to stop him now. She was going to die. Her time had finally come.

No, the voice cried. *Listen, Sara. It's me, it's Josef.* It was suddenly loud and clear, urgent and insistent. It was, it had to be, Josef. Somehow he was still alive. The man who had saved them from the sligs was still alive and was calling out to her for help. Golkar must have heard it too, for in the same instant that she realised where the voice had come from, the wizard broke off his attack and a moment later she heard Josef cry out in pain, only this time it was a real scream, not just words in her head.

It was her fault, she realised with a sickening feeling in the pit of her stomach. Though he must be on the verge of death, he had sent out a plaintive call for help and all she had done was allow Golkar to switch the point of his attack from her to him. She hadn't even tried to stop the monster. Just as she had feared, her ineptitude in this one-sided battle was only dooming her friends to more pain and anguish. How much more would they have to endure because of her? She was floundering. She had to do something: equivocation was worse than inaction. She had to resist him, or die trying. She had to fight him, or stand by while he destroyed each of her friends in turn.

Without any further hesitation, Sara responded in the only way she knew how, by resuming her attack on the wizard. With her new-found resolve fuelling her efforts she quickly fended Golkar's assault away from the old man. This time she stood firm when the Guardian renewed his attack on her, throwing herself back into the fray with reckless abandon.

She was too bewildered to even consider what was happening any longer. She just went with the flow of it all, running on pure adrenaline and instinct. A blind fury seemed to take hold of her as she pushed back the wizard, parrying wave after wave of energy that came coursing across the space between them as he too lifted his game in the face of her renewed vigour.

That's right. This time Josef's thought was as clear as a bell, though even in her mind his voice sounded weak and faltering. *Push him back Sara, push with all your might. Try to force him backwards. Put him on the defensive.*

Somehow, she found that she could, push him back that is, both physically and mentally. Josef's unexpected appearance had given her a new sense of purpose. Sara dug deep now, drawing on all of her hatred for the wizard, remembering what it was that he planned to do to her, and to Rayne, and to all of the inhabitants of Ilythia, remembering all of the things that Josef had told her of what was to come should she fail. She felt the fury steadily rising within her. He was evil, so evil she couldn't even contemplate where such malice had sprung from. He had to be beaten. He had to be defeated. He couldn't be allowed to complete his cruel plans.

She watched in wonder as the wizard's body began to recoil as he gave ground in the face of her furious counter-attack. This time it was his turn to try and weather the storm that had suddenly assailed him. He was grimacing himself now as he struggled to resist her, trying vainly to brace himself against the floor of the chamber as his slippers slowly but surely slid back across the rough wooden planks of the floor.

Not for long though. Golkar had no intention of being defeated, not here, not in his own chamber, nor anywhere else for that matter, and certainly not by her, not by a girl not even versed in the ways of the use of the arcane arts. If anything, the reversal only seemed to spur him on to an even greater effort. For the first time, he seemed to comprehend that his opponent was a closer match for him than he had previously realised, that the duel they were engaged in really was one to the death, that his precious source of power may just have to be destroyed to ensure his own survival. Sara's new found hope quickly turned into shock as a ball of fire suddenly appeared in the wizard's hand and he hurled it in her direction. It all happened in the blink of an eyelid.

For Sara, all hell seemed to break loose and the world seemed to slow on its axis. She watched like a detached observer as the fireball careened across the room towards her, slowly but surely cutting through the force she was throwing at her opponent. While that was happening, she gaped in shock as she felt a second and even more unexpected assault on her senses. She shuddered as a set of what felt like cold and icy fingers took a hold of her skull and slowly begin to twist her head around and away from the fireball, thwarting her efforts to deal with its inexorable fiery progress and sending cold slices of pain spearing down into her cranium at the very same time.

Though she had to fight to suppress her mounting panic, Sara knew that she had no time to deal with this second and more insidious assault. The fireball, though slowed considerably by the fierce battle of wills that still continued unabated between her and the wizard, was clearly the more immediate and deadly threat. Its steady but obdurate progress towards her only added to its horror. It was like someone had thrown a switch to slow-motion and everything now was moving as if they were wading through treacle.

Disregarding for the moment the vicious pains that seemed to stab right down into the very core of her brain, Sara concentrated all of her effort on maintaining her focus on the fiery object that was rapidly filling her field of vision, on slowing it even further and desperately trying to steer it away from its original and murderous path. Somehow, she managed to do it. She looked on with wonder as the fireball spun past her shoulder, watching it turn lazily on its axis as it did so. The scorching heat of its passing signalled how perilously close the wizard had come to destroying her. When it shattered against the wall beside her, unexpectedly spraying a hot stinging liquid all over the side of her face and her neck, her assessment was only too painfully affirmed.

Once more she tried to ignore the pain in order to concentrate more fully on the task at hand. Though the stabbing pains in her head had continued unabated throughout the whole incident, she was surprised to realise that her decision to disregard them while she dealt with the fireball seemed to have had the effect of diminishing both their frequency and their intensity.

That was it. For the first time since the battle with Golkar had begun, Sara began to think that she might actually be able to beat him. Even pain, it would seem, could be subdued by the strength of her will. She was better at this than she realised. Somehow, she was doing something right.

Slowly, but surely, she mentally prised the icy grip away from her forehead and flung it across the room and away from her body. With the pressure on her neck relieved, she hastily resumed her assault on the wizard with a new found confidence fuelling her efforts. She was wary now and alert for any more of his surprises.

The nagging doubts quickly returned, however, nibbling away at her confidence again, like termites steadily undermining the foundations of a building. She was forcing Golkar back, but to what avail? And what would he throw at her next? Her skin still stung painfully where the remnants of the fireball had splattered against the side of her face. His goal had now become all too painfully clear.

He would stop at nothing now . . . nothing short of her total destruction. And what's more, he knew how to achieve that. One look at the wizard was enough of a reminder that her foe was no novice to this deadly form of combat. His robes, his maturity, the resolve etched on his face, they all spoke of an experienced and determined foe not used to losing. She may be stronger than she had previously thought possible, she may even be able to force him back and to deflect his blows for a time, but how could she possibly win?

As if to confirm her doubts, the wizard began yet another of his fearsome assaults. Sara felt a dread anticipation build within her as she watched him draw back his hand, clearly preparing to hurl some new and deadly object in her direction. Though she could see no hint of the fireball that had formed in his open hand in his previous assault, she guessed that whatever it was he intended to do it would be something she would rather he didn't. Striving to maintain her own assault on him as she did so, she quickly tried to focus a part of her will on resisting his efforts to bring his arm forward again from its raised position.

The fresh clash of their wills ran through her like a shudder as their two minds wrestled, each fighting to subdue the other. Though an observer would never have known it, they were locked in a deadly duel now, Sara focusing more and more of her effort on stopping the wizard from unleashing his mysterious new missile, and Golkar struggling to free himself from the restraint which she was trying to impose upon him. As their two wills locked in a grim struggle, each sought for a weakness in their opponent's resolve, an opening or a lapse which would give them the ascendancy they so desperately sought.

Sara began to wonder how long she could keep going. She sensed that her focus was wavering again, that she was struggling to maintain the intense level of concentration their battle was now calling for. She had never experienced anything like this before in her life. And it was taking its toll. She was tiring now, struggling to stay focused.

Too many new things kept happening; there was too much to deal with, too much for her mind to absorb, no time to plan the next step. To add to her woes, yet another unexpected development abruptly emerged, demanding even further division of her attention. Though her eyes were focused on Golkar, she suddenly became aware of a flickering light from the very periphery of her vision. Then Josef's thoughts intruded on her mind once again.

Push him towards the mirror, Sara. I've opened the portal. You must force him through. Hurry. I can't hold it for long. My strength is failing.

You've got to be kidding, thought Sara. She was already having the greatest of difficulties in simply maintaining the status quo.

As she tried to absorb the import of the new message from Josef, and how best to achieve what he suggested, she noticed her opponent risk a quick glance over his shoulder. It was clear that whatever was being said to her by Josef was also being heard by Golkar. Unfortunately, there wasn't much she could do about that. She had no idea how to shield those thoughts from him and now was not the time to start taking lessons.

Sara allowed herself the luxury of glancing where Golkar was looking as well. She felt her pulse quicken as she saw the shimmering light she had seen in her room the night she had been abducted. It looked just like it had on that fateful night, like an opening into another place, a rough tear in the fabric of their world that led to some distant oblivion. Just where this opening led to she couldn't even begin to guess.

Despite its familiar appearance, however, there was one significant difference to the portal that had been opened to bring her to his world. Unlike the one Golkar had created in her room, this one seemed to be an opening on the very surface of the mirror itself, the same mirror that Golkar had used to leave and return by earlier that day. Though the inside of the rent was filled with a brilliant white light, just as she remembered the one she had been taken through had been, this one was also less substantial. It kept fading in and out of focus, there one minute, as clear as could be, and almost disappearing from view the next, before reappearing again once more as bright as ever. Sara guessed that Josef was having some difficulty keeping it open. Not surprising for someone she'd thought had been dead!

Now she could see a way of ending their grim struggle. With a renewed sense of purpose, she began to turn the whole of her mind to the task of pushing Golkar towards the mirror.

It was a fatal mistake, however. In her haste to achieve her new goal, she forgot to maintain the restraint she had put on his outstretched arm. Suddenly finding himself free to complete his intended action, the wizard seized the initiative she had so foolishly relinquished and flung his new spell at her with all the force he could bring to bear. Sara watched in horror as a bolt of lightning materialised in the space between them and shot like an arrow across the short distance that separated them.

Though she opened her mouth to scream as the bolt tore into her midriff, she never actually heard the sound she made. Her senses were suddenly flooded with such an agonising pain they began to shut down from the overload. What little control she had left deserted her. The room spun wildly before her as she thrashed against her bonds, jerking and twisting as her muscles spasmed and flexed uncontrollably in an involuntary dance. A dark veil descended over her eyes and the pain that only a moment before had threatened to consume her senses began to rapidly recede from her awareness. In its place came an overwhelming sense of well-being. The room and all of its confines slipped out of her awareness as surely as if she had died.

As her awareness began to return, Sara felt confused and disoriented. Wherever she was it was dark, so dark in fact that she couldn't even see her own body when she looked down at where her hands and feet should be. It was also cold, so very cold. She felt a shiver course through her as she tried to make some sense of where she was and what had happened to her, of what was going on.

She had been in a room, she thought, and something terrible had happened to her . . . .she had a feeling that that was so but no actual memory, no mental picture, no details to give any substance to the feeling . . . but . . . but that was before, anyhow . . . what about now . . . where was she now?

As she reached out with her senses, trying to get some sense of her surroundings, she realised that it wasn't just that she had no idea where she was; she couldn't remember how she had got there either . . . or what she had been doing before she came to this place. Yes, she had been in a room, that was a strong feeling, and something terrible had happened to her, that much she also felt sure was right, though she couldn't explain why, but any further detail completely eluded her.

As she struggled with these thoughts, an awareness began to grow within her of a dim glow that was forming, where before there had only been darkness. She could definitely see a dim glow in the distance now, up ahead of her. Though why she thought it was 'ahead' she wasn't sure. Until she had become aware of the glow there had been no more ahead than there had been behind, or up or down. There had only been the utter darkness. But now . . . now there was . . . something . . . a glow. A glow that was slowly but surely growing. A light. Something to focus on. Something to guide her.

A thought that perhaps she should move towards the light started to form within her mind, and slowly it strengthened. A light had to be better than utter darkness, that seemed patently obvious. The thought to move towards it grew. Within moments the thought became a desire. More than that . . . it was a need. She *had* to move towards it.

Without any further ado, she began to move . . . towards it, towards the comfort the light seemed to be offering. She didn't know how, but somehow she was moving now . . . towards the light . . . or was it moving towards her? It didn't matter. It felt right. She could almost feel the comfort and warmth that it seemed to offer.

No. Don't go. Sara, not that way. You must return to your body, quickly.

It was a man's voice that suddenly broke the utter silence, startling her. She thought she had been alone. Where had that come from? And what was that name he had called her? Sara? She hadn't realised till now that she had forgotten her name too. Was that who she was? Was that her name? She hoped so. It sounded like a good name.

She felt a tugging then. Something was pulling at her, pulling her away from where she was. Away from the darkness . . . and the light. It felt strange, but somehow it also felt right. For some reason, she decided to let herself go with it. *How interesting*, she thought as she felt herself slipping away.

Sara opened her eyes and blinked. She was back in her body. She knew instantly that she had just had some sort of out-of-body experience, though how and why she had no idea. Memories of what had been happening to her flooded into her mind in just a fraction of a heartbeat.

The first thing she saw was Golkar. Though he was standing right where she had last seen him, she knew instantly that something had changed. Something was different about him. She looked him over from head to toe, searching for some change in his appearance. Then it suddenly dawned on her. She couldn't sense anything coming from him. He wasn't even looking at her. For some reason, he had stopped attacking her.

Before she could digest that thought, a wave of excruciating pain suddenly coursed through her body, like a subway train suddenly and unexpectedly roaring through an abandoned station. *Where did that come from?* she thought to herself as she struggled to cope with the realisation that the intense pain she was experiencing was coming from many parts of her body at the same time.

Pain was too soft a word. She was in absolute agony. Unbelievably agonising pains were racking her body. Though she was sure she was suffering from multiple injuries, her left side, in particular, felt like it had just been doused in acid. She could even smell the acrid odour of burning flesh. For a moment she thought she might pass out.

Golkar, he did it, she realised as a whole batch of further memories came flooding back to her all at once, triggered by the pain and pushing it aside as they jostled for attention within her mind. He threw that bolt of electricity or lightning or whatever it was at her and she had been sure that her time had come.

Well, I'm not dead yet, she thought to herself grimly as she pushed the pain aside and focused her attention on the wizard. She could feel her hatred for him welling up within her like hot lava surging within a volcano. What had been anger before, rage even, was now a hatred, unlike anything she had ever experienced before in her life. She had no idea how she had managed to survive his attack, but one thing was certainly clear: for the moment he seemed to be completely unaware that she had regained consciousness. From the look of things, he probably thought she was dead. The very thought of the vile creature gloating over her death pushed her emotions into the red.

I'll make him sorry he didn't finish me off when he had his chance. I'll give him a fight like he's never seen before in all of his days. Knowing that to delay would only aid her enemy, Sara gave full vent to her reinvigorated rage, hurling it from her in a sudden torrent of raw and unfettered energy, driving straight at Golkar as if she was wielding some almighty battering ram. This time she was determined to break down his defences and drive him right out of this world.

Though the force of its impact, coming as it did from a foe he thought he had finished, nearly knocked him from his feet, amazingly the wizard recovered quickly enough to weather the initial storm. The very strength of Sara's blow had rung out a warning that had given him the chance to prepare for its impact. Even so, a lesser opponent than he would never have recovered in time. The fact that he did was proof, if ever she needed it, both of the extent of his power and the depths of the malice he drew on as its source. The tide of the battle, however, had changed.

This time the doubts that had hobbled Sara's earlier attacks were nowhere to be seen. Sheer unadulterated revulsion, combined with furious anger, fuelled an attack the force of which had never before been seen in Ilythia. Bearing down on the wizard in an extraordinary display of power and determination, Sara drove him before her like a lamb to the slaughter. Before he could begin to mount a more orderly defence than the hasty one he had first contrived, he found he had been driven a full pace closer to the edge of the mirror.

The whole focus of Sara's attack now centred on one thing and one thing alone, the portal. It was still open, its ragged edges clearly visible along the surface of the mirror behind Golkar. And that was her goal. That was where she intended to drive the monster that stood before her, and this time she was determined that nothing would divert her from achieving that end.

Pain is nothing, she thought to herself dourly, refusing to her allow her brain to respond to the frantic signals the nerves in her body kept sending. Fierce thoughts coursed through her, bolstering her will and fuelling her determination. *Pain I can endure; but I cannot abide the presence of this monster in Ilythia for one more day, not even for one hour, not for one minute.* Though the strength of her feelings startled her, she held to her purpose with grim resolve, wincing as the wizard joined battle with her once more. This time she would finish it. This time there would be no second chances.

Though Sara knew that he was desperately trying to resist her, she could tell that Golkar was worried. The look of desperation on his face told its tale. He had the appearance of a man who had looked his own fate in the eye and who had quailed at what he saw there. She guessed that the uncertainty etched across his harrowed features was sapping his strength now, just as her own doubts had sapped hers earlier. His self-assurance had deserted him, and for that, she had no pity.

Sara felt her own hope surge within her, fuelling her efforts to defeat him even further. This time she would see it through, though she knew that she had to hurry. The portal kept shimmering in and out of existence behind him. Josef was obviously fading. If he died, presumably the portal would close with him. And if that happened before she could force Golkar through it, then she wouldn't know what to do to beat him.

And it wasn't just Josef that was wavering; she knew that an attack the likes of which she had just unleashed couldn't be maintained forever. Her reserves of energy were not unlimited. And yet still she was somehow winning . . . for the moment at least. Slowly, but surely, she was forcing Golkar back.

He didn't seem to be able to muster the same capacity for resistance he had shown earlier. Perhaps his bag of tricks was empty. Maybe he had given her everything he had. The earlier battle must have drained him considerably. Perhaps whatever he had been up to while he had been away had also taken its toll. It didn't really matter. The question was: would she be able to outlast him?

Sara refused to succumb to her own weariness, though she desperately felt the need to. She had to keep going. One slip now and all would be lost. She watched as Golkar almost stumbled as the back of his heel bumped into the base of the wall behind him. The portal was right behind him. She increased the pressure, digging even deeper than she already had. Somehow, incredibly, she began to force the wizard into the gaping hole behind him. It was unbelievable, but she was doing it. Despite his frantic attempts to resist her, Golkar was being driven into the portal.

The look of horror on his face told her that he knew the end was close. The portal seemed almost to be helping her now, drawing him in as if it had a will of its own, as if it was attracted to his energy. Within a few moments, he was almost through. He was holding on to the edges now in a last desperate attempt to stop her from achieving her goal. The main part of his body was swinging wildly behind him, already through the portal but starkly outlined against the bright light coming from wherever it led. He looked so bizarre, like a rag doll being sucked into some huge fan.

It was all so unreal. He was holding on to nothing now, a nothing, however, which he refused to let go of, a nothing that was his only remaining link with this world. The edges of the rent that had been opened by Josef were simply the edges of this plane of existence. They weren't solid; they were just the air that bordered the portal. And yet, despite that, Golkar had a firm grip on them with both of his hands and was using them to stubbornly resist Sara's attempt to push him right through and out of Ilythia. Try though she might, she couldn't find the extra effort to dislodge him.

She was tiring rapidly now. She couldn't keep this up for much longer. If she didn't finish him soon, she would be spent. Her head began to spin and she felt the energy sapping from her limbs as she struggled vainly to maintain the pressure. Her vision began to blur as she struggled to keep from passing out. A vague shape suddenly hovered into view from the right side of her rapidly narrowing field of vision. It was Rayne. He was crawling towards the mirror.

"No, don't," she cried out. *What did he think he was doing?*

She watched in abject horror as Rayne slowly struggled to his feet beside the mirror. He and Golkar seemed to be locked in some battle of their own. They were staring at each other, each seemingly unable or unwilling to tear his gaze away from the other. Golkar was doing something to him, she realised, compelling him in some way that she couldn't fathom. She had to do something. But what? She had barely the strength to stay conscious, and to keep pushing. She couldn't divert her attention. Not now. She had to keep pushing, no matter what.

Slowly, Rayne moved closer to the edge of the mirror. As he did so, Golkar suddenly let go of one of the edges of the portal and reached out towards Rayne with his free hand. Sara's heart seemed to stop beating. He was going to drag Rayne in with him. She was powerless to stop him. She was too weak now; it was too late for her to help him.

She watched in dismay as Rayne lifted his own hand. For the first time, she noticed the black crystal shard which hung from a chain around the wizard's neck. While the main part of his body was being drawn back into the void, beyond the opening, the crystal, along the chain which held it, both of which had hitherto been hidden from view beneath the wizard's tunic, was pulling in the opposite direction, back towards the room, as if it didn't want to leave Ilythia, or some strange power connected to it was resisting the countervailing force which threatened to take it into the void.

"Begone," Rayne hissed in a rasping voice as he suddenly and quite unexpectedly reached out and grabbed a hold of the dark crystal, snatching it and breaking the chain that held it around Golkar's neck.

In that same instant, the Guardian lost his remaining hold of the edge of the portal and his body disappeared with an almighty rush into the piercing brightness of the void behind him. He was gone. Finally, he was gone. The portal snapped shut, closing off any chance of him finding a way back.

Rayne collapsed to the floor at the foot of the mirror as the portal winked out of existence, his hand releasing the crystal shard as he did so. The shard bounced across the wooden floor and came to rest only a few paces from where Rayne's still form now lay. The reflection of the wizard's chamber on the surface of the glass gave no hint that the mirror had ever been anything else than a simple looking glass.

CHAPTER 15

Grartok roared mightily as he raised his hands above his head in exultation. His brother's blood dripped down from the blade of the axe that he held suspended above him and onto the dull surface of the hardened leather breastplate that covered his broad and muscled torso. The roar of voices around him as he stood there, gloating over the bloodied carcass of his meddlesome brother, was music to his ears. There was no finer sound to a slig warrior. If ever any had doubted his right to lead them, his victory over his brother had effectively silenced even his harshest critic. The lifeless body at his feet presaged a similar fate for any who dared to challenge him.

"Sound the attack," he shouted as he pushed his way through the throng of surrounding warriors and beckoned for his horse to be brought to him. As he climbed up onto the back of the beast, he could hear the horns ringing out across the open field below them. The roar that followed as the Sagath host surged forward in response to the signal sent another surge of blood-lust through his veins. He raised his axe again as he steadied his mount below him.

"Come," he cried to his fellow warriors as they rushed to mount their own steeds. "Let's put an end to these troublesome Algarians once and for all." With that, he spurred his horse forward and raced down the slope in hot pursuit of his charging army, not bothering to wait for the rest of his entourage to follow.

As he urged his horse on, eager to join in the slaughter that was about to begin, he knew that his finest moment was upon him. The culmination of all his plans, of all his dreams, would be here on the field of battle before the walls of his enemy's most prized possession, their capital, Keerêt. Nothing could stop the Sagath now. Nothing could stop him from achieving his destiny. Everything had gone just as he had known it would.

He counted off his achievements in his mind. He had risen to become First Warrior of the Sagath, the bravest of all of the slig tribes. He had waged war on the most hated of all the slig's enemies and had driven them relentlessly back across their territory until they could retreat no further; and now . . . now he was about to lead the Sagath to their final victory. His scheming brother was dead, by his own hand in single combat. He had an heir, a male child that would one day take his own place at the very pinnacle of the slig nation, as First Warrior of the First Tribe, as the first King of the sligs, perhaps even as Lord of all Ilythia.

And when he was done here, he thought, as the hand of spite gripped and squeezed his heart, he would deal with Norag, the one remaining blot on his record. It wouldn't do to have the lad grow up thinking he had put one over on his leader. If Golkar had known about it sooner he'd be lying in a dung heap right now. And once Mardur had borne his child, he would kill her as well. He would let her live, for now, let her think she was safe and free from danger, let her think he knew nothing of her treachery. Then, when she had served her purpose, he would . . . replace her . . . with someone more respectful, someone more accommodating, someone . . . someone like Varna perhaps, or one of the others.

Grartok's dreams were swept aside as his mount crested the rise he had watched his army sweep over only moments beforehand. Below him, not far from him now, the bulk of his forces swept on. He could see that there had been precious little resistance from the Algarians here at their first line of defence. They must have turned and fled at the first sign of the charge.

Down through the rolling hills below him and out into the plain below, the Algarians were running before his warriors now in a wild panic. Once again, Grartok spurred his mount on, slashing down with his axe to bring down an Algarian straggler who had somehow survived the initial assault and was struggling to rise from where he had fallen. There seemed to be too few of them though. Where were all the dead bodies? The position his warriors had overrun must have been manned by only a skeleton force. Curse the Algarians; they must have known they couldn't hold this position.

Looking out beyond the van of his host, Grartok could now see, way off in the distance, the plain that surrounded the great city. Even from here, he could see it was full of Algarians, scurrying for the safety of the city walls. They must have withdrawn the bulk of their force long before the charge had begun. It would be a race now, a race to see how many they could cut down before they got inside the city. This would be even better than he had thought it would be.

Spurring his horse on again and veering slightly to his left, Golkar leaned over in his saddle to slash at a Ranger who was frantically limping towards a small ditch in which a few of his wounded companions had already taken cover. As the slig leader did so, he heard a strange whooshing sound from behind him, as if a bird were about to swoop down low over his head. Ignoring the distraction, he swung at his foe, catching him a glancing blow across his shoulders and bowling him over as his horse swept past him. Suddenly, a huge shadow swept over both him and his mount, disappearing again as rapidly as it had appeared, leaving them drenched in the light of the burning sun once more. Turning his eyes skyward, Grartok was startled to see a huge winged beast sweep past him, only a metre or two above his head.

As a swirling wind buffeted both him and his mount in the aftermath of the winged creature's passing, Grartok struggled desperately to keep a tight grip on his rein and to stop from falling from his saddle. When another of the massive creatures swooped over his shoulder, his horse reared up in panic, throwing him to the ground and almost trampling him as it frantically tried to escape.

Grartok fell heavily to the turf, feeling the breath rush out of him as his own weight added to the force of his impact. Panting for air, he struggled groggily to his feet as quickly as he could, one hand still firmly gripping his axe while his other tentatively reached for his throbbing temple. His horse had caught him a glancing blow with one of its hooves as it danced about wildly in its desperate bid to escape from the strange winged creature that had appeared so suddenly, as if out of nowhere.

Pulling his hand away from his forehead, he wasn't surprised to see it was covered in blood; his head was still ringing with an ache that befuddled his thoughts. The ground beneath his feet was swaying about alarmingly, as if the whole world was rolling about wildly on its axis. Somehow he managed to stagger drunkenly away from where he had fallen as several more of the winged beasts glided over his head. Their hideous screeches wailed through the sky above him. They were like huge eagles, he thought as he stumbled across the uneven turf, only misshapen in some terrible way he couldn't discern in his current condition.

Realising that he was wandering aimlessly across the hillside, Grartok stopped and tried to steady himself by leaning on the haft of his axe. A wave of nausea swept over him as he concentrated on regaining his composure. After a few moments, he felt that he had recovered sufficiently to stand without falling. Turning slowly and unsteadily towards the field of battle, he looked in horror at the scene unfolding before him.

The winged beasts had begun to attack the Sagath. He could see what seemed to be a dozen or so of the fell creatures from where he stood. They were circling above his army and swooping down to drag warriors from their mounts, tearing them limb from limb or simply letting them fall back to the ground as they effortlessly climbed back up into the air with just a few flaps of their mighty wings.

Grartok had never seen their like before. The sun glinted from their plumage as they dove down on his hapless army, sending panic and confusion throughout his force and bringing the attack on the Algarians to a sudden and grinding halt. Though he could see that the Sagath were desperately trying to fend off the foul beasts, their spears and axes seemed to be having little effect. Here and there, he could see crossbows being aimed at the beasts, but once again, with no apparent success. It was as if they were impervious to his warrior's weapons, easily fending off their feeble attempts to defend themselves from this deadly airborne attack.

As Grartok began to stumble down the slope in the vague hope of joining the battle, an arrow suddenly thudded into his left thigh, sending a sharp stinging pain shooting up into his groin. He slowly sank to one knee, grappling groggily for the missile with the aim of pulling it from his flesh. Before he could complete the task, another arrow thudded into his chest. He grunted as yet a third of the missiles pierced his skin.

The slig leader slumped to the ground. Dimly, way off in the distance, he heard the sound of trumpets. He knew what it was. As the darkness descended over him, he knew that Zar's acolytes were sounding out their clarion call. Another slig warrior was making his last journey, to his final resting place, to the Halls of Gollohim. His time on Ilythia was over.

~~~

Elissa let the tears run unchecked down her cheek as she gazed out across the plain before the city walls. Even from where she stood, on the balcony of her private apartments, high up in the royal palace, she could still smell the stench of the dead and the gagging fumes from the funeral pyres. Reaching out with her hands, the queen steadied herself against the intricately carved stonework in front of her. Leaning against the balustrade, she closed her eyes for a moment, hoping to blot out the memory of the painful scenes she had witnessed over the last few hours. It was no use. Opening them again she saw that nothing had changed. The same dismal scene confronted her that she had been watching for the last hour or so. She guessed that the memory of what had preceded it had been indelibly etched on her soul.

"So much death, so many horrors, so many broken and shattered lives. For what?" she lamented, making no attempt to conceal her bitterness. "To feed the egos of two men? Is that all this was for? So that Grartok and Golkar could both pursue their obscene dreams of glory?" Her heart was empty. There was no rejoicing in Keerêt, neither here in the royal apartments nor down in the city itself, there was only sorrow, sorrow and anger.

The Queen of Algaria wept silently as she stared out across the plain that spread from the walls of the city to the distant hills beyond. Though the battle was over, the signs of the carnage that had taken place only a few short hours earlier were still there for all to see. Other than an occasional sob or gasp from those around her, for several minutes, all were silent. The enormity of the situation could not help but weigh heavily on every observer.

"So many lives," she finally exclaimed in a hoarse whisper, struggling to keep her emotions in check as she spoke. "Such senseless slaughter, and for what purpose? This morning as I watched the ranks of our soldiers as they assembled I was so proud of their courage. I couldn't help but feel their vitality their vigour, their hope. Now . . . now it's like a forest floor covered in dead and decaying leaves. So many dead, from both sides. So many who will never return home again."

After a few moments of silence, she finally gave vent to the anger that was quickly displacing her grief.

"This is Golkar's doing," she exclaimed more loudly, turning her face away from her companions as she spoke to hide the tears welling up in her eyes. "What will he do when all of the leaves have fallen? What further horrors will he inflict on Ilythia then?"

"The Guardians failed us," she continued after a few moments, turning to look at Regulus as she spoke. "The bodies of countless Algarians are burning this evening because the Guardians failed us."

"The Guardians didn't fail us," Regulus replied wearily, returning her look. She could see from the harrowed look on his face that he was equally as gutted as she was by what had befallen their city. "One of the Guardians failed us. The other two died valiantly trying to defend us. Let's not let our bitterness besmirch their memory. They gave their lives for us Elissa, without question and without hesitating, I suspect. Perhaps it was us that failed. Perhaps we were too complacent, too willing to let the Guardians watch over us and to not be ready to defend ourselves. For how many generations have we relied on them and them alone for our safety? Now we will have no choice. Now we will have to stand on our own feet. Maybe that will be a good thing."

"Maybe it will," Elissa responded, sighing. "It's hard to see things right when you look out from the walls of your city and see the bodies of so many of your subjects heaped upon the funeral pyres. I'll think more clearly on the morrow, I'm sure, but tonight . . ." She took a long deep breath as she paused. "Tonight all I can do is weep."

Regulus moved a step closer to his queen and drew her to his side. With their hands about each other's waists, they stood silently, looking out from the balcony above the city at the remnants of a fateful day. The count could still hear the horns ringing in his ears. He would never forget that moment, the turning point in the fortunes of the Algarians, when they had seen the wondrous winged beasts come in over the hills and begin to destroy the slig army.

They had all stood there, stunned, all of those that had taken to the walls to watch what would become of their army as it rushed to get back to the safety of the city. When the winged beasts had turned up, the gryphons as they now knew they were, they had thought at first they were something conjured up out of nightmare, some demons or monsters that the sligs were somehow in league with and which had come to join in the slaughter.

The cries of wonder as they had turned on the slig army had sent a thrill through every single Algarian there. Regulus would never forget that moment and the exhilaration he had felt as certain defeat had been so abruptly swept aside. After wheeling above the slig army, the gryphons had suddenly and unexpectedly attacked the Algarians' foe in a vicious and deadly airborne assault, picking them off like a flock of eagles would pick off their prey, herding them together like sheep, then darting down to snatch them one by one, and all the while the sligs had milled about, frantically trying to defend themselves.

It was hard to conceive that so few of them, just seven he had counted, though it had seemed like many more at first, could have turned back a whole army. He hadn't known then that they were magical beasts, possessed of awesome powers and abilities, though even watching them it had been clear that the sligs were unable to do them much harm, that there was a power within them, unlike anything anyone had ever seen in a beast.

Then Brassilius had sounded the trumpets and the Algarians had turned and rallied. The horns had rung out and the seemingly routed Rangers had checked their headlong flight for the city walls and bravely turned and stood their ground. Slowly, the tide had turned. Men who had been consumed by fear had found courage again. Soldiers who had forgotten all of their training had suddenly regained the discipline their training had taught them. The fleeing remnants of the Algarian militia had become an army once more.

Eventually, together with the gryphons, they had driven the harried sligs before them, back into the hills, back finally to the very edge of the Sarrowmar River. The battle had gone on well into the afternoon. Finally, it had ended. What was left of the sligs had fled, or was left dead or dying on the field of battle.

Then, despite their exhaustion, the army had reformed and Brassilius himself had led it northwards into the dusk of a dying day to head off the threat from the sligs on the northern front. There would be more fighting on the morrow, but the outcome of the war had been decided here today. The bulk of the slig forces had been defeated and scattered. The second slig force by itself could be contained. Once the outcome of today's fighting was known, it would probably dissipate and move eastwards as quickly as it could in an attempt to cover the retreat of the remnants of their forces. The war was as good as over.

It had been a great victory, but at such a cost. As Elissa had said, too many good men had died needlessly. Too many of Regulus' friends would not come back. The clean up would go on for a long time. The pyres would burn all through the night, and tomorrow again, no doubt, there would be more of them. Though the city was relatively quiet now, many of the wounded were still being brought in. It was an unnatural quiet that had descended on the city, a quiet borne of grief, not of inactivity or sleep. Many would not sleep at all tonight.

"You were brave," he said To Elissa, breaking the silence that had fallen between them. "It must have been quite a sight to see you stand your ground when Kaladyr came to the city." Like everyone else, Regulus had heard the tale of how the gryphon had come to the city and spoken with their queen, how it had hovered with great flaps of those monstrous wings a short distance beyond her balcony while she had spoken with it. He wished that he had seen that. If he had waited on the walls, he would have; but he had been too anxious to reach her side once he had seen that the battle had turned in their favour. He had missed what must have been one of the greatest moments in the history of Algaria.

"No. I don't think it was bravery. More like stunned awe, I think. I could feel the good in him right away. Somehow, I knew that there was nothing to fear from him. I didn't think of him as a beast at all, you know. It was like speaking to a person, even though the whole conversation took place in my head. I even knew his name, though I don't recollect him ever saying it. It was so strange. Perhaps it was all just a dream after all."

Elissa stopped for a moment, shaking her head at the memory. "I know that I was scared after he'd gone, though. I couldn't stop trembling for a long while. You saw how I was. It must have been a delayed reaction."

"Call it what you will, the bard's will turn it into a legend before the night is out, mark my words. The tale of Elissa and the King of the Gryphons."

Regulus smiled as he saw the broad grin that came to his queen's face as he spoke. It was the first light-hearted comment he had dared to venture. It had been too solemn a day for jesting.

"He never said he was their king, or even their leader. He just told me that they had come at the request of a friend, and that the Guardians were all dead, that Golkar had killed both Tarak and Kell, but that we were safe now, and that Golkar was gone. He didn't say how he knew all of this, but he made it clear he was sure that Golkar was gone, that he had been forced out of Ilythia. Then he said that the gryphons had fulfilled their promise and he sort of dipped his head, as if he was bowing to me.

"I wasn't sure what to do, so I thanked him. I said it aloud, so I hope he understood me. I told him we were in their debt . . . and then he left. He flapped those huge wings of his and just rose up and away, so effortlessly. Then I went back into my room and I collapsed, right into Brina's arms. Then you and the others turned up. It really wasn't anything glorious, certainly not the stuff that legends are made of."

"Who summoned them to our aid?" asked Regulus, still wondering at her words, despite having heard her story once already. "Did he say? And how did you know it was a he?"

"He never said who and I didn't get the chance to ask him. He didn't wait around long enough. I don't even know how I knew he was a 'he'. I just did, that's all. I hadn't even questioned how I knew that until you just asked me."

"Well, if Golkar killed Tarak and Kell, and if the gryphon doesn't know how or why Golkar left, then there's a couple of big chunks of the story missing somewhere."

"I know. But quite frankly, I'm too tired to think about it any more right now. I just give thanks to Mishra that they turned up when they did."

"Yes. I'm sorry. We should both get some sleep. There's going to be a lot to do to sort this mess out. And we still have to deal with the threat from the north. I don't think this will be truly over for some time yet. For many, I guess, it'll never be over."

"Yes. I'm sure you're right. But before I go to sleep I must go down into the city. I want to visit the sick and wounded again before I allow myself some rest. Will you come with me?"

"Of course."

"Good. I was hoping you'd agree. It isn't a task I would like to undertake on my own. I must show them a strong face. I may need an arm to lean upon. By the way . . . thank you."

"What for?"

"For being here, for letting me lean on you, for understanding, for caring about me."

"I don't *care* about you, Elissa. I love you."

"I know. And you know that I love you too. It feels like I always have and always will. Maybe it's time for me to acknowledge that."

With that, the two friends turned and walked back, hand in hand, through the open doors behind them. They had been simple words, casually spoken, but they had both understood the depths of the feelings behind them. They both knew that they could go on now. They both knew that there was still something to live for, something to hope for.

~~~

Jinny's thoughts were elsewhere as she slowly made her way back to the campsite, scanning the ground as she went for dried pieces of timber to add to the pile she already held within her arms. The day was rapidly coming to a close and they would need to get the fire lit and their meal cooked before darkness fell. Though they felt safer now that they had left Kurandir, they would still have to be cautious. The ridgeline above the town allowed them a good view of the surrounding area, but an open fire at night would also leave them exposed to sight should any sligs still be about.

As she picked her way across the stony ground, she wondered at the closeness that had grown between Thom and her over the past few weeks. The friendship that had existed between them before the war had blossomed now into something much more than that.

Thom had visited their farm often over the past few years, always ostensibly as a result of some errand or message from his father to hers, and he had always made a point of seeking her out and spending some time with her before he would leave. At first, she hadn't known how to respond. Even when she could think of something to say in response to his kind words or his gentle enquiries, her shyness seemed to prevent her from contributing to what inevitably became very one-sided conversations. She would nod and smile at his comments and keep her eyes on her sewing or whatever it was she had been about until eventually, he would say it was time for him to go.

Nothing ever seemed to deter him though, and she found that she began to look forward to his visits. Somehow, she began to find the courage to speak up and even to risk the occasional glance in his direction.

She thought him handsome and kind and, over time, she began to count him as one of her closest friends. Although after a while he also began to figure prominently in her daydreams, it had never really occurred to her that he might be as fond of her as she found she had become of him.

She knew now that he cared about her very much. They had become as close as friends could be, though she still didn't dare to tell him what she really felt about him. Perhaps he guessed. From the way he held her to him when he hugged her, she could tell that he liked her, that he liked being close to her, and she knew that he liked to kiss her. Jinny felt her face going red with embarrassment at the last thought, pleasant though it was. Thank goodness he couldn't see into her mind.

Reminding herself that she needed to hurry and get back to the camp, Jinny turned her mind back to her task. Bending down, she took a hold of a large piece of bark that had fallen to the ground beside an old rotting tree. Once she broke it up, it would make an ideal addition to the load she had already collected.

As she lifted the flimsy material from its resting place, she suddenly gasped in alarm and jumped backwards, dropping the bundle of faggots she held in her arms and bringing her hand up to her mouth in an involuntary response. When she saw the scaly foot which had come into view as she had lifted the timber move, she squealed with fright and turned and bolted in the direction of their campsite.

Looking back over her shoulder as she ran she saw the slig scrambling out from underneath the fallen timber. Within only a few moments her worst fears were confirmed when another glance established that it had risen from its hiding spot and had quickly given chase. Though it was a female, it looked big and just as frightening as one of their warriors. When Jinny glanced back a third time she stumbled as her leg crashed into something hard and unyielding, a log or a branch she assumed, though she had no time to look and check.

For a moment, she thought she would fall for sure, but somehow she managed to stay on her feet and keep moving. As she recovered her gait and began to pick up her pace again, however, she suddenly felt something grab a hold of her ankles. In the blink of an eye, her forward motion was brought to an abrupt halt and her upper body crashed heavily to the ground, her forward momentum merely adding to the force of the impact as she desperately reached out with her hands in an instinctive attempt to break her fall. Ignoring the searing pain as her arm scraped across the rough ground, Jinny desperately scrambled to pull free of the slig who had crashed to the ground with her and was frantically trying to grab a hold of her flailing legs.

When she looked back and saw her assailant drawing a long blade from her belt with her one free hand, Jinny screamed and began to twist about wildly, frantic to free herself from the beast before she could manage to use her weapon. She felt the blood in her veins turn to ice as the slig's grip on her trousers tightened and, with surprising strength, she began to pull herself up into a position where she could use her blade and put an end to their grim struggle. Jinny felt herself freeze with terror as she saw the slig lift her deadly weapon up with her free hand while she held her in a vice-like grip with the other.

"STOP," a voice suddenly screamed out from nearby. It was Thom. "Stop, or your child dies right now."

Turning her head while nervously trying to keep an eye on the blade poised above her, Jinny could see Thom slowly approaching them. He had his own knife out and was holding it over a bundle of old rags he was cradling in his other arm. It had to be the slig woman's baby. She must have left it back at the spot where Jinny had found her. Perhaps they had been hiding there, or sleeping, seeing out the daylight hours and waiting for the darkness, just as she and Thom had done over the past week or so. Who knows where they were going or what they were doing out here alone.

Jinny felt a chill run through her as she suddenly realised there may be more of them close by. Surely a slig woman wouldn't be travelling alone through enemy territory like this. She must have a companion or a mate, perhaps even a whole group she was travelling with, nearby.

"Put the babe down or the girl dies," the slig replied in a thick guttural voice, pulling herself up on top of Jinny and bringing her blade down to rest against her throat as she did so.

Jinny dare not move from where she lay. She felt paralysed with fear. Even could she have found the courage to move, the way the slig was now lying across her upper body, with the whole of her weight pressing down on Jinny's abdomen, there was little she could do but await her fate.

"I don't think so," replied Thom, moving to his left slowly as he spoke. He still held the slig infant in the crook of his arm with his knife poised over it, point down. The tip of his blade was resting against the infant's swaddling. "I don't want to hurt your child, or you for that matter. You hurt the girl and I'll kill you both, I swear it. Let's think about this. We don't need to do this. Let's find a way that we can both go on about our journey without anyone getting hurt."

"I'm not that stupid, putok." The slig woman spat as she said the last word. Tightening her grip on Jinny and pressing her cold blade even more firmly against the skin of Jinny's neck, she continued. "I'm not ready to die yet. If you want this little one here to see another dawn, then put down your blade and put the child on the ground there in front of you. Then step back away. Do it now, or else."

"It's not gunna happen like that," said Thom coolly in response, though Jinny could sense his nervousness. He was still circling them as he spoke, forcing the slig to keep twisting around to keep her face to him as he did so. "I give you my word. There's been enough killing."

With that, he stopped circling and began to back away from where Jinny and the slig woman lay. He was speaking very slowly and deliberately now. "We're both going to back off. I'm going to give you the space you need to get up. Then I'm going to put the child down. And you're going to let the girl go. Then we're all going to go our own way, like we never saw each other in the first place. I don't want to see the girl hurt and you want your baby back safe and sound. Let's be calm about this so we can all live to see another day."

Thom, who had been slowly backing away as he spoke, was now some twenty or so paces away from them. When he finished speaking he stooped and lay the bundle in his arms down on the ground. As he did so the child began to cry. Slowly, Thom backed away a few more paces. "I mean it," he said. "You hurt the girl and I'll kill the child before you can stop me. You let her go and we all go our own way and forget we ever saw each other."

Jinny swallowed nervously in the silence that followed Thom's speech. She felt the slig woman's hold on her ease off ever so slightly and the pressure go off the blade against her throat. When the slig began to rise, Jinny knew that she had to stand with her. The slig made no attempt to remove the knife, despite her more relaxed attitude.

"How do I know I can trust you?" sneered the slig once she and Jenny had risen. "You expect me to take the word of an Algarian?"

"Yes, I do. I tell you, I have no desire to kill you. I just want my friend back safe and sound. Besides, I've seen enough killing for a lifetime. I want no part in any more of that. But I will do it if I have to. My name is Thom. I give you my word. Let's both pretend we never even saw each other."

Jinny could sense the slig was nervous. After a few moments, she replied. This time her voice was less threatening. "I am Mardur. I will trust you, Algarian, though it goes against my grain." With that, she began to move towards her child, keeping a firm hold of Jinny with one hand and her knife at her throat with the other as she frog-marched her across the intervening space.

As they approached, Thom backed away even further. Jinny could feel her own heart racing. She knew that the critical point was approaching. As they reached the spot where Thom had laid down the bundle, she suddenly felt a shove in her back. As she stumbled forward she suddenly realised that the woman had released her. With a cry of relief, she raced across to Thom and threw herself into his arms.

Turning her head, she saw that the slig had picked up the child and was slowly backing away from them. At the same moment, she heard a noise from behind Thom.

"What are you doing?" a male voice cried out. It was Dain. "Don't let them get away boy. C'mon. We can take her easy."

Dain had his sword in his hand and was about to rush past them, in the direction of the slig woman, who had stopped and placed the child on the ground again, ready to defend herself from this new attacker. As Dain came level with them, Thom reached out with his arm, barring his way.

"No," he said firmly. "I gave her my word. I told her she could go without any fear of pursuit."

"Forget it, boy. She's a slig. You don't go makin bargains with sligs. Not unless you wanna wake up with your throat cut. I said we kill her, and kill her we will."

"No," insisted Thom, grabbing a hold of Dain's jerkin as he made to move towards the woman again.

Dain spun around angrily in response. "Who you think you are, boy? You're just a kid. You don't know nuthin about it. You didn't see the butcherin that went on at Kurandir. You didn't see what those murderin scum are like. Your folks teach you no manners, boy? You listen when someone older'n you tells you what to do. If you're too squeamish for it, not a problem. Leave it to me, boy."

As Dain went to turn towards the slig yet again, Thom grabbed a hold of him one more time. "No," he said, maintaining his grip as Dain tried to pull free. "I gave my word. I know what happened between us and the sligs. I got eyes in my head. By Mishra, I know. But I also know I don't want to see any more of that. I've seen enough of death. We all have. Besides which, we ain't sligs, we're Algarians. We don't butcher, least of all women and children. And when we give our word, it means something. One woman and a baby are no threat to anyone. The killing has to stop somewhere."

Finally, something he said seemed to get through to Dain. Jinny watched as the old man slowly lowered his sword. Looking back at Thom and then across at the slig woman who still crouched nervously, with her knife at the ready, he let his breath out in a long sigh.

"Okay," he finally mumbled in a subdued voice. "Okay."

"Here you are, Mr Danarson. The first one's for you."

Jinny watched as Thom's father took the skewer of meat from her hands. She could see the flickering firelight reflecting in the soft sheen of his eyes, eyes that were fixed greedily on the golden strip of glistening meat in front of him. It was almost tragic to see the anticipation in his face as he unconsciously smacked his lips with his tongue. As he brought the skewer up to his face, he held it beneath his nose for a moment and drew the savoury smell of the meat deeply in through his nostrils. Obviously satisfied with its rich aroma, he quickly opened his mouth and hungrily began to devour his food, tearing the meat from the stick like a dog that has just been given his favourite meal.

As she returned to her own spot beside the fire, Jinny glanced across at Thom. The grin and accompanying wink he gave her made her turn her head away quickly in an embarrassing attempt to suppress her own smile. She didn't want his father to think she was laughing at him.

As she looked out at the trees beyond their campsite, she wondered at the transformation in their lives. She and Thom had been kids when all this had started, and she still was, she knew that. But Thom . . . he had changed. She wondered if any adult could have handled that situation with the slig woman any better than he had. It had taken a cool head to get her out of that. Even now, the mere thought of how close she had come to death sent a shudder through her. And that altercation with his father. He would never have dared to speak to him like that before all of this. Either of them would have been lucky not to get a whipping if they had even thought about defying their parents so brazenly. But Thom had stood up to Dain like a man.

Thom's voice interrupted her thoughts. He was speaking to his father.

"Umm. Mr Danarson? I think we should go back down to the town tomorrow. If the refugees are starting to come back then that'd be the best place to wait for your wife. She'd have to come back through Kurandir."

"Yeh. You're probably right there, boy. Good idea. I'm not goin in, mind you. We can wait somewhere outside, near the road."

"Okay."

It must be so hard for Thom, thought Jinny. Having your own father not know you any more. He must have seen terrible things in Kurandir to end up like that. Maybe Thom was right, though. Maybe he would be all right in time. If Thom's mom was okay, and if they could find her again, maybe she could help him remember the life he had had before all of this began.

Jinny wiped her nose on the side of her sleeve as she felt her eyes moisten at the thought of the life they had all left behind. She didn't expect to ever see her father again. Thom had skirted around the issue but she knew what he was avoiding saying. It would have taken more than a miracle for her father to survive the attack on Brand's Ford. And if he had, he would have come back to the farm to look for her. Nothing would have kept him from doing that. Nothing . . . except . . .

She felt Thom's arm upon her shoulder as he sidled up next to her. "Are you okay," he asked, reaching out and wiping the tears from her cheeks as she turned to face him and looked up into his gentle eyes.

"Don't you be cryin now, girlie," she heard Thom's father call from across the fire. "Your boy there, he'll look after you now. Heard him say so the other day, and I reckon he meant it. We all lost ones we loved. Least you still got someone who cares about you girlie. Just don't let him get away." Dain cackled a bit at his last comment, then fell to mumbling unintelligibly to himself.

"You've got someone who cares about you too," she responded, pushing her emotions back down where they were safer, where they couldn't stir up her memories. "Thom's going to look after the both of us. Aren't you Thom?"

"Yep." Thom pulled her closer in to his side as he spoke. "I think those of us that are left are going to have to stick together. Isn't that right, Mr Danarson?"

"Mmmm." Dain was clearly being non-committal. After a pause, he spoke again. "Can't promise what Khared will say about that. Guess you could have Thom's room though. You and ya girlfriend. Have to marry her though, boy. Not gunna sleep under my roof together otherwise. And don't go telling me she's too young for that. She ain't any younger than Khared was when I married her. No point in waitin once you found the right one."

Jinny watched in amusement at the grin the two men shared at his comments.

"Haven't asked her yet," replied Thom.

"Well. What'ya waitin for, boy?"

Jinny looked up at Thom again and gave him a look that said, 'have you two had enough fun yet?' She could feel her face reddening. Couldn't they see how embarrassed they were making her?

"Too scared," said Thom suddenly, taking Jinny by surprise and keeping his eyes locked to hers as he spoke. "Would've already asked her but I'm too scared she might say no."

Jinny felt her jaw drop. She didn't know what to say. Had she heard what he had said right? Frantically she tried to think over what he had just said, what the exact words he had used had been.

His father's voice cut into her thoughts as her mind whirled in turmoil. "Sounded like a proposal to me, girlie," he cackled. "Sounded like somethin my Thom might'a said. Round and about, and comin at it sideways, but askin ya as clear as could be just the same. Reckon you should give 'im an answer."

"Yeh Jinny," said Thom. "Reckon you should."

~~~

The soft patter of the drizzling rain on the roof of the crypt seemed appropriate to Sara. It was almost as if the very land itself was weeping in honour of his memory. Pulling the thick cloak about her shoulders, she slowly rose from where she had been lying, hunched over the cold stone of the marble sarcophagus, idly tracing her fingers over the graven image carved with such skill into its unyielding surface. The slow drizzle in some way seemed to take a part of her grief with it as it trickled down the granite walls and puddled about the steps that led up into the open air.

To have lost him after knowing him for such a short time seemed to her a cruelty beyond all the others she'd had to endure in the course of her stay in this strange and bewitching land. With a long slow sigh, she turned away from his tomb. Taking the hand her companion offered, she slowly made her way up the steps and through the iron gates that led back to the world of the living.

"I wish you'd told me who he was while I still had a chance to know him," she said wistfully, hugging the sorrow that always accompanied these visits to her like a much-cherished friend.

The gentle squeeze of Rayne's hand against hers lifted her spirits and she stopped and turned to face him, not wanting to go any further until she had said what she planned to. Now was as good a time as any. Throwing back the hood of her cloak, she reached out and gratefully accepted the warm embrace he offered as her eyes began to swim.

"I want to repay his selflessness, Rayne," she sniffled, burrowing her face into the warmth of his tunic. "I want to give him the chance to live again. Only, this time I want to make sure he lives a life that is long and happy, with both of his parents there to watch over him, to love him, and cherish him."

"Does this mean that you're going to stay?"

Sara felt her heart wrench as she recognised the trepidation in her companion's words. The question had sat between them for so long now, neither of them daring to raise it, both afraid to confront the consequences of the decision she knew she would eventually have to make. Now, she had finally made her decision.

"Yes. I want to stay. If you'll have me. I couldn't stay here without you to look after me. I wouldn't want to."

"Of course I'll look after you," he laughed, unable to restrain his joy and hugging her tightly to him. As he swung her around and off her feet, he cried out in his happiness. "Oh, Sara. You don't know how much I've dreaded your answer."

"Yes I do," she managed to get out between his kisses. "Put me down. Someone will see us."

He chuckled again as he gently placed her back on her feet. "Let them. What do I care anymore."

"What about Josef?" she asked, returning to a more serious tone. "Do you think we could do that? It's a bit scary. Having a baby, I mean. Do you really want to be a father?"

"I already am, or was, or will be. I don't know; it's all so confusing. Yes. Yes, I want to be a father. Somewhere, in some timeline, Josef already was our child. Without him, you'd never have been able to defeat Golkar. And without us creating him, he wouldn't have been able to come back and help us. It's all pretty confusing, but I agree with you. We owe it to his memory to give him another chance; a chance for a better life than the one he was forced to endure last time. Besides, it could be fun."

The smirk on his face as he turned away and began to stroll down the pathway brought a smile to Sara's lips and a lump to her throat. There must be a god somewhere, she thought. How else could such happiness have come her way?

Pulling the hood of her cloak back over her head, she hurried to catch up to him, knowing there would be much to talk over on the long ride back to the city. An image of her parents formed in her mind as she walked through the rain. It was hard to accept that the life she was choosing would be one in which they couldn't play a role. Life's choices were like that, she guessed. Pathways opened before you and you had to make choices. You couldn't always have all of the things that you wanted.

Still, she wouldn't let them go through their life despairing of what had become of their daughter. She would have to tell Rayne eventually. Not now, but soon. He would understand, she was sure. He would have to. She was going to stay, she had made that decision, but that didn't mean that she was going to stop trying to find a way back home. There had to be a way to go back and tell her parents what had happened to her, to tell them how much she missed them, to tell them that she was happy, and about Rayne and everything else. Golkar's diary, the one that Tanis had written, the answer was in there. Josef had worked it out and so would she, no matter how long it took.

As she reached the tree where Rayne stood waiting for her with their horses' reins in his hand, she realised that she felt better than she had for weeks. There was so much to do, so much to plan, so much to look forward to now, both for her and for the rest of the country. Taking Rayne's hand, she climbed up onto Nell and together they set off on the long journey back to Keerêt.

THE

END

ABOUT THE AUTHOR

Mark McCabe was born in Brisbane, Australia, later moved to Sydney and then to Canberra, the Australian capital city, where he completed a career in the Australian Government and Australian Capital Territory's public service agencies.

Upon retiring, Mark and his family moved to New Zealand and took up residence near Dunedin.

Mark holds a Bachelor of Arts majoring in Classics, Latin and English from the Australian National University.

Mark's favoured genres are fantasy (predominantly epic and high fantasy) and science fiction, although he does hope to write a series of crime novels at some stage in the future. He cites David Gemmell, Jack Vance and Ursula Le Guin as key inspirations and influences.

In his spare time, Mark is an amateur photographer and a keen student of the classics, with a particular focus on Rome as well as ancient myths and legends such as the Trojan Cycle.

Author website: https://markmccabeauthor.com